Rewind

Because part of us will always be
seventeen years old ...

A FIVE DIRECTIONS PRESS BOOK

Rewind

A NOVEL

Denise Allan Steele

ISBN-13: 978-1947044029
ISBN-10: 1947044028

Published in the United States of America.

A Five Directions Press book

Cover images: front—Polaroid frame © RusN/iStock; cassette © Wouter Tolenaars/Shutterstock; lip gloss © BeautyImage/ Shutterstock; "Coal not Dole" button © Denise Allan Steele; back and spine—"Early Evening, Sauchiehall Street" pastel on paper by Jamie Simpson © www.simpsonfineart.com.

Book and cover design by Five Directions Press

Five Directions Press logo designed by Colleen Kelley

FIVE DIRECTIONS PRESS

*For Anyone Who's Ever
Had a Best Friend*

Contents

1. Abide with Me

CAROL AND I SAT HUDDLED TOGETHER ON THE COLD HARD pew of Kilbrannan Parish Church. The weak sunshine coming through the huge stained glass window above our heads illuminated the figure of Saint Andrew, the ruby red of his gown beautiful and rich against the sapphire blue of the Scottish flag behind him. I had always loved that window, the way it gave me a feeling of peace and God and benevolence and contentment, the colours precious and magnificent in the austerity of the chilly old Presbyterian church. I had last seen the window from the inside in May 1977, when I had just turned fifteen. That was the day that Carol and I had been thrown out of the Girl Guides for refusing to say out loud the Brownie Guide promise that we would serve our God and our Queen. We felt that the Queen had enough servants and we definitely didn't want to serve God, so we were asked to leave. We didn't tell our mums and every Friday evening for months we had put on our Guide uniforms and gone to the amusement arcade at the beach, got changed in the toilets and hung about at the slot machines looking at boys and buying candy floss with our Guide money. Our sham was over when Mrs. Howie, the Guide leader, met Carol's mum at the bus stop and our mums made us go the next Guide meeting and apologise.

I put my hand in Carol's. "You okay?"

I hadn't seen her since the last time I was home a year ago, and it felt like we had been together last week. Every time I came back to Kilbrannan, even after twenty-five years, it felt like I had been gone for a few days, and Carol and I just slotted back in to our lifelong friendship.

"Remember the last time we were in here and we got chucked out of the Guides?" She snorted, trying not to laugh. "And we had to go and apologise to that old bag Mrs. Howie. I still see her in the town, and she still glares at me, after thirty years!"

"Do you think that might be because you shouted 'God save the Queen, the fascist regime' at the top of your voice as we were running out of the church?"

I couldn't stop the little snort. It was still funny. We had lain on the roundabout in the swing park that night and laughed and screamed until we could hardly breathe, then for days we had laughed whenever we thought about it.

"But right now, you should be sad. Grandpa Jimmy is dead. This is a funeral. Why is no one sad? Your mum's not even crying, and it's her own dad—he's not even my real grandpa, and I'm the saddest person here!" I gestured around the church. People were chatting and whispering as if it were a wedding or a christening. Even the minister had been cheery when he talked about Grandpa Jimmy's life and how he was in the war, and about his family and eternal rest and Heaven. When we had sung his favourite hymn, "We Have an Anchor," the voices had been spirited and loud, not mournful or grieving. I could hardly sing with the big sad lump in my throat.

"Karen, I am sad, but my grandpa was almost ninety years old. He never had a day's illness in his life and died sitting on his girlfriend's couch with a cup of tea in one hand, a cigarette in the other and a plate of chocolate digestive biscuits on his lap. He had just had his favourite dinner—pork chops, chips and peas—and was watching the horse racing. He had a good long life—it's not that sad."

"Carol! It's tragic. I was looking forward to visiting Grandpa Jimmy and now I'll never see him again, never." A big tear plopped down onto my hymn book.

She gripped my hand. "He was looking forward to seeing you too. He had bought Jaffa Cakes and Chocolate Mini Rolls especially. He didn't actually mean to die before you were all supposed to be coming over next month. But he had a good, full life and it was his time. I see tragedy every day at the hospital, Karen, and this is not one. I do miss him and I feel sorry for Mrs. Fleming and my mum and Uncle Jakey, but it was his time, you know. And today is not the day, but you are going to tell me what this nonsense is about you leaving your husband."

Carol's mum turned to shush us as the burnished mahogany coffin, completely covered with beautiful white flowers, was lifted onto the shoulders of the six pallbearers. The cortege slowly made its way down the aisle as the organ played "Abide with Me." I sobbed quietly.

As they passed the third pew, two very old men wearing tartan trousers, tartan berets with cockades and dark regimental jackets covered in highly polished medals on ribbons stood up and walked slowly behind the coffin. Their bodies were sore and bent and they were leaning on walking sticks, but their bearing was noble, their pale rheumy eyes dignified and proud as the old soldiers stared straight ahead and marched with their brother-in-arms for the last time.

I heard a loud sniffing beside me. A big man in front of me blew his nose loudly. Handkerchiefs appeared from pockets and handbags and were passed from pew to pew as the sniffling, sobbing and nose blowing spread through the church. Carol linked her arm through mine.

I looked up at Saint Andrew as the sunlight illuminated his robe and flooded the church with light.

2. My Way

AFTER THE BURIAL, WE ALL GATHERED IN THE CHURCH hall, apart from the two old soldiers who, amidst much handshaking, were picked up by the ex-servicemen's minibus at the graveyard. It turned out that they were the last of their Black Watch regiment, many lost as young men in wartime France, the rest taken by time. For the past sixty-five years, the entire regiment, including Grandpa Jimmy, had turned up for every funeral. Now there were only two of them left, and at the next funeral, there would be only one. Then none. It seemed unbearably moving and dignified and inspirational and sad.

The church hall still smelled the same—musty, dusty and of wax floor polish. The Women's Guild ladies had arranged the room nicely, each trestle table adorned with a starched white table cloth and little posies of fresh flowers. Carol's mum and Auntie Julie were surrounded by well-meaning sympathizers as her Uncle Jakey and nephew Christopher lurked in the doorway having a smoke. I was still jet-lagged; it was dinner time in California, or breakfast time maybe; and there were huge piles of the kind of sandwiches I loved and hadn't tasted since I was home last year. Fresh white Mothers Pride Scottish bread with the hard crust, filled with a selection of pink tinned salmon, peppery eggs mashed with butter, and grated Lockerbie cheese with tomato, all cut into tiny delicious rectangles and piled high on huge white oval plates. The white-haired, big-bosomed, well-meaning Guild ladies were circling the room, bustling around with massive teapots, pouring strong hot tea into china cups, and I was desperate. I took my chance when Carol got waylaid by two elderly ladies and filled my plate with the soft full sandwiches, picked up a cup of tea and was making my way to the corner when I saw Mrs. Fleming, sitting on her own. I thought about making a detour, but she had seen me.

I sat down beside her, putting one hand on her arm and the other on an egg sandwich. She was as neat and elegant as ever, in a smart navy dress with pearls in her ears and around her neck, her fat little feet squashed into very high heels, her old sweet face covered in beige powder and pink rouge. She gladly accepted my cup of tea. It was a huge sacrifice for me to hand it over but the poor woman had just lost her companion. And I had just lost my cup of tea.

"I'm so sorry, Mrs. Fleming, I know how much…"

"Yes, dear, we were together for over thirty years, Jimmy and me. I don't really know what I'm going to do without him. It was such a shock. One minute he was enjoying his tea and his chocolate digestive biscuit and the next minute he was gone. He was just about to go out and water the sweet peas and then he was dead. He never did finish his cup of tea…"

Her eyes filled and so did mine. I was so grateful when an ample lady in a floral pinny, her hair in a neat bun, interrupted us to pour us tea.

"Karen, dear!"

Oh no, she knew me. I couldn't place her and definitely didn't want to talk to her. But the tea was so welcome and she was holding a plate of grated cheddar cheese sandwiches, so I forced a smile. "Hello Mrs…"

She leaned forward. I could clearly see where her thick makeup stopped in a straight line on her jaw. Very orange face, very white crinkly neck. I tried not to stare. Nice pastel Marks & Spencer's cardigan and sensible beige tartan pleated skirt, like almost all her other Guild pals with the teapots. Quite a posh voice, did she used to help at the church youth group? Tufty Club? Library? Definitely from a bought house, not the council scheme like us.

"When did you get back, my dear? How long are you here for? Have you seen your mum and dad yet? Are they here? How are they enjoying their retirement in Spain? Oh my, Spain! Lucky things, well apart from the Spaniards and the funny food, and they don't speak English there, do they? And they didn't support us in the war either, humph. Does your dad still play bowls? I bet your mum loves the sunshine; she could dry her washing outside every day, oh my. You must be cold here after you living in America for so long. You're a right Yankee, so you are! Look at your nice teeth and lovely hair. I remember when you and Carol were a right pair of wee rascals running around on your bikes with that daft dog of yours. You two have been best pals your whole lives, haven't you? How old are your children now? They must be getting big! And that husband of yours, I heard he designed that big tower in Dubai, oh my, it must be grand, and you a teacher, you've done well for yourself, you were such a cheeky wee lassie, so you were, a right wee besom! Your granny was demented with you, so she was. Oh hello, Mrs. Fleming, I'll go and get you a wee biscuit, you'll be needing it after that terrible shock with Jimmy." And she was off. Neither of us had said a word and we half-smiled at each other.

"Who was that?" I whispered.

"Mrs. Montgomery, from the Post Office." Mrs. Fleming rolled her eyes.

"Oh that old busybody! My husband didn't design the tower, Mrs. Fleming. He's working on a project in Dubai Airport. I don't know where that tower story came from. I've heard it three times today."

"Where do you think?" she said slyly, nodding her head towards Uncle Jakey. "Jake McMillan, fifty-nine years old going on fourteen. I don't know how Julie puts up with him. His father spoiled him rotten, dear, especially after his mother died. But he was already in his late twenties by then, and Jimmy wouldn't listen to me. I miss him so much, Karen."

Her old hand freckled hand was shaking as I took it in mine.

"Me too. You two were together for so long. I must have been about fifteen the first time I saw you together."

"That's right, dear. Carol was fifteen when her granny died and I started stepping out with Jimmy six months later. My Thomas had been gone for a long time then, I was only forty when I lost him and I never thought I would find happiness again. But I did, with Jimmy. We were so happy, dear."

"I always thought you would..." I stopped myself.

"Get married, dear? Everyone thought that. But we were happy the way we were. I had a nice gentleman friend to twirl me around the dance floor. Can you imagine what it's like sitting at the side all the time? And I made his tea every night, we went to the dancing on a Friday and Saturday, had our nice holidays in St. Anne's and in Berwick, had a wee kiss and a cuddle. But I never had to wash his socks and shirts, never had to listen to him snoring, never had to see him without his teeth in the morning, never had to bother with him coming back drunk from the bookies or the pub. And every night I got my warm bed to myself with a wee cup of tea and my magazine. I got what I wanted, dear. Thomas was still my husband—he wouldn't have wanted me changing my name. Besides, I would have lost his Post Office pension. Yes, my dear, we were happy the way we were, me and Jimmy."

We were interrupted by a commotion on the small stage at the end of the hall. Uncle Jakey was standing there, in his thirty-five-year-old "good suit," the brown lapels almost as wide as his yellow tie. His hair was still long but not so dark or thick any more, in fact not there at all in some places. He clapped his hands to get our attention.

"Oh dear God, what is he doing. He's drunk. You have to stop him. This is his father's funeral." Mrs. Fleming was frantic.

My eyes desperately searched the room for Carol or her mum, or Auntie Julie, but I couldn't see them. The room went silent.

"Stop him," Her voice was urgent.

I was frozen to the folding seat. I raised my hand and opened my mouth but nothing came out.

"Ladies and gentlemen!" he shouted. He had a spoon in his hand.

He looked ridiculous as usual—his clothes, hair, teeth, platform shoes, all stuck in a terrible 1970s time warp. This was horrific. But hysterical. People were looking frantically around the room. There was a horrible silence. Julie was sitting with her head in her hands. I knew what Jakey was going to do and tried so hard to stifle the inappropriate laugh that was bubbling inside my throat.

The silence grew thick. Jakey stomped his shiny plastic platform boot three times, put the spoon to his mouth like a microphone and closed his eyes, his voice loud and clear as he started to sing "My Way" in a ridiculous Frank Sinatra impersonation.

The smokers in the doorway scuttled back inside to see what was going on. The Guild woman in the back kitchen scurried through to form an outraged huddle with the teapot ladies.

His eyes were closed, his head slowly nodding up and down, as he sang his signature song.

As he reached the crescendo, he paused, gesturing for us all to join in, which no one did apart from his son Christopher, who still had a lit cigarette in his hand and was wearing his usual *Miami Vice* outfit of a pink T-shirt underneath a baggy cream suit, sleeves rolled up and slip-on shoes with no socks, an outfit that would have looked fantastic thirty years ago. Christopher's cigarette waved a gesture of support to his father, who stamped his huge platform boot, shut his eyes, lifted his head and wailed the next verse.

Then it got even louder and there was a dramatic pause between each word.

Auntie Julie had covered her eyes as her husband continued. Carol was nowhere to be seen. Mrs. Mackenzie and Jennifer were hiding in the kitchen and everyone else was frozen with horror. Except me. I had to bite my knuckles to stop myself laughing. This was a man of almost sixty years old, dressed like an Empire catalogue page from 1975, holding a spoon to his mouth and singing his heart out as if he were Frank Sinatra in his Vegas heyday.

He looked solemnly around the room, his head nodding in time to the imaginary orchestra, then he put the spoon back to his mouth and spoke sincerely in his best Elvis Tennessee accent about having his regrets and his fill of losing.

"Aye, at the horses, big man!" shouted a fat man in a cheap suit from the back of the hall.

Jakey gave him the thumbs up and continued singing at the top of his voice into the spoon.

Carol appeared at my side, her eyes red and watery with trying to hold in the laughter. She sat beside me. We couldn't look at each other, my seat was shaking, and she was letting out little snorts.

Jakey was building up to his finale, one arm reaching to the ceiling, the other holding the spoon to his mouth. The singing was really loud by now as Christopher, who actually did have a good voice, picked up a teaspoon and joined in the crescendo about doing it their way.

For the last lines, Jakey's boot stomped in time to each word as Christopher pumped his fist in the air.

We spent the next forty-five minutes hiding in a toilet at the back of the church hall, trying to control our laughter and compose ourselves sufficiently to rejoin Grandpa Jimmy's funeral tea. Ever since I had moved to California twenty-five years ago, I had come back to Kilbrannan every single summer, and every summer, it felt like I had been gone for about a week. And this was what I missed most, being seventeen years old again with Carol.

3. I'm Not in Love

IT HAD BEEN ANOTHER SCORCHING, SUNNY DAY AND THE evening air was warm and still. Rather than the usual cold lashing rain and low grey skies that routinely marked the beginning of the school summer holidays in the West of Scotland, we were having what passed for a heatwave. The *Daily Record* had marked the occasion of the 70 degree temperatures with headlines of "Scotland Sizzles" above photographs of grinning wee ginger-haired boys in their swimming trunks digging holes on Ayr Beach. Carol and I spent our days lying on our mums' scratchy towels on Kilbrannan Beach, me unsuccessfully trying to eke out a tan on my freckly pale skin, Carol slowly turning golden brown, listening to Radio One on her tiny orange plastic radio, looking for boys and daring each other to put our feet into the frigid sea. Then at six o'clock, I went to work on the ice-cream van and she helped her mum. The warm evenings always brought crowds to the van and I could tell that Mr. Ross was panicking that we would run out of ice cream like we had last Thursday when there had almost been a riot on Arran Avenue with some swearing and heckling. I thought it was amazing that grown women the same age as my mum planned their evenings around the television and a ten pence cone.

The gathering at the ice-cream van was growing restless as Mrs. McNamara chattered on as usual, her fat pink elbows blocking the window. She stood there in her fuchsia fluffy slippers, her hair dyed as black as coal and pulled into unflattering curls as small and tight as her face. I knew the factory early shift got out at 3 PM. It was now eight o'clock in the evening and here she was, still in her blue shiny work overall. All the factory women did that. They got out of the early shift when the horn blew at 3 PM, came home on the bus together, smoking and chattering loudly, brought in the washing, went to the shops, made the tea, did the dishes, then came out to the van in their shiny overalls. It never seemed to occur to them that they could get changed.

"I saw your mum in the butcher's shop, Karen. She was buying some nice gammon steaks. Did yous have them for your tea?"

"We did, Mrs. McNamara."

Mr. Scott shot me a look of displeasure as he scooped the ice cream onto the four cones he held in one hand—I could only hold one at a time but had just been working on the ice-cream van since school stopped for summer three weeks ago. He should help me get rid of her, but nobody ever did; they all just sighed and shuffled and rolled their eyes as she blethered on and made us late. Ever since Mr. McNamara had been killed at an explosion in the factory, she was above reproach and she knew it.

"Was it tasty, your gammon steak?"

"Lovely, thanks."

No, it was horrible. It was a dead pig. I want to become a vegetarian but my mum won't let me.

"Did yous have it with pineapple?"

"We did, Mrs. McNamara. And chips."

"Oh, I'm no a chip haun myself. I prefer those new potatoes."

The gathering tried to shuffle across to Mr. Scott's side of the queue.

"Would you like some ice cream, Mrs. McNamara? It has been hot today."

"Effing roasting. Aye, a wee cone with raspberry, hen, and twenty Benson & Hedges. And a Raisin and Biscuit Yorkie; they're dear, them, but I like a wee treat on a Monday night."

She said that every night.

Behind her, two women in matching factory overalls were talking about Emily and Ernie Bishop going on holiday to the Lake District, discussing Gail working in Elsie's shop and debating the twenty quid that Albert had won at the bingo. They were talking about *Coronation Street*, not about real people they knew. It was unbelievable.

Then I saw him. Bobby Henderson, sailing around the corner on the skateboard he had made from an old roller skate nailed onto a length of wood with a bit of old carpet glued on top.

My heart stopped as the crowd disappeared before my eyes. Carol and I had stolen a single from Woolworths last summer, 10 CC's "I'm Not in Love," and I had been singing it to myself all day. I was not in love with Bobby Henderson. It was just a silly phase. I took Latin and French and was in the school choir and Bobby Henderson was in remedial and smoked. He turned and skated back into Harbour Road and out of sight. He knew I worked on the van. He must have been looking for me.

"How much is that, hen?"

"Sixty pence, please, Mrs. McNamara."

"Twelve bob! That's scandalous!" cried a voice from the back.

The crowd laughed quietly. Mr. Balfour came to the van every night with his wee scruffy dog, Winston, in his arms. He was a very old retired railway man with a shiny head and white flyaway hair above his huge giant waxy ears that I always tried not to look at, and he always came to the van in his string vest with his trousers pulled almost up to his armpits and tied with an old belt. Why did people around here not get dressed? Winston was friendly though and I always gave him broken wafers.

"It's what it costs, Mr. Balfour."

Mrs. McNamara always stood up for us. She put her hands on her ample hips and turned to scold him.

"And you have to start using the new money, Mr. Balfour. Decimalisation," she continued, talking over the heads of the dozen or so amused people gathered around the ice-cream van window.

"It's been years since they brought in the new money, isn't that right?" She appealed to Mr. Ross to back up her argument. His neck grew red and his long face grimaced.

"You just have to get used to it." She continued. "Things are dear now since the decimalisation."

"Well, it's a damp scandal, so it is." He glared at Mr. Ross. "A wee cone used to be a shilling. Now it's ten pence. That's three times the price! Daylight robbery."

I could see Mrs. McNamara trying to work it out as she stuffed her cigarette packet, Yorkie bar and purse into her overall pocket while trying to keep the lit cigarette in the air. Mr. Ross drummed his fingers on the Formica counter. I tried not to laugh.

"A shilling is five pence, and two shillings is ten pence, so a wee cone is two bob now, not three." She sucked on her cigarette in triumph then shuffled back to her telly and fags as Mr. Balfour grumbled about Ted Heath and the Common Market while Winston licked the window.

Bobby Henderson was standing at the back of the queue.

My cheeks burned. My hands were shaking.

He was gorgeous. He was the most gorgeous boy in Kilbrannan. Light silky brown hair down to his shoulders flicked back like Woody in the Bay City Rollers. Light brown eyes. Looking right at me. He smiled. I dropped the ice cream scoop into the tub.

I'm not in love with Bobby Henderson.

I tried to breathe normally and get through the customers. Bobby Henderson was definitely standing in my half of the queue.

Finally, there he was looking up at me and smiling, beautiful in his brown tank top, yellow shirt and brown bellbottoms—and I was horrible in my blue overall which looked like Mrs. McNamara's.

"Hi, Karen."

"Hi, Bobby."

It came out quieter than planned.

"One Embassy Regal and a match please."

Our hands touched briefly as I handed him his change.

He grinned then skated down the street. I stared after him. He was gorgeous. He knew my name. I loved Bobby Henderson.

4. Love Me Tender

"PUT YOUR LEFT FOOT RIGHT BEHIND YOUR RIGHT FOOT, and swivel round. No, to the left! Follow the foot at the back!"

Carol's Uncle Jakey was teaching us the Hustle. Although he was quite old, nearly thirty, he liked the same records as us—Queen, ABBA, Showaddywaddy and Rod Stewart—and he always gave us money to go to the pictures. Carol thought he looked a bit like Rod Stewart, as did many of the young girls and mums on our street, but I thought he looked more like Paul Nicholas who sang "Dancing with the Captain," although I don't think that Paul Nicholas nor Rod Stewart sat about their sisters' fake leather couches drinking Tennent's lager, eating tomato sauce crisps and laughing their heads off at *The Banana Splits* and *Scooby Doo*, and pretending to play a guitar to *Bohemian Rhapsody*.

Carol and I had our fifty pence tickets for the Civic Centre Disco on Friday night and I knew that Bobby Henderson was going to be there. I could hardly wait and had already carefully picked out my outfit: my new black high waisted bellbottoms that went right down to the ground over my four-inch-high red platform shoes with the three buckles, a red ribbed vest

17

top and red and black love beads. Bobby was sure to notice me wearing that fantastic outfit and dancing the Hustle with my hair flicked out like Farrah Fawcett Major. He always stood at the back of the hall with his group of rough remedial boys, all of them swearing, shouting crudely at girls and pushing each other around. They only left their dark sweaty corner to go out for a cigarette and a swill of vodka from the bottle they had hidden round the back, or to pogo and push each other around the dance floor to The Clash, The Boomtown Rats and the Stranglers, loud angry music that I didn't like. I knew his favourite group was The Sex Pistols as he always wore a black Sid Vicious T-shirt, but they never played their records at the disco. Even Radio One had banned them. Bobby had never spoken to me at the disco nor asked me to dance, but he always watched me, nodding his head a bit when I caught his eye, so I thought that he secretly fancied me but was too shy to approach me. That's what Carol and I had decided in the many hours we spent lying on opposite sides of my bed in the darkness, our legs on the brown velvet bean bag in the middle as we listened to Radio Luxembourg, burning musk incense, eating Jaffa Cakes and watching my lava lamp make slow fantastical ghostly orange shapes.

I had been in love with Bobby Henderson for eighteen months, and he still hadn't made his move, even though we followed him home from school three days a week. On the other days, we ran to the nearby Catholic school to follow Dan Capaldi, the boy from the chip shop that Carol loved. I had read an article in *The Jackie* magazine about how to tell if a boy secretly likes you, and all the signs were there— Bobby Henderson looking at me, pushing his pals when we passed in the school corridor, shouting a bit louder when I was there, looking to see if I was watching him as he kicked his pals on the dance floor. I just needed to encourage him to approach me. It was time for Bobby Henderson to make his move and it was time for me to give him the opportunity; that was all he was waiting for. If I danced the Hustle really fantastically on Friday night, he might be so amazed and impressed that he would ask me for a slow dance at the end—my heart thumped every time I thought of being that close to him.

Mrs. Mackenzie was at work, so we had pushed the couch against the living room wall to give us more room. Jennifer sat on the armrest watching us while her raspberry ice lolly dripped all over her chubby little legs, her Tiny Tears doll, and the yellow leatherette cushions.

I lifted the arm of the record player and put it at the beginning of the LP, then rushed back to my place on the swirly brown and orange carpet. We stood in line with Jakey in the middle and this time we were fantastic, it was amazing. We turned in unison, we clapped and changed direction, the swivels were perfect. I loved dancing and it was thrilling when we got it right.

"Lassies, that was brilliant! Yous could be in Pan's People on *Top of the Pops*—I'm going to phone Jimmy Saville and tell him! Yous two are definitely going to get lumbers at this disco. Want me to pick you up at the end?"

We definitely did not want him anywhere near the Civic Centre Disco after the debacle at the school Christmas dance, where he had volunteered to come as a helper and when all the other normal mums and dads were giving out juice and crisps, he was dancing in the middle of the school assembly hall in his yellow Simon shirt, brown bellbottoms and platform shoes with several hundred fourteen-year-olds copying his every move.

The Rector was blustering and angry, stalking up and down the stage in his black gown, stomping his black shiny shoes, insisting that the D.J. play "The Military Two Step" that we had all been practicing for weeks at gym, but the D.J. was Mandy Miller's uncle who had been in the same year as Jakey at this school and had also been expelled, so he just laughed and played the records from the list that Mandy had put in his pocket.

Jakey was in his glory. He had organized the entire third year, including the remedial boys, the rugby team, and the cool group who liked Genesis and Yes into lines for Showaddywaddy's "Under the Moon of Love"; he had put everyone in a huge circle with him in the middle for The Real Thing's "You to Me Are Everything" and had danced a spectacular solo to The Bay City Rollers "Bye Bye Baby." Well, that is what we heard, as Carol and I had spent the evening cringing in a locked toilet by the science lab.

Everyone knew that we had brought him and even though it was embarrassing, it had done wonders for our social life. Two boys had asked me out after it, but not Bobby Henderson. Carol had also got an A+ for French as Miss Callan obviously fancied her Uncle Jakey and kept asking us how he was and if he was at home or on his oil rig. So after all that, we didn't want him anywhere near the Civic Centre on Friday night, especially if Bobby asked to walk me home.

"Okay, okay, I get the hint. You don't want your big tough uncle to get in a fight with your boyfriends. Let's have one more practice. D.J., music! *Do the Hustle!*"

I put the record back on and ran back to complete a perfect, thrilling Hustle, which was just finishing when Carol's Auntie Julie burst in the front door. She ignored her husband as she looked frantically around.

"Is Jeanette in? Put that music off!"

Jennifer ran to the record player.

Julie was wearing her red nylon supermarket overall as usual. Every day, I wondered why women around here did not get changed after work.

"Is Jeanette here?" Julie's voice was urgent.

"Where's your mum, Carol, where is she?" Julie had started to cry and was fumbling in her overall pocket for her cigarettes.

"She's at work, Auntie Julie. She'll be back in half an hour. What's wrong?"

I could sense Jakey's rising panic. He hated anything emotional or womanly and was desperately thinking of a reason to leave. He put his hand stiffly on Julie's shoulder. She shrugged him off.

"Oh just go, ya daft gowk, go on, get out!"

He grabbed his cigarettes and lighter from the mantelpiece and ran out the door and up the street in the direction of the bus stop. Julie threw herself onto the couch, too distraught to notice her ample backside landing on the ice lolly. We sat on either side of her. Unlike Jakey, Carol and I loved nothing better than a good drama and one was about to happen.

"What is it, Auntie Julie?"

Her hands were shaking, her eyes red, her breathing laboured.

"It's Elvis. He's deid, hen. Elvis is deid!"

The last word came out as a high-pitched, almost silent squeal as she burst into copious tears, causing Jennifer to run upstairs with her doll.

"Elvis the Alsatian next door?"

"Naw, hen," she sobbed. "Elvis Presley. The King. Fae Memphis Tennessee."

I made Auntie Julie a cup of tea and lit her cigarette for her, which she sucked on desperately while Carol comforted her by rubbing her hand. We really did love all this although we couldn't understand why she was so upset about an old singer in America that she had never met. When Carol's mum burst in ten minutes later, in her blue nylon factory overall, she was already bawling as someone on the bus had told her about Elvis. She threw herself into Julie's arms as they rocked backwards and forwards on the yellow couch, inconsolable and hysterical. We had to light a cigarette for her too as her hands were shaking too much to open the box. It was the most tragic thing I had ever seen, two grown women in their nylon overalls and American Tan tights, huddled together wailing and crying, smoking one cigarette after another, with mascara trailing down their faces.

We sat on the yellow couch all evening—me, Carol, her mum, Auntie Julie and Jennifer, watching it on the telly— the huge sobbing crowds gathering outside Elvis's big fancy house, the shocked newsreaders, the police on motorbikes, the long black shiny cars with dark windows. Even the reporter in America was trying not to cry and had to stop and blow her nose in the middle of telling us about how Elvis's daughter had found out that her dad was dead. She was only Jennifer's age. That just made them worse and the crying got louder and more high pitched, the cigarettes smoked more urgently. Every time they showed a clip of Elvis singing, especially the really old black and white ones when he was young, the two women howled and bawled and clutched each other's hands. When he sang "Love Me Tender" they wailed with grief. Carol and I felt really important making cups of tea and lighting cigarettes. We were fascinated—all that raw emotion, the grief, the drama and the relief that no one we actually knew was dead.

At five o'clock, Carol's mum sent William to the chip shop as she was too distraught to make the tea, and they needed extra cigarettes and Anadin, so I got a black pudding supper and Vimto, and we got William to get us a Fry's Five Centre chocolate bar and a quarter of midget gems each with his mum's money, she was never going to notice. He bought two extra packets of Benson & Hedges too—one for himself and one to sell at school the next day.

We were still sitting there watching the telly, the room lit only by the television and two points of orange glowing from the cigarettes when my mum came over for me at half past ten, and even Carol and I were crying by then. My mum said that the chip shop had been empty all night and no one had gone out to the ice-cream van. It was sad that he had died. People had really loved Elvis. I wondered why I had never noticed him before.

5. Tonight's the Night

CAROL STOOD WITH HER HANDS ON HER HIPS, HER EYES searching the lines of clothes I had laid out on my bed. She had already rejected my red vest top as too plain for the night that Bobby Henderson was going to become my boyfriend.

"Not the gypsy skirt. I'm wearing mine tomorrow and we can't match."

She lifted my flowery layered skirt with attached lacy petticoat and folded it over the back of the little white wicker chair that we had carried home from the church jumble sale and painted, leaving white marks all over the back step and the grass.

"And that pinafore—" She lifted my new beige pinafore dress that tied at the back. "—needs to go to Oxfam. You don't suit it. Your face is pale, your hair is light, and with that beige dress on you'll look naked. You shouldn't buy clothes without me."

"But I like it."

"Oxfam." She replied emphatically, folding the dress onto the brown shag pile carpet.

"Now this—" She picked up my new cheesecloth shirt. "—is perfect. The blue and brown vertical stripes will be slimming, and you could tie it up at the waist, it'll be a bit sexy but not tarty."

She picked up and discarded my black cords, then homed in on my Wrangler jeans.

"With these! The shirt tied up and unbuttoned at the top. These jeans make your bum look great. My narrow gold belt, the blue espadrille wedgies from the market, the high ones, your new blue love beads tied around your neck to draw his attention to your boobs, all your silver bangles, and you can borrow mine too to make a stack on your arm, looks good when you dance, and I'll do your nails. Then the chamomile rinse in your hair, and I'll flick it out like Farrah Fawcett Major. Bobby Henderson will not be able to resist you! This is it, Karen. It's time."

At the mention of his name, my heart skipped a beat. I knew he was going to the disco on Friday. He had been looking at me at school and had smiled at me when we passed in the corridor, although we had only passed because I ran around the A block between English and German so I could casually be walking past the remedial class when he was going in. He had smiled right at me as he pushed a wee first-year boy into the wall. I loved him. I sat on the shiny yellow eiderdown and picked up the jeans.

"Do you think he likes me, Carol? I mean, you're not just saying that?"

I picked some wood chips out of the wallpaper and flicked them into the flowery plastic bin.

"Karen, I know he likes you. Everyone can see it. He always stares at you because he fancies you! You will be gorgeous tomorrow, and you know what to do. Look him in the eyes for exactly three seconds, then look away. Count to three, then look at him again. That's how a boy knows you want him to come over. I read it in *The Jackie*."

We started to get ready straight after school the next day. I was so excited and could hardly eat my chips, fried egg and beans or even hear what my mum was telling me about her and my dad going out to a dance that night. First I had a peach-scented bubble bath with orange peel floating in it to make my skin soft, for when Bobby touched my arm, but it wasn't very relaxing as my mum kept shouting through the door that my dad needed to get into the bathroom to shave. I pretended I couldn't hear her, turned the radio up, wiggled my bright pink toenails above the bubbles and sang along to Rod Stewart's "Tonight's the Night."

Tonight really was the night.

I was tingling with anticipation, holding strands of my hair in front of my face to admire the blonde highlights brought out by the chamomile rinse. It had really worked and was well worth the ten pence it would have cost if I had bought it rather than slipping it into my blazer pocket in Boots the Chemist.

"Karen, this is ridiculous! I know you can hear me! You've been in there for an hour and a half now. Your dad needs to shave, we're going to the dance at the Masonic. Turn that racket off and get out right now! Karen, do you hear me?" She rapped noisily on the door as I pulled the plug. The last time I wouldn't get out the bath, my dad had turned off the electricity, which meant I couldn't dry my hair and had to go about looking like Crystal Tipps.

"I'm out. Sorry, Mum, didn't hear you!"

I had to lie on my back on the floor, bum in the air, to get my Wrangler size ten jeans on, easing the zip up very slowly, very carefully, a tiny bit at a time, one hand pushing in my tummy, the other pulling on the wooden coat hanger I had threaded through the zipper to give me more grip as I breathed in and sucked my tummy in as far as I could.

Finally, it closed—they were on! The size ten jeans were on! I had to roll around on the floor and hold onto my bed, then the chair, to pull myself upright as they were so tight, and I could hardly walk or breathe but my tummy looked really flat and the cheesecloth shirt did look great tied above the thin gold belt at my waist. Grabbing my blue clutch bag and curling tongs, I ran down the stairs and across the road to Carol's house, shouting "bye" as I slammed the front door behind me and kicked Carol's gate open.

I sat in front of the mirror at Carol's dressing table as she did my hair, rolling it round and round the hot tongs, then pressing the button to steam into place the big giant flicks. We were playing a tape of the charts we had recorded from Radio One on Sunday—our favourite songs were "Yes Sir, I Can Boogie" by two Spanish girls, and "Silver Lady" by Hutch from *Starsky and Hutch*. Everyone had to pick one—I picked Starsky and Carol fancied Hutch and we had stolen the single from Woolworths. Jennifer sat on the bed and watched as we danced around, the room filling with our excitement, the steam from my hair, my Charlie perfume and Carol's Moonwind scent that her mum had bought from the Avon lady.

We were ready. Carol looked fantastic in her black vest top and red and black gipsy skirt, her dark hair shiny and smooth in her new pageboy cut. I couldn't stop looking at myself in the mirror. Even Jennifer said that I looked fancy. My hair was flicked out so wide and really did look like Farrah Fawcett's. My blue eye shadow was thick across my eyelids, like how the blonde girl in ABBA did it, and I put on loads of black mascara and eyeliner, all pinched from Woolworths the day before, when we were there to steal the record. I had wound the love beads around my neck and the silver bangles were piled high from my wrist almost to my elbow, to jangle exotically when I danced.

The jeans were more comfortable as they heated up and I felt fantastic as I sprayed on some more perfume and slicked on my orange-flavoured lip gloss. We stood side by side, admiring ourselves in the mirror, grinning, then before we left, played Donna Summer's "Love to Love You, Baby" and danced with Jennifer around the tiny room.

The disco started at seven o'clock, but we didn't want to appear desperate so got there at ten past, waiting in the queue to pay our fifty pence entry fee to Mr. Anderson from my dad's Rotary Club. I hated it when he was on the door.

"Well hello, young ladies."

He was about a hundred and twenty years old and always wore his bowling club blazer, even to do this. It was pathetic. He took so long to count out the money and give the change but no one said anything to him or he wouldn't let them in.

"You both look particularly lovely tonight. But don't be talking to any young gentlemen or I will be forced to tell your father at our next meeting, when we will be discussing the tidal patterns of the Clyde Estuary!"

It was embarrassing, and everyone in the line behind sniggered, especially Kelly McNicol, who hated me. I hated her too, and was a bit scared of her as she was rough and loud. She was in all the thick classes like cookery and sewing and typing and was very thin with big boobs that everyone said was her bra stuffed with socks, and her long stringy bleached blonde hair had black roots. Her tight black drainpipe cords with punky zips all over them, low, tight black T-shirt and high pointy sandals made her look even more tarty than usual. I tried not to look at her.

"Thank you, Mr. Anderson."

Kelly McNicol snorted and flicked her cigarette ash at me but I just ignored her and we were in the door. She wasn't—Mr. Anderson wouldn't let her in with her cigarette so she went away in the huff. I was so relieved. I didn't want anything to spoil this night. I knew Bobby Henderson would be there, he was going with his pal Kenny and Kenny was in Alison Scott's gym class and he had told her they were going and she told me.

No one was dancing yet, even though they were playing "Jive Talking" and everyone loved that song. The room was dark and crowded and the music was thumping and exciting, I could feel it going right through my feet and into my tummy and my heart. I couldn't wait to dance. People stopped to look as Carol and I walked in—we were famous for starting off the dancing everywhere we went, so we walked carefully down the stairs as our wedgie shoes were high and the carpet sticky, and strutted right to the middle of the dance floor. We started right away, twirling, clapping, spinning around, standing back to back like the ABBA girls then facing each other and shaking our shoulders, spinning around holding hands and standing side by side to do our pointing move.

By the end of the song, the dance floor was half full and they were all looking at us. At me. And they were laughing. Frantically I looked around the room to see what they were laughing at. Kelly McNicol was standing on a chair pointing at me and jeering, screeching with delight. Then I saw it. My white bra shining brightly in the ultra violet light, illuminated in the darkness. My bra. My huge unsexy granny bra. A crowded room, with half my school in it and my horrible elastic Marks & Spencer's bra glowing in the middle of it. I put my arms in front of myself and walked quickly through the laughing crowd to the toilet where it became invisible again. I didn't cry until Carol and I were sitting upstairs on the bus going home ten minutes after we arrived.

The next day, Mr. Anderson came round to my house and gave me back my fifty pence. It was the worst day of my life.

6. The Hustle

October 1977

IT WAS A MONTH BEFORE I COULD FACE GOING BACK TO THE Civic Centre Disco after the Great Bra Debacle. I was hugely relieved to discover that Bobby Henderson hadn't been there as he had spent that terrible Friday evening in Kilbrannan Police Station after he and Kenny had been caught stealing a bottle of vodka and a hundred cigarettes from the minimarket. Thank you, God. Thank you, Jesus and Mary and St. Christopher and Mother Teresa. Thank you, Buddha and the pope. Thank you, Hari Krishna and the Dalai Lama. It was still humiliating to think about that evening, especially when Kelly McNicol pulled her school jumper into peaks and laughed whenever she saw me, but I had actually cried with relief when Alison Scott told me that Bobby had not been there. I lay low for four weeks, not calling attention to myself at school, working extra shifts on the ice-cream van and watching the telly with Carol until the raw crushing embarrassment started to fade. I would rather have frizzy ginger hair and thick National Health glasses and be fat and have acne forever than face that kind of social humiliation again, but I didn't die and Bobby Henderson had actually

31

talked to me in the school dinner queue when he asked me what time it was. That was clearly just an excuse to be close to me as it was obvious what time it was. I thought about it all day and was glad that Carol had seen it so we could talk about it on the way home, how he had picked me out from the 1,499 others in the queue and had stood so close to me that I could see his little fuzzy moustache and smell the Polo Mints and stale tobacco smoke on his breath. I was so overwhelmed with his gorgeousness that I had to hold onto the wall to stay upright. Then when he was walking away, he had turned and looked back at me. I could hardly breathe. He was so handsome in his grubby school shirt, his tie in a tiny rebellious knot. I had loved him for so long now and felt that something was finally about to happen.

So we went back to the Civic Centre Disco. I wore the same outfit as last time but with a tan-coloured bra, and although I still looked fantastic I was a bit nervous and didn't dance until the third record, which was "Jive Talking" again. No one laughed, no one pointed, and I saw Bobby Henderson watching me. My life was back. I didn't want to draw attention to myself, but when "The Hustle" came on and three older, nice-looking girls took to the dance floor, we joined them in a line. We were all great at it, the choreography was perfect and people actually clapped at the end. It was fantastic. It got even better when Bobby stood and watched Carol and me do our "Dancing Queen" routine. The dance floor was mobbed so he had to push his way through to see me and never took his eyes off me. He was definitely going to ask me tonight. I could feel the electricity between us, an invisible static thread between him and me. His pals pushed and kicked each other around to The Stranglers' "No More Heroes" and The Sex Pistols' "Pretty Vacant" but I couldn't see Bobby, he must have gone out for a cigarette and a swill of vodka to pluck up the courage to ask me.

Eleven different boys asked me to dance that night, and one called Joe with nice black hair and a clean ironed white shirt asked if I would be at the next disco, which I think was his way of asking me out, but Bobby was watching and my heart was racing so I pretended I couldn't speak English. I really couldn't think of anything better to say to get him to stop talking to me, and I didn't want Bobby to think I was interested in Joe.

Although the disco was really dark, they always dimmed the lights even more at the end to make it more romantic for the slow dance. Carol and I sat on top of a table watching the couples on the dim dance floor. A boy was walking towards us, smiling right at Carol. She gripped my hand—it was Dan from the chip shop, the boy she had loved for ages, the cheeky boy with the brown curly hair who always gave us extra chips and called Carol "babe."

"Go!" I hissed. "I'm waiting for Bobby."

We had this rule that neither of us could leave the other one sitting at the end of the disco, but tonight was different. I could see him, Bobby, my soon-to-be boyfriend, standing in the doorway searching the room for me. He saw me. Carol landed heavily on her platform shoes as I nudged her off the table. I had read in *The Jackie* that it was easier for a boy to approach a girl on her own rather than in a group, so she had to go. She looked at me nervously, then let Dan take her hand and lead her onto the dance floor. It was our favourite Leo Sayer record.

When I need you.

Carol slipped her arms around Dan's neck and smiled at me. She was beaming. She had loved Dan for so long. Tonight was the night for both of us; it was perfect. I could see Bobby walking into the hall towards me, beautiful, radiant, in his black leather jacket and drainpipe jeans.

He's coming over, don't look, don't look, do something. Look cool, look busy.

I fumbled inside my clutch bag, pretending I was looking for something. I could feel my knees shaking and I was struggling to breathe. I felt a tap on my shoulder.

"Want to dance?"

I spun around. It was Joe. Out of the corner of my eye I saw Bobby Henderson on the dance floor. His eyes were closed and his arms were around Kelly McNicol's horrible skinny waist, his beautiful hands on her ugly scrawny bum.

I felt the hot tears sting my eyes. Kelly McNicol did it with boys. She was going to do it with Bobby. His mouth was on hers, his hands in her horrible bleached stringy hair. The room spun. The voice came from very far away.

"Dance, please?" Joe was still there. I grabbed my bag and ran, called my dad at the Masonic Hall reverse charges from the phone box in the hallway and told him I felt ill, then I hid in the side porch crying my eyes out until I saw his Morris Maxi. I told him that Carol's mum was picking her up, but as we were driving off, she ran up to the car, banged on the window and jumped in the back. She was still beaming and didn't even notice my heartbreak and distress, then whispered to me that she and Dan had kissed and she had given Joe my phone number. So she got to kiss a boy before me, I obviously meant nothing to Bobby Henderson and he was going to do it with Kelly McNicol, the ugliest, tartiest girl in our school. It was the worst night of my life. My dad put my hand under his on the gear stick all the way home.

7. Ally's Tartan Army

"A QUARTER OF MIDGET GEMS PLEASE, A QUARTER OF Italian Creams and a Sherbet Fountain."

I looked at the Yorkie bars, lying in neat blue rows between the Twixes and the Toffee Crisps. Thick solid blocks of smooth delicious chocolate. They were fourteen pence each but I really wanted one.

"Oh go on, Karen, just get it, we're loaded!"

Carol was right. We were loaded. Carol's Uncle Jakey had been living with them for a few months, since his wife Julie had chucked him out. He had somehow got a job as electrician with an American oil company—two weeks on, two weeks off. The first two weeks of the month he spent sprawled on Carol's mum's yellow leatherette couch drinking lager, eating crisps, reading the *Daily Record* and watching the horse racing and the children's programmes with Jennifer—*Magpie, Blue Peter, Scooby Doo* and *How* were his favourites. When he lay on the couch or sat right back, his spare change would slip out of the huge pockets on his bellbottoms and gather underneath the cushions. Even though he was twenty-nine, he liked to rub his bum from side to side to make farting noises just to annoy Carol's mum and make Jennifer laugh. When he did that, even more money fell out so we always pretended to laugh to get him to do it more. After two weeks of that, Uncle Jakey went back to the oil rigs, leaving behind a pile of washing for her mum, a bin full of empty Tennent's lager cans and a stash of coins down the back of the couch.

Every fourth Thursday at eight o'clock in the morning, a taxi arrived to take Jakey to Kilbrannan Station. At 8:15 he got the train to Glasgow, where he always met some pals from Liverpool in the Station Bar. After a few pints, they would pile into taxis to the bar in Queen Street Station, get the train to Aberdeen, meet up with their pals from Newcastle in that Station Bar, then somehow they got themselves to Aberdeen Airport and onto helicopters to get back to the oil rigs. Carol and I joined the small crowd of neighbours in their dressing gowns who always gathered to wave him off. Carol's Auntie Julie usually came too, with a lot of makeup on for that time in the morning. As the taxi drove off, with Jakey hanging out the window waving while the driver beeped the horn, Carol and I would run back into her house, roll up the sleeves on our school shirts and thrust our hands down the back of the couch, gathering money. We didn't bother with the one pence and two pence pieces, the fifty pences were what we were after, their shape obvious to our well trained fingers. By the time Carol's mum and brother came back in and the women in dressing gowns had gone back to their kitchens, our pockets were full. Today had been a good day, reaping us almost sixteen quid.

After school, we told my mum that we were going to the swing park at the beach, then to the China Palace for our tea. Jennifer was swinging on the gate in her shorts, T-shirt and bare feet when we ran across to Carol's house to tell her mum. The front door was lying open. Jennifer just pointed into the house and wiped her nose on her wrist.

Carol's mum and Aunt Julie were sitting in the kitchenette at opposite ends of the tiny fold-down table, the ashtray between them overflowing. Their faces were ashen and Auntie Julie had been crying. Carol clutched my arm. We said nothing, waiting for the terrible news. Julie looked right at us, her eyes red, her face streaked with mascara. Carol's mum sobbed quietly as she stirred her tea. Someone must have died. This was horrible, but at least we both knew it wasn't Jennifer who had died as we had just seen her swinging on the gate.

I found Carol's hand and held it. She tightened her grip and we were ready.

"What is it, Mum?"

Julie stubbed out her cigarette and spoke, her voice quiet and raspy. "It's Jakey. The daft bastard has went and ran away."

"He just went back to the rigs, Auntie Julie."

"No, hen, he didnae. Me and your mum have been frantic all day. All day, haven't we, Jeanette?"

Carol's mum nodded gravely and took a deep draw on her cigarette.

"Your mum got a phone call this afternoon from a big Yankee who said that Jakey hadn't turned up at Aberdeen Airport and they didn't know where he was."

I wondered how she knew that the Yankee was big just from his voice but thought I better not say it.

"We were frantic. Eric the taxi driver said he dropped him off the station as usual and Fiona in the pub in Glasgow Central said he was there until eleven o'clock with his Liverpool pals and had a pie and a pint, and she thought he was just going back to the rigs. But Margaret at Queen Street and Angela at Aberdeen Station said he hadn't been in, and all his Geordie pals were waiting for him, so we were worried sick, weren't we, Jeanette? We thought he had fell off the train, isn't that right, Jeanette?"

Carol's mum nodded solemnly again and took a sip of her tea.

We phoned the polis and every hospital in Glasgow and Aberdeen. And in Perth and Stirling as that's where we thought he might have fell off. Fiona phoned all the pubs around about George Square but no one had seen him. Then our William and his pal came in from school laughing and ceckling.

"Look at this!" She thrust the newspaper at us.

There he was on the front page of the *Evening Times*, Carol's Uncle Jakey. He was wearing a disheveled red kilt which hung almost to his ankles, blue football socks, his Scotland football top and no shoes. On his head was a giant yellow tartan hat and in his hand a can of lager raised triumphantly in the air. He was surrounded on all sides by dozens of similarly dressed men and one dog in a Rangers top.

I felt a snort try to escape from my nose. Carol's hands were shaking with mirth. I could feel her nipping me to stop me from laughing.

"He's ran away to the Argentine. He's joined Ally's Tartan Army, the daft bastard. Look at him, he's steaming! And what a brass neck for me. How can I ever go back to work? Black affronted, that's what I am, hen, black affronted."

Julie's outrage just made it worse. The snort escaped from my nose but I skillfully turned it into a cough.

"Where is the effing Argentine anyway?"

"It's Argentina. It's in South America, Auntie Julie. Underneath Brazil." Carol's voice was a high squeak. I couldn't look at her.

Julie's rage was growing. She thumped her empty cup onto the Formica table.

"South A-fucking-merica!? I'll South America him!"

She was going to South America him.

It was too much. Carol's snort exploded and mine came out as a kind of strangled scream as we turned and ran through the living room, past Jennifer on the gate, across the road, through my living room, then finally we burst out of my back door and threw ourselves onto the safety of the grass under my mum's washing. I screamed with laughter as the tears ran down my cheeks, lying on my back and kicking my feet hard on the cold grass. Carol lay on her tummy, thumping her fists and honking out each breath. Every time she caught my eye we screeched and guffawed afresh. When my mum came out to take in the washing and chased us away, we ran to the swing park and sat on the seesaw so we could see each other, and laughed until it started to get dark. When she silently pointed to her head, we screeched about the big yellow hat. When I helplessly pointed to my feet, we laughed about his missing shoes. When a wee dog ran past we howled about the dog in the Rangers top. It was the best laugh I have ever had in my life.

8. Rat Trap

"AMO, AMAS, AMAT, AMAMUS, AMATUS, AMANT," WE chanted, as the teacher beat the rhythm on his desk with a long wooden ruler.

Christine Bell leaned over to me, the loose knot in her tie the biggest I had ever seen, a small sign of rebellion at Kilbrannan Academy.

"Amant going to do any homework tonight."

"Amant wearing any knickers," I replied.

We stifled our giggles and continued to chant. "Amabo, amabas, amabat…"

It was warm and sunny outside, the sky clear and blue against the tops of the trees that brushed against the ancient creaky windows. Far away, someone was cutting their grass and a dog was barking. Last period of the day. Twenty minutes to go. I really wanted to be outside and not stuck in here. No one had spoken Latin for thousands of years. The ordinary Romans probably hadn't even ever spoken it: how could they ever have had a conversation with all those verbs and conjugations and declensions? How could you ever just say I'm late or Bobby Henderson is gorgeous? Except for the pope and some monks, I really couldn't see the point in anyone learning it, but Mr. Morrison the guidance teacher had said it was good for getting into university. It had some great words though, like *amabamus* and *homo* and *virginus*, and it was a laugh to say them out loud in class, especially the time we got to say homo erectus and Mr. Reid had had to whip his belt out of the sleeve of his gown and lash it against his desk to restore order to the hysterical class.

"Amabamus, amabatus, amabant."

"You're a bamus." Christine giggled.

"And you're a batus!"

Mr. Reid shot us a look and we straightened up, looking pointedly at the books in our hands, published by MacMillan & Co in 1953. 1953! My mum was probably still at school then. I tried to work it out in my head, counting back my mum's age from now.

"Miss Alexander!" Mr. Reid's voice was raised. He shuffled through some papers on his desk.

"Sorry, Sir."

"Miss Alexander, I have a note here stating that you have to go to the Rector's office right away. Off you go now. And Martin, I don't care if Kenneth did call you a homo, get back to your work."

Christine raised her eyebrows at me, and I shrugged my shoulders—I really didn't know why the Rector would want to see me. I loved getting sent messages for the teachers and walking along the wide silent corridors by myself, but this was a bit worrying. I knew I hadn't done anything wrong. Maybe they were going to pick me as the Dux. That would be fantastic and would definitely get me into university and out of Kilbrannan forever.

Miss Fraser the secretary made me wait in the dusty hushed corridor outside the Rector's office—I really hoped that no one would pass as it would look like I was in trouble.

My hands were sweating. From the music wing I could hear the school choir sing "Ye Banks and Braes o' Bonnie Doon" as Miss Harris thumped on the piano. Outside, a class was coming back from the hockey field shouting and laughing. Miss Fraser's typewriter was clacking rhythmically. I strained to listen to the muffled voices coming from the other side of the carved wooden door that said in gold "Dr. Euan F. McNab, M.A., Rector."

A chair scraped. Footsteps. The door swung open.

"Please do come in, Miss Alexander." Mr. McNab looked distracted as he ushered me in, smoothing his Brylcreemed grey hair into place. Carol was sitting on a chair in front of his huge wooden desk, looking at her feet. Beside her was her wee brother William, with a big smirk on his ugly spotty face. Mr. McNab didn't ask me to sit down so I just stood there, feeling stupid and awkward as he arranged his black gown and slowly sat on his throne.

"Now, Miss Alexander." He looked right at me. The Rector had always liked me. He liked the pupils who took Latin as he used to teach it. "William Mackenzie here has been found with a large sum of money on his person and he says that you gave it to him. Is this true? Yes or no."

I hated William. We both did. "No, Mr. McNab, sir. Definitely not, sir."

"Well he claims most emphatically that you and his sister—" He struggled with her name. "—Carol here gave him one hundred and fifty pounds."

I gasped. "No, Sir. Mr. McNab Sir. We did not. I only make fifty pence an hour on the ice-cream van and Carol doesn't even have a job, she just helps her mum with Jennifer."

William smirked right at me, his freckly face sneering and red. "You did sot. You gave me the money last night, you told me to hide it for you. You probably nicked it from the van."

"I did not!"

"You did sot!"

I appealed to the Rector's reason rather than argue with a stupid spotty ugly first-year. "Why would I do that, Sir? I never steal anything."

Carol coughed, her eyes avoiding mine.

"Well, that's what we are trying to find out, Miss Alexander. I have called Mrs. Mackenzie and asked her to come to my office first thing tomorrow to sort this matter out. So do both of you girls deny any knowledge of this sum of money?" He held the thick pile of five pound notes up for us to see.

"Sir, it definitely wasn't us. We were at the pictures last night and never even saw that thieving little ... boy."

"I am inclined to believe you, Miss Alexander. Both of you girls have exemplary records, whereas William here—" He pointed the money at William. "—does not. William, you stay here and these two young ladies can go back to their classrooms. I will speak to all of you tomorrow first thing sharp. Off you go."

We wanted to kill him, the sneaky lying wee bastard, trying to get us into trouble like that, and ran to the school gate at home time to kick him in and get the truth, but he must have jumped the fence and run home along the railway line. We found him with Snottery Mark outside the chip shop later that evening and ran at them, catching them by the hair and throwing them up a close that led to the bins at the back of the shops.

"I know where he got it!" sniveled Snottery Mark. "And I'll tell you if she lets me feel her boobs." He pointed at me.

"You grubby little pervert." I twisted his ear until he started to cry. "Where did you get the effing money?"

Carol had William on the ground, her knee in his back.

"Did you steal it from Mum's purse?"

"Leave me. I can't tell you, I promised."

"You'll tell me right now, you thieving little bastard!"

"I cannae tell. I'll get into trouble."

"Get in trouble? The effing Rector knows. You're already in huge trouble, you stupid little bastard!"

He was really crying now as Carol and I pummeled on his back as he crouched in a ball on the hard concrete. She pulled his leg straight and dug her fingers deep into the back of his knee as he howled in pain. I aimed a hard kick at his arse, my heavy wedgie shoes giving me a good swing at him. I was surprised by how much I was enjoying this.

"Uncle Jakey gave it to me yesterday."

"You lying wee bastard. He's away to Argentina. Where—did—you—get—the—money?"

Each word brought a hard kick to his backside.

"Stop it! It really was Uncle Jakey. He gave me the money. It was him, honest."

Snottery Mark ran away and Carol and I stopped our onslaught. William rolled over, covering his head in case we weren't really finished. We stepped back. He sat up, his horrible spotty freckly face bright red and covered with dirt. "He's no in Argentina. He's in Glasgow, staying with a wummin. He went to London on the train with Ally's Army but when he got to the airport, they wouldnae let him on the plane as he didnae huv his passport. His new pals flew to Spain and they're waiting for him there. They're going to Argentina on Saturday, except the one who's in the jail in Spain."

We were shocked, our jaws hanging open. It was bad enough Jakey running away with Ally's Tartan Army but now he was with another woman. Carol's Auntie Julie was going to kill him.

"He phoned me at Snottery Mark's house the other night, telt me where to find his passport. It was underneath all they dirty magazines under his bed. Then I dogged school, walked to the station with the passport and sneaked on the train to Glasgow. Uncle Jakey met me off the train, took me to Burger King and gave me two hundred quid so I wouldn't tell anyone. And he said I can keep his dirty magazines. I wanted to go to the World Cup too but he says I couldnae as Mum would kill him. He's still steaming, by the way."

"What about his girlfriend? Did you see her?"

"She's no really his girlfriend as he's married to Auntie Julie. She's called Mary, and he's just staying there 'til tomorrow. Then he's going to Spain. It's her husband that's in the jail there. She's dead fat but she's nice. She gave me a cigarette. Yous better not tell Mum."

If William still had the money, we would have split it three ways and never told anyone. But the Rector had it, so the three of us had to go home and tell Mrs. Mackenzie. She was raging. She didn't say anything but her face went tight and she was really sucking on her cigarette. We all sat there watching her, not really knowing what to do.

Finally she spoke, the words quiet and angry. "The daft bastard. Well he's just went too far this time."

That night, she put all his stuff into black bin bags, except for his dirty magazines, which she burned in the fire, put it all into Jennifer's old pram and wheeled it round to Julie's house.

The next day, Julie put it all out for the binmen.

9. Only the Lonely

IT WAS SO STRANGE HAVING NOTHING TO DO ON A SATURDAY night. Carol was going to the pictures with Dan again and I really didn't have anything to do or anyone to see. She had kind of been going out with Dan since last year, but still mostly going about with me, but now they were seeing each other every weekend, and I still didn't have a boyfriend. Carol and I had been going about together since Primary 5, and I hadn't bothered with anyone else. I did know other girls to sit with at school and have a laugh with, like Christine Bell in Latin and Lynne Hunter in P.E., but I had never seen them outside of school. I didn't even know who they went about with, maybe no one, maybe this was how it was for other girls who didn't have a best pal. It must be terrible for them to be like this all the time. I had always had Carol, and that had obviously been a big mistake. I had put all my eggs in one basket. My best friend had abandoned me for a boy. I would probably have done it to her if Bobby had ever asked me out, but we had never thought about this; we just thought we'd always go about together. I needed back-up pals. I couldn't just call Christine or Lynne now, at 5 o'clock on a Saturday and see what they were doing, it would be obvious that I was desperate, but I resolved to start the new campaign at school on Monday. We were Carol and Karen, Karen and Carol, some of the teachers and the dinner ladies didn't know who was who, people called me Carol all the time and I just answered to it. Carol's own mum had even called me Carol a few times. Now I was just Karen and I didn't know what to do. I sat on my bed and read some old *Jackie* magazines but they seemed silly and childish. I had an essay on *Macbeth* to finish, but homework on a Saturday night would just be tragic.

What I really needed was a boyfriend. It was obvious that Joe still liked me, after him tracking me down to the ice-cream van the other night, and Carol had said that Dan gave him my number and he would call me over the weekend. I hoped he would, and I had run to the hall every time the phone went, but it wasn't him. Maybe he had changed his mind or lost my number. Going out with Joe would solve everything—me and Carol, Joe and Dan, all going about together instead of me sitting in with my mum on a Saturday night. She kept asking what I was going to do. She obviously wanted to sit and watch the telly by herself. I started to clean out my drawers, putting all my pants and bras on the bed then folding them and putting them back in nicely, but I got fed up with that—I didn't even have any nice underwear— and threw everything into the drawer. It wasn't even tea time yet and I wished it was bedtime. This was unbearable. Was this lonely? Did other people feel like this? Was Christine in her bedroom reading a book right now? Should I call and find out?

It was still sunny. After tea, I would stop being pathetic and would go to the shops and buy chocolate and a magazine. At least I had money. Then I would have a bubble bath and paint my nails, listen to Radio Luxembourg, keep my spirits up.

I wished that Joe would call. I wished I had the courage to call Christine. I wished I had been nicer to her. I think she had actually hinted at us going to the pictures and things together but I had never really been interested. Now I was really interested. I would definitely talk to her in Latin on Monday.

Just as my mum shouted me down for my tea, there was a loud knock on the front door. It might be Joe! He might have lost my number and tracked down my house, and I sprinted to the door, stopped, and casually opened it, my heart thumping.

It was a policewoman and a policeman. They showed me and my mum a photo of a wee four-year-old boy, Aiden Townsley, who lived at the bottom of our street, and asked if we had seen him. I said yes, I had seen him that morning in the swing park when I was going to the shops for my mum. He was on the roundabout with the group of big and wee boys that he always went around with, his brothers and cousins. I told the policeman and he wrote it down and asked me what Aiden was wearing but I couldn't remember. I just remembered his curly blond hair going round and round. The policeman told us that Aiden had been missing for seven hours, which was just after I had seen him. He said that a lot of people had seen him in the swing park but they didn't know where he went after that. He just disappeared and the other boys couldn't find him. The policewoman asked us to check the garden hut, but he wasn't there. They gave me a card and asked me to call if I remembered anything else, like if I had seen anyone that I didn't know at the swing park or had seen Aiden again.

My mum put on her coat and went out to look for him but wouldn't let me come.

I was quite relieved, in case Joe called. She didn't even eat her tea, which was macaroni and cheese, so I had some of hers too. The loneliness was making me hungry. My mum had made my favourite Bird's Eye trifle, the kind that came in a box and you made up the jelly then the custard then whipped up the cream from the sweet-smelling powder and sprinkled Hundreds & Thousands on the top. I loved it and had only planned to eat a third but I just couldn't stop—the green jelly, the delicious cold cream, and I really did have nothing else to do. I knew my dad would be mad as he loved the trifle too but surely he would take pity on my loneliness.

I checked the hut again, and the coal bunker in case Aiden was hiding there, but he wasn't. I shouted for him and could hear other people shouting too. I was getting worried about him, and felt nervous in my stomach. It was a horrible evening, having nothing to do for the first time in my life, waiting to get into trouble about the trifle, waiting for Joe to call and now the wee boy missing. He should have been home by now, it was getting dark and he was only four. I remembered a few years ago it was the same thing with Snottery Mark's wee brother, everyone out looking for him and his mum about to phone the police when he turned up for his tea. This would probably be the same. Wee boys did that: they followed dogs and went to the beach and went away on their bikes.

Police cars went up and down the street all evening, and all the neighbours were out looking for him and shouting his name. At eight o'clock they brought in some police dogs from Glasgow, Alsatians that jumped out the back of the police van and sniffed urgently up and down the street.

Joe still hadn't called and I checked the hut again. I was really hoping Aiden was there but he wasn't.

The police dogs found him just after midnight in the woods a few miles into the country.

The whole town turned out for the funeral, lines and lines of people on the pavement. We all got the morning off school. There was complete silence—no cars, no boys out playing, just hundreds of people standing still on the pavement. My dad wore his fire brigade uniform and held his hat in his hand. He put his hand on my shoulder and held me against his rough jacket. Mr. Kirk across the road wore his policeman's uniform and took his hat off too. Mr. Stevenson even wore his janitor's uniform. When the cars slowly passed our house, I saw that the tiny white coffin was covered with flowers and teddy bears and Aiden's wee Celtic top, and I started to cry. He was only four. Most people just stood still, quietly sniffling, with some women sobbing—it was horrible to hear all those people I knew crying like that. Even the shops shut and put the shutters down and the buses stopped when the funeral cars went by. There were so many of them. It was the saddest day of my life.

We all went back to school in the afternoon and that evening Carol and I took Jennifer to the swing park. We had never done that before. We even bought her an ice lolly and pushed her on the swings. My mum and dad never mentioned the trifle.

10. Man in Black

EVERY WEDNESDAY, WHEN CAROL'S MUM WENT TO THE bingo with Auntie Julie, Carol had to go to her Grandpa Jimmy's house to make his tea. We used to love going there when her gran was alive. Grandpa Jimmy called us Anna and Agnes—he meant Anna and Agnetha from ABBA—and when we arrived, he would shout to his wife, "Quick, put the kettle on, Isa, hen. Anna and Agnes, the international superstar singers fae ABBA are here, all the way fae Sweden."

He said that every single week and we loved it. Carol's gran would bustle about in the kitchen and come through with a plastic flowery tray carrying a big stainless steel teapot, a milk jug in the shape of a Jersey cow with the milk coming out of the cow's mouth, a crystal bowl of sugar lumps, a butter dish, a jar of her bramble jam and a plate piled high with delicious warm homemade sultana scones. Then Grandpa Jimmy would bring through a plate of Jaffa Cakes and Cadbury's chocolate logs that he'd bought just for us.

"Wire in, lassies, wire in," urged Grandpa Jimmy every week. "Yous are far too skinny. Ye'll never get boyfriends in that state."

We really loved it when he said that as we thought we were quite fat.

Carol's gran and Grandpa Jimmy lived at the other side of the scheme in a council house which Carol's gran kept spotlessly clean. The garden was the nicest in the street, the letterbox the shiniest, the net curtains the whitest. She even swept the pavement outside the house to keep the leaves and cigarette butts away.

"My wee palace," she called it. I called Carol's grandpa "Grandpa Jimmy," but her granny I called "Mrs. McMillan," as she was old-fashioned and quite severe. She never smiled and always tutted, and I knew she didn't like me as she always scowled at me. I didn't like her either, but she was a great baker and I really loved Grandpa Jimmy. He was always smartly dressed when he wasn't at work at the harbour, always in a black suit and he had thick jet black dyed hair which he slicked back with Brylcreem. According to him, Johnny Cash's dad was from Glasgow and the singer was his cousin, and Grandpa Jimmy himself had given Johnny his first guitar and taught him everything he knew. He was always telling rubbish jokes and stories, talking about the time he had killed one hundred German soldiers with his bare hands, how he had brought down a Luftwaffe bomber over Clydebank by throwing rocks at it, and how he and his two army pals had been on the last boat out of Dunkirk, rowing it all the way to England with German bombs going off all around them. He always gave us money when he won at the horses, sometimes as much as ten quid. He had always liked to drink, but he was the funniest drunk I knew.

But then Mrs. McMillan died. I heard my mum say that Carol's gran was just walking up to the shops to get a loaf with her purse in her hand when she dropped dead on the pavement. That's what I heard as no one ever talked about it.

I was just glad that we hadn't seen her lying on the pavement dead with her big fat belly and wee skinny legs.

I didn't see Carol for two weeks after that. Their curtains were closed all day and my mum said that I had to stay away and give them peace to grieve. Then one day, Carol came to my door, we went and got a cone, Carol cried for a while, and that was that.

It was terrible going to Grandpa Jimmy's house after that. The garden quickly became overgrown with dandelions and the grass was as high as my knees. The flowers in the tubs had died as no one had watered them all summer. The gate was broken and hung on one hinge, and the curtains were always closed. The house was stinking of beer and cigarettes and B.O. and the telly was on night and day, but the worst thing was the state of Grandpa Jimmy.

Now he was smelly, miserable and unkempt and he looked like the tramp who lived in Glasgow Central Station, the one with the wild hair who walked about with a rope tied around his waist. Grandpa Jimmy had not cut his hair for months, nor shaved, and he had not gone to work for one day. The harbour had kept his job open but he wouldn't go, and wouldn't even leave the house. His eyes and nose were red with all the beer, and his house was dark, filthy, stinking and depressing. Carol's mum and Auntie Julie took turns cooking for him every night and when Uncle Jakey was home, he would take him fish suppers and beer, but Grandpa Jimmy didn't care, he just lay around all day watching the telly and stinking, ignoring all the people who came to the door. He didn't even put his false teeth in so he even sounded like a tramp.

One Wednesday, Grandpa Jimmy looked worse than ever.

"Sit down, lassies," he said somberly. "I have something to tell you."

We sat together on the couch while he stood in the middle of the cluttered dark room.

"The thing is, Carol, hen, I'm not long for this world. It's nearly my time, I can feel it." He wasn't drunk for the first time in months, and he spoke clearly and decisively as he had put his teeth in. "I'm not going to do anything daft. I'm just going to turn my face to the wall and wait for God to take me. I've had enough of this life. So, lassies, yous two are the most sensible people I know, so here…"

He handed me a plastic Lipton's bag. "Look in it, Karen, hen. I know you're not my real granddaughter, but I want you to have my records. These here are originals, signed by the Man in Black himself. I want you to have them, hen. Oor Jeanette never liked Johnny Cash, Jakey is daft, and young William would sell them at the Barras for a fiver. But I know that you'll look after them for me. And there's some Frank Sinatras in there too, signed by Old Blue Eyes himself in 1969. Worth a fortune."

I could feel my heart thumping with sadness and tears stinging my eyes. I couldn't look at Carol as I cradled the precious records.

"And you, Carol, hen, you're the only sensible person in this whole family, so I want you to have these." He handed her two tiny boxes, which she did not take.

"You're not going to die, Grandpa! I don't want them." She was really breaking her heart. We were both crying hysterically by now.

"It's my time, hen, take them."

One box, the black velvet one, had her granny's engagement ring in it, and in the flat wooden box were Grandpa Jimmy's two war medals on ribbons.

Carol's mum was raging when we ran in the door howling and crying. She put the ring and medals in her pocket, and then she threw the records into Jennifer's old pram, along with a plastic bucket, a bottle of bleach, a mop, rubber gloves, her plastic work apron, a pile of black bin bags and the hoover.

She was sucking on her cigarette, really annoyed. "Right, that's it. I've just about had enough of that daft bastard. He's just gone too far, upsetting you lassies like this for a piece of nonsense. I just lost ma mother, I'm on ma own, three weans, nae man, nae money, and yet every morning I manage to get us all up and out the door. He's a stupid, selfish drunk bastard is my faither, and I've had enough. Ma mother would be black affronted, so she would, with the state of that garden. It would break her heart, so it would, and her lovely wee hoose looking like a pack of manky tinkers moved in; it's ridiculous. Yer granny would be ragin' if she saw that. If that daft old bastard can survive pleurisy, one hundred Germans, Dunkirk and all that alcohol, he can survive this. He needs to give himself a good shake. Turn his face to the wall, my arse! He's fifty-nine years old with a good job waiting for him and it won't wait much longer. Make the wean's tea, hen, and bring the washing in. Phone Julie and tell her to go to your grandpa's house right now. I'll be back in time for *Coronation Street*. I'm going round there to get him telt." And at that she marched out of the door with the pram.

She came back in just as *Coronation Street* started and sat and watched it without saying a word.

The next time we went to his house, which was straight after school the next day as we were desperate to see if Grandpa Jimmy was dead, the garden was trimmed and neat. The flowers were still dead but the pots had been watered. Grandpa Jimmy was fixing the gate and he was clean, with no straggly beard. He had had his hair cut, his nails were trimmed, and the house was spotless and smelled like bleach and polish.

"Cup of tea, Grandpa?" suggested Carol.

"That would be lovely, Agnes, hen," he replied.

11. You're the One That I Want

"IF YOU WERE CHOCOLATE, YOU'D EAT YOURSELF. YOU'RE supposed to be going out with Joe, you know." Carol was making a big point of not being happy with me and was looking out of the opposite window, avoiding my eye. We were sitting on the high bench seat at the back of the bus on our way to the new ice rink in the next town, where I had arranged to meet a boy I had met there last week, on the first night of skating. It had been fantastic, so exciting, crowded with people our age, loads of gorgeous boys from other schools, loud music, a D.J. who took requests and coloured lights that flashed across the ice. The boy had skated right up to me as I stood at the side, gripping onto the rail to keep my balance. He was singing "You're the one that I want" as he held out his hand. I took it, we smiled at each other and skated round and round all evening, hand in hand, laughing and talking. He was gorgeous with flicked-out reddy-brown hair and was wearing jeans, a white T-shirt and a black leather jacket like John Travolta. He didn't kiss me at the end, even though I was desperate for him to and kept putting on lip gloss to encourage him, but he had asked me to meet him at the same time the next week, and that was today. Now that I had kissed Joe and knew how to do it, I wasn't nervous about it any more and knew that tonight would be the night that the ice-rink boy would ask me out. I was going to say yes and chuck Joe.

I had been thinking about him all week, he was so confident and funny and had picked me out from all the girls who were watching him. He was showing off a bit, skating backwards really fast and spinning around in the middle of the rink, holding his leather jacket above his shoulders like John Travolta in *Grease*. He was gorgeous. I would love to be his girlfriend and was so excited despite Carol's bad mood. She was still annoyed that I had left her at the side of the rink last week and hadn't talked to her all evening, but the boy was so funny and good-looking that I had forgotten about her and had to give her my blue clutch bag to apologise, even though I didn't feel sorry at all—it had been a boy emergency and she had gone to the pictures once with Dan when she said she would go with me, leaving me stuck in with my mum and dad all night, watching *The Sweeney* and doing her homework as well as mine.

The bus lurched around the roundabout. I had another look at myself in the dirty window and smiled—with my hair flicked out, my blue rugby shirt, blue eye shadow and my favourite orange-flavoured lip gloss, the boy would definitely ask me out tonight.

"You don't even know his name, because he didn't tell you. You don't even know what school he goes to, if he even goes to school. He might be engaged or have a girlfriend or be a psycho or gay or on probation, and you're supposed to be going out with Joe."

I *was* supposed to be going out with Joe. I really liked him. He was good-looking with black hair, he had nice clothes, I liked kissing him, and he never tried anything else. I was relieved to finally have a boyfriend and to have kissed a boy at last, but I didn't really love him, not even a bit even though he was perfect and kind and loved me. I wished I loved Joe but I just didn't. It was quite sad as he wanted us to get engaged at Christmas, but I could never ever imagine wanting to do it with him—never. Carol really loved Dan. She loved him as I had loved Bobby Henderson.

"Two best pals going out with two best pals. It's perfect, why are you spoiling it?"

We had been having this same conversation for a week now, but the truth was I didn't really want to go out with Joe. I just didn't have anything else to do when Carol was with Dan. Joe made me feel important and gorgeous and always told me I looked lovely and that he loved me, and bought me bars of Dairy Milk chocolate. Even my dad liked him and said he was a decent young man and that Joe's dad was the best roofer in the town, so I didn't really have a reason to chuck him. Until now.

"You're one to talk." I retorted. "Going out with a boy called Dante. Dante Capaldi, what a poofy name."

We both laughed.

"It really is poofy. I just call him Dan. His mum hates that. I really love him, Karen."

"Yes, you said. I wonder if that boy's name is Johnnie or maybe Paul. Johnny-Paul, or Paul John."

She was back.

"If he does ask me out, I'll tell Joe right away. We can still be pals and all go out together." Joe was so pathetic that I knew he would probably do that, and that's probably why I would never love him.

"So what do you think his real name is?"

"Liberace."

"David Cassidy."

"Nigel, probably. Or Arsehole Wank Bastard."

We both laughed, then gasped in unison as Bobby Henderson got on the bus.

With Kelly McNicol.

She was horrible in a tight black pencil skirt that only emphasized her skinniness. I wanted to think that Bobby was horrible too in his red tartan punk trousers covered in zips, but the truth is he was still gorgeous, although my heart didn't beat as it used to, because of the boy at the ice rink. He lifted his hand in a half-wave but Kelly ignored us. Carol was outraged.

"Cheeky bitch! They both smoke so why are they sitting here? They should go upstairs with the other smoky scumbags. She just wants to annoy us. What does he see in her? She has no boobs, and her hair is dyed and stringy, and look at what she's wearing!"

"But don't you think he's quite good-looking?"

She looked at me aghast.

"Karen, Bobby Henderson is horrible! He's uncouth, rude, disgusting, loud, smelly, drunk, thick and scummy. How can you even say that? Joe is good-looking and so is that ice-rink boy, whatever his name is. Bobby Henderson is ugly. Always has been, always will be."

Kelly's hair really was horrible. They sat a few seats in front of us so I got a good look at how bleached it was with her dark roots. My hair was naturally blonde—but he had picked her. Two stops later, when we were whispering a list of all the other scummy boys that Kelly had gone out with and probably done it with, Carol grabbed my arm and pulled me onto the stinky floor of the bus.

"Get down! It's my Grandpa Jimmy and Mrs. Fleming!"

We crouched in the small space between our seat and the seat in front, curled up with all the smelly chip papers and chewing gum. It was horrible. I was desperate to keep my rugby shirt from touching the sides. I peeked up to have a look.

After Carol's mum had bleached Grandpa Jimmy's house from top to bottom that day he said he was going to die, he had started to look like himself again. He had got a haircut, shaved, cut his nails, dyed his thick wavy grey hair jet black again, got new false teeth and a new shirt and suit from Julie's Empire Stores Catalogue and started to go to the dancing. He went to the Masonic Club on a Thursday, the Dockers' Club on a Friday and the Unionist Club on a Saturday, then usually the Railwaymen's Club on a Sunday night. And he had started to go out with women, lots of them, until he met Mrs. Fleming at the Masonic Bingo.

Carol's mum hated her and had had a big screeching argument with her in the middle of the Co-operative when she told everyone that Mrs. Fleming was a gold digger who had started chasing her dad when he won a lot of money on the horses. The fight must have been fantastic and Carol and I were really sorry that we had missed it. Now Carol wasn't allowed to talk to Mrs. Fleming, even though we thought she really did like her grandpa—Mrs. Fleming didn't need his money. She had a nice tidy house with a green porch and lots of flowers in the garden. She used to have her own husband but I heard my mum say that he was dead and had left her well looked after.

Now here they were coming onto our bus, him in his cheap black suit with shiny marks all over it where he had ironed it on too hot a setting, and Mrs. Fleming in a nice green dress, her fat little feet squashed into her stilettos. Her hair was dyed blonde too, but nice and soft, not like Kelly's, and she had a kind face with lots of powder and lipstick and she always smelled like flowery perfume. Grandpa Jimmy smoked but Mrs. Fleming didn't, so they sat downstairs too, right behind Bobby and Kelly. It was a nightmare. If they had gone upstairs as usual, we could have run off the bus and got the next one.

"They'll get off at the Masonic Club." She hissed, "Just keep your head down. I'm not allowed to talk to them."

We stayed crouched on the floor as the bus lurched from the stop, holding onto each other and the sides of the seat. I couldn't help but peek, but no one else on the bus had noticed us. Bobby and Kelly stood up and went to the door, they were getting off. He didn't hold her hand. I hoped they wouldn't look round but knew they would.

"Bye Carol Mckenzie, bye Karen Alexander. Are you two mingers under the seats again looking for cigarette butts?" Kelly McNicol shouted as she walked to the front. I hated her. Bobby had the cheek to laugh as they jumped off the bus before it had stopped properly. I hated him too. Carol was right, he was scummy. Carol's grandpa and Mrs. Fleming looked around, then to my horror, he stood up and walked towards the back of the bus. Carol hid her face in her hands. I crouched behind her.

"Carol, hen, what are you lassies doing down there?" Carol's Grandpa Jimmy was standing there looking down at us. He smelled exactly the same as Uncle Jakey—cigarettes, lager and too much Brut aftershave.

"Oh hi, Grandpa!" her voice was too loud and too high. "We dropped fifty pence under the seat. We're just looking for it. I didn't even see you, Grandpa!"

I had no choice but to go along with it, groping under the filthy seat for the pretend fifty pence.

"Let me help yous." He hitched up his shiny trousers and with difficulty crouched down beside us, fumbling in his inside pocket for his lighter. "I'll find it. Just let me have a look."

Carol was panicking. "No, Grandpa, it's okay, we don't need…"

With his backside in the air, he reached under the seat and flicked his lighter on.

He jumped back. "Christ! It's went on fire. The seat's went on fire!"

The flame had touched a bit of plastic that was hanging under the seat and had melted it, letting off a pungent burning smell that soon filled the bus. Grandpa Jimmy took off his slip-on shiny shoe and hit the underside of the seat. Everyone was turning round to look at the three of us. Some people stood up. I crouched down as far as I could go, there really didn't seem to be anything else to do. The driver stopped the bus and was looking around. Thank God Bobby had gone. This was beyond humiliating.

"Whit's that smell?" shouted the driver. He was really annoyed.

Carol's grandpa rubbed his hands on his jacket, slipped his lighter back into his pocket and pulled himself to his feet.

"It's okay, driver!" he shouted back.

People were coming down the stairs to see what was going on.

"These lassies here wiz playing with matches, but I stopped them."

We couldn't believe the cheek of him, her own grandfather.

"Thanks, Mister. Right lassies, aff the bus."

Carol's grandpa slipped her a tenner as we did the walk of shame down the middle of the bus. Two old bingo women tutted as we passed. Mrs. Fleming shook her head and gave us a little smile. She knew.

We couldn't face getting on another bus in case the driver had radioed the other drivers, so we walked to the China Palace and had chicken Maryland and fried rice with bamboo shoots and water chestnuts. I never saw the ice-rink boy again. He never called me even though he knew my name and what school I went to. And Carol never told her mum about Mrs. Fleming and the bus incident.

12. Delilah

AFTER THE ARGENTINA DEBACLE, WHEN MARY'S HUSBAND got home from jail in Spain and kicked him out, Carol's Uncle Jakey decided that he wanted to move back in with his wife. He had been living with his big sister on and off for two years and knew that she was getting fed up with him. Carol's mum had liked the company at first, with Carol's dad working down in England and never getting home. Jakey was an electrician and could fix things with the tools that Carol's dad had left hanging meticulously in the hut. He got them a big telly from Radio Rentals and paid for Mrs. Mackenzie to have her hair done every Saturday at Ritzie's Salon. However, every day he left a mess—piles of empty lager cans and crisp packets, dirty washing, shoes, Custard Cream packets that Carol or her mum had to clear up, and he gave Carol's wee brother cigarettes and left ash all over the carpet. After Julie went to the pictures with Big Douglas the bus driver, Jakey was determined to win her back, so he enlisted us, two sixteen-year-old schoolgirls, to help. We were sitting on Carol's living room couch, me doing her English homework for her, when Jakey burst in the door. He stood there with a delighted grin on his face, waving his cigarette around and leaving trails of white wispy smoke.

Carol waved the air in front of her face. "That's disgusting, Uncle Jakey, you have to stop smoking. It's bad for your health and you stink."

"I know, hen, I know. I'm stopping on Monday, but wait til you hear this!"

He stubbed out his cigarette and lowered himself onto the armchair opposite us, pulling up his enormously wide bellbottoms to reveal his giant platform shoes. Last year, Carol and I had thought that his clothes were fantastic, but now they were just old-fashioned and he was starting to look ridiculous. It was time for a new image for him, so we had cut pages out of her mum's Grattan catalogue men's section and left them on his bed, but he was sticking with his 1973 style.

We were both looking disdainfully at his Gary Glitter shoes when he made his announcement. "Lassies, I've decided to have a lovely party for Julie. It's her birthday next Friday and I want everything to be perfect. Yous lassies are quite posh—well, compared to me—so could yous get her a nice present?" He fished in his pocket and handed Carol a bundle of five pound notes. "And help me with the party?"

We looked at each other, trying not to laugh. "Why don't you just buy her flowers, go round and make her tea, and ask her if you can move back in?" Carol asked.

"I tried that, Carol, hen, the flowers and that, but she telt me to get to eff, can you believe that?"

"Well, she said you could move back in when you stop drinking lager and talking shite, and she's still really angry about fat Mary and the Tartan Army and you being in the paper steaming. Anyway, I don't think that Mum would let you have another party, not after the one you had to celebrate the deaths of the two popes when the police were at the door and all the neighbours came out to watch."

Carol's Mum had been humiliated and raging when she heard about that and had threatened to throw him out.

"That was just one of the old greetin'-faced Catholic neighbours moaning about the music. How could they not like Showaddywaddy? And I never went to Argentina, did I? I came back. Just as well. Some of them are still there, so they are, stuck in Buenos Ayr with no money and no passports. And fat Mary is just ma pal, hen. Her husband is a pure psycho and she never fancied me anyway. I did try my luck but she said I kept talking shite."

"That's unbelievable, Uncle Jakey. How could any woman not fancy you? I mean, look at you! And you so good-looking, responsible, considerate and mature. A real gentleman. You even have some of the original Wembley turf from the pitch invasion that you started last year, growing on your mantelpiece in a flowerpot, and beside that a piece of the Wembley goalpost you swung from and broke that same day. The 1690 tattoo over your knuckles is just the icing on the cake. What a catch you are!"

"I know, hen, I know." He smiled humbly.

It had been my mum who had phoned the police at two in the morning after they had played "Under the Moon of Love" really loud for four hours, with all the windows and doors open. Carol and I had loved that party, and my mum had never found out that I was there. It had started when Jakey's pals came round after the pub shut, one of them pushing an old pram piled with crates of Tennent's lager, another carrying a box of tomato-sauce-flavoured crisps, all playing records and dancing because two consecutive popes had died within months of each other. Jakey had paid us twenty quid each to clear up after it, and two of his pals had paid us too, so it was a great night for us, hiding in the kitchenette, eating the crisps and Custard Creams, laughing our heads off at all these drunk pathetic thirty-year-old men without a wife between them, dancing with each other and occasionally bursting into spontaneous shouts of "No Surrender." They had all scuttled home when the police came, so the party was short but very profitable for us, and we had left the house spotless, except for the smell of smoke.

"Mum won't let you, Uncle Jakey, she really won't. And Julie won't come."

"Your mum will never know, will she, lassies? She's going to Ayr Butlins for the weekend with Jennifer's playgroup, and Julie said she'll come. Me and Julie are going to get back together. I know it, she knows it and that big fat poofy bus driver knows it."

As soon as Jennifer and Carol's mum got picked up in the social work minibus the following Friday, we got started. We pushed the couch against the wall so they could all dance, we made plates and plates of gammon and tomato sandwiches and we put out every ashtray we could find. Jakey asked us to make posh fancy food too, so we threaded wooden skewers with chunks of gammon, pineapple and cheese, popping a maraschino cherry on the top of each one then displayed them artistically by sticking the ends of the skewers into raw potatoes that we had covered with silver foil. Jakey was thrilled and couldn't wait to show Julie. There were also the usual plates of crisps, but because this party was supposed to be posh, Jakey had bought Quavers and prawn cocktail Skips as well as the usual tomato-sauce flavour.

Carol and I had spent half of the birthday present money on ourselves and half on Fiji perfume for Julie from the posh chemist shop, where they had gift-wrapped it with dark blue paper and a purple ribbon. It looked really lovely, we decided, as we smelled the box. Julie was going to be thrilled. To complete the posh theme, Jakey had bought the funniest thing I had ever seen. It looked like a six-inch upside-down silver umbrella, and when you pushed the handle down, it opened out like a tropical flower, displaying an array of thin cocktail cigarettes in a circle, all in pale pastel colours—yellow, pink, blue and green. He was entranced and kept opening and closing it but we thought it was pathetic.

"Fancy cancer sticks," whispered Carol as she rolled her eyes.

Nine of them came to the party, in two taxis, straight after the pub shut at half past ten, spilling onto the pavement, up the path and into the house where Jakey greeted them like long-lost relatives and told us to run and get them drinks, even though they each held a carrier bag from the pub, bulging with cans of Tennent's lager. Seven of them were his usual pals from the darts team, all dressed embarrassingly in bellbottoms and platforms like Jakey, but two were women that we hadn't seen before. There was a quiet, smiling woman with long straight light brown hair, in a green Laura Ashley maxi dress holding onto one of Jakey's pals' arms. I think his name was Craig. The other woman came screeching out of the taxi, in a cloud of Tabu perfume, wearing a ridiculous 1960s style mini dress as black as her long dyed back-combed hair, thigh-high white plastic platform boots and layers and layers of bright makeup—orange on her face, blue on her eyelids and hot pink on her lips. Carol and I were aghast but it was obvious from the way that all the men stared at her that they didn't agree.

She screeched when she saw Carol. "Carol, hen!"

She opened her arms and lurched towards us. I could tell that Carol didn't have a clue who she was but she politely held out her hand as the woman enveloped her in a drunken bear hug. "Carol, hen, last time I saw you, you were toty! Now look at you."

She held Carol at arm's length to get a better look, her eyes unfocused, her balance unsteady, her breath stinking of whisky. "You've grown into a lovely big lassie! Your dad will be so proud of you when he gets out!"

"Sandra! Her dad's down in England, remember?"

Jakey was panicking as he ran towards the kitchenette and I knew in that instant that Carol's dad was in prison.

Craig and the woman in the green dress were hurrying towards us too, as part of the drunken damage-limitation exercise. The woman grabbed Sandra and led her into the living room.

"When your dad gets out of his contract, that's what she meant, hen, ha ha!" Craig laughed nervously as he stood next to Jakey.

"Aye, his contract!" repeated Jakey, his eyes darting from me to Carol.

They needn't have worried. All Carol heard was the word "big." Sandra had called her a lovely big lassie and Carol was outraged.

"She called me big!" she hissed to me as we took the silver paper off of the sandwiches. "Did you hear that? She said I was big!"

"Carol, she's steaming."

The sandwiches looked horrible. The juice from the tomatoes had soaked into the thin white Wonderloaf bread, leaving soggy pink circles. Carol picked one up and dropped it back onto the plate in complete misery.

"You are eight and a half stone and a size ten, you're not big! Look at you! Dan thinks you're gorgeous, and boys fancy you."

"But she said I was *big*!"

I couldn't believe that Carol had not picked up on what else Sandra had said and vowed never to mention it. "When's Julie coming anyway?"

"She's on a back shift so will be here about half past eleven. Look at them, they're all pathetic."

They really were. Jakey was standing in the middle of the living room, stamping his platform shoes on the brown flowery carpet and raising his fist in the air. "Come on, come on! Come on, come on! Come on, come on, come on!"

"Can you believe he is thirty years old? Julie will never let him back in."

Jakey was on a roll as his pals roared their encouragement.

"Oh yeah!" they all chorused, even the quiet woman, as Jakey sang to the record about being the leader of the gang.

He really was the leader. Of the most pathetic gang in the world. After that resounding performance, he pulled over a bar stool which had arrived with the group in the first taxi and sat on it, looking around the suddenly quiet room for dramatic effect.

Seven of them were squashed onto the yellow couch, the two women sprawled across several knees and the other two men on the floor at their feet, surrounded by empty lager cans and full ashtrays. From the kitchenette, we could see Sandra's white elastic support girdle, as her tiny dress rode up her huge thighs. It was disgusting. Jakey was looking too. They were all waiting to see what he was going to do.

"Come on, Jakey boy!"

He started quietly, then the chorus from the couch joined in as Jakey led the sing-along to "Delilah." Sandra was on her feet, taking centre stage with Jakey, her arm thrown around his neck as they swayed together.

The living room door slammed. Carol and I saw her before everyone else did. Julie was standing in the doorway in her new jeans, high shoes and a pink floaty top, her hair newly permed, her face like thunder.

The room was silent.

"Julie, doll, happy birthday!"

"Don't you happy birthday me! Just what exactly is going on here? What is *she* doing here?"

She was striding towards Jakey and Sandra. Carol and I had never seen Julie this angry before. It was amazing. She was really raging. We looked at each other in delight. This was going to be good. Even the couch chorus was silent and open-mouthed.

Julie grabbed Sandra by the throat—it was even better than we could have hoped—then she screamed, really screamed, at her. "Get yer filthy hands off ma man, ya manky scabby mingin' old whore!"

We ran into the living room to get a better look. It was brilliant. Sandra grabbed Julie by the arms, ripping her top as they tumbled around the room.

"*Your* man? How is he *your* man? You huvnae did it with him for years, you frigid bitch! You don't even like the boaby! But I do."

"Right, that's it, ya whoring cow." Julie was livid, her rage increasing her strength as she lunged at her rival.

The couch chorus started a new refrain, led by Craig, as the two women lurched around the room.

"Lassie fight! Lassie fight!" They chanted, clapping their hands and stomping their platform shoes in unison. Jakey did not join in but he didn't try to stop it, watching in glee when Julie pushed Sandra onto her knees, pulling her dress up around her waist, revealing her twenty-four-hour girdle and fat pink thighs to the delighted audience. Sandra grabbed the bar stool to pull herself up, cursing and swearing, while an equally cursing Julie kicked her back down and grabbed at her hair, pulling out lumps.

Jakey pulled himself together enough to make a halfhearted attempt to stop the fight. "Right, ladies, eh, that's enough."

"Enough, my arse!" screamed Julie. "That mingin' bitch was after my man, at my own party, manky bitch that you are!"

Sandra used the diversion to pull herself to her feet and run to the door. Julie screamed at her, picked up the bar stool, and threw it at Sandra. In slow motion and watched by everyone, the stool sailed through the air, crashed through the living room window and landed at the feet of the two Strathclyde police officers who were walking up the path.

That was when Carol and I had to hide behind the chair. The entire street, including my mum and dad, came out to watch the two disheveled women being led in handcuffs to the police car. I had to hide in Carol's room until all the lights went out in my house and I could sneak home through the back door, my T-shirt stuffed in my mouth to control the laughter.

Jakey moved back in with Julie when she got home the next day.

13. Independence Day

WE COULDN'T DENY IT ANYMORE—CAROL'S PERIOD WAS two weeks late. She was probably pregnant. She lay in a crumpled heap on my bed, face down, bawling into my yellow cotton pillowcase which was now wet and streaked with black mascara. I had been trying to pack all day while running up and down the stairs with tea and hot chocolate for her. She hadn't said a word, only stopping to sip a tiny amount, then throwing herself onto the bed to resume the loud sobbing. My mum and dad and her mum thought she was upset because I was about to leave for university, which had given her an excuse to hide in my room all week. I was sitting beside her, stroking her arm as she ignored me, trying hard to be sympathetic, but my duffel bag, tape recorder, mix tapes and Blondie poster were in the car, my dad was stomping about downstairs, and it was time to go.

I picked up my new scarf that I had got in the university shop—rough wool, royal blue with a thick gold stripe running along the middle from end to end. I wound it around my neck again and looked in the mirror. Me—a student! Even though my best pal was distraught, I couldn't help smiling at my reflection. I looked fantastic in that scarf. I looked like a student. I wondered if it would look better with long ethnic-style earrings or plain studs. There had been an earring stall in the Students' Union when I had been there a few days ago for my books and my sweatshirt and scarf. I had bought three pairs, one feathery pair which would definitely be too much with the scarf, one long gold pair which would go great with my new black university sweatshirt and some small blue studs, which might go better with the scarf, but first I had to get Carol to move. Or start her period.

Slowly, painfully, she turned around and sat up. I took her hand, using the other hand to slowly unwind the scarf and place it on top of my new Adidas bag. She hugged her knees to her chest, still gulping and sobbing but obviously trying not to.

"I can't believe you're going now. This is the worst thing that has ever happened to me and you're going away."

The sobbing started afresh. I did feel terrible about the timing and wished I could do something about it. I wished she wasn't pregnant. I wished that my boyfriend Joe hadn't been ignoring me for three days, since I had gone to Glasgow by myself when he had wanted to come with me. I wished Carol's period would start, that it would all be a miscalculation and we would laugh with relief then go to the Chinese restaurant to celebrate. But we really had got the dates right, we had drawn calendars and charts and worked the dates backwards and forwards and always got to the same conclusion. I knew that she was pregnant and had secretly worked out that she was due in June. At least I would be home by then.

"I promise I'll come back on Friday night. I'll buy a test (I couldn't bring myself to say pregnancy) at the corner Boots and we'll do it together, here in my house. Then if it is true, we'll go and tell your mum. Then we'll tell Dan."

"I can't tell my mum, Karen."

"You have to tell your mum. She'll notice soon anyway."

"No I can't tell her. She'll kill me, she'll die, she'll be so disappointed. She's told everyone at the factory that I'm going to be a nurse, that I did really well at school and that I got accepted to train at the hospital in Glasgow. She'll be so let down." Carol's words struggled out through her racking sobs.

I knew all that was true and was really struggling to find things to say, but everything I said sounded patronising and not sincere. Not sincere at all. "It's not the end of the world. You can still be a nurse. You'll only be twenty-two when the baby goes to school, and in the meantime you can go to night school and work part time. Or Julie might help you with the baby. She's due in a few months and will be at home anyway. Maybe you can start nursing next summer. And Dan's a good guy, he'll stick by you."

"I don't want him to stick by me. I want him to be with me because he really wants to. I want to go to Glasgow now, like you. And I don't want to be a nurse in five years, I want to be a nurse now. I want to move into the nurses' home with all the other nurses and go to see bands and go to cool shops and pubs. I want to live in Glasgow too. I want us to hang about together there. I don't want to be stuck here. I hate it here, we've been planning our escape from Kilbrannan for years, and you're going and I'm staying. You know what's going to happen, don't you? Dan has been going on about us getting engaged at Christmas. He'll ask me to marry him and I don't really have a choice, do I? I mean, I probably would marry him anyway, after I became a nurse and had a flat in Byres Road and a car and loads of clothes from Top Shop and loads of shoes and a job at a big hospital, but not now. His mum will blame me. She hates me already because I'm not a Catholic, and she'll think I've trapped him. He can't leave here. His dad wants him to run the chip shop on his own soon so that Mr. Capaldi can go back to Italy more. He'll want a big wedding in the chapel before I start to show. All his family will come from Italy but my Uncle Jakey and my grandpa won't come because it's in a chapel and priests will be there. You know how much they hate priests and nuns and the pope. Then Dan will take over the chip shop and I'll get a job in the factory with my mum and we'll go to work together on the bus, get a pie from Greg's for our dinner and then we'll come home together on the bus wearing our nylon overalls. I'll start to smoke and me and my mum will have chips and beans for our tea every night, then we'll light up our cigarettes and sit and watch *Coronation Street* on the yellow couch, with a cup of tea and a Tunnock's Teacake. The highlight of my evening will be going out to the van in my slippers and my blue overall."

We both laughed weakly at the thought of Carol in a blue nylon overall and smoking.

"Then I'll get a short curly perm, like Mrs. McNamara. And you, in the meantime, you'll go to see bands and pretentious French films with your new posh snobby best pal Anna, and you'll smoke dope, and late at night you'll sit in cafés in Byres Road with poofy sarcastic smart-arse posh boys who wear eyeliner and long black velvet coats down the ground, and you'll talk about philosophy and the universe and how you all hate Maggie Thatcher, and I'll be here in my blue overall with my cigarettes and chocolate biscuits, watching Vera Duckworth and Ken Barlow."

"Carol, you're my best pal and always will be, always."

Anna was my new roommate that I wished I hadn't told Carol about. We'd met when I went to see my room on Tuesday—I couldn't believe my luck at getting a place in the huge student hall of residence in Sauchiehall Street. It was exactly where I had wanted to live, with hundreds of other students, right in the middle of the busiest street in Glasgow. I felt tingly every time I thought about it, ever since I got the acceptance letter last week. I couldn't wait to see my room and had stood outside in the rain for half an hour before it opened to let the new students sign in. Me, a new student. Standing on the street in Glasgow by myself, wearing my new university sweatshirt and scarf. I thought I was going to die of excitement. It was right next to the cinema and pubs, cafes, shops, taxis, buses, and there were hundreds of students, and I was one of them. Anna and I had walked into room 330 at exactly the same time, both wearing our new black university sweatshirts. We laughed and hit it off right away—I knew we were going to get along really well. On my way back to Central Station, I had gone into Littlewoods to buy chocolate buttons and lip gloss, and I had laughed out loud as I walked along in the drizzly rain, eating my chocolate buttons and wearing my new lip gloss and my scarf that told everyone that I was a student. At university. I stopped to listen to two fantastic buskers playing guitars and gave them fifty pence. They both winked at me. It was the most exciting day I had ever had, especially when a long line of girls and boys my age, all dressed in black, ran past me holding hands and shouted hello at me in made-up accents, then they ran into the building where I was going to live. I thought I was going to burst.

"Karen!" The voice from downstairs sounded impatient. "We need to leave in five minutes. You need to sign in by three o'clock, and I don't know where I'll park in Glasgow. There might be traffic on the Kingston Bridge. Are you about ready?"

"I really need to go, Carol. I'll call you tonight, and I'll be back on Friday."

"You won't be back on Friday." She was looking at the brown shag carpet on my floor. "You'll go out with Anna on Friday, to the Students' Union. You'll wear your matching sweatshirts and go to the bar and talk to smart-arse posh boys called Ewan and Fraser who play rugby and talk Latin, then you'll go back to your room with the smarmy boys and play your Simple Minds albums and smoke dope and talk shite all night, then you'll go to bed at seven o'clock in the morning and you and Anna will go to a café and have your breakfast at four o'clock in the afternoon."

That would be fantastic! I tried not to smile and sat on the bed beside her, rearranging my face to look sad and sincere. I really had to go. "I'll come home on Friday. We'll tell your mum, then I'll take you to the Chinese restaurant, we'll have chicken Maryland, then we'll go and tell Dan. Both of us. Together." I squeezed her hand and she clung on, her nails jagging into my palm.

"Carol." I whispered. "We're set up for free fish suppers and ice cream and chocolate for life!"

She forced a weak laugh and handed me my bag. "You better go. Your dad is about to shout 'for Pete's sake.'"

I nodded.

"Karen, for Pete's sake! Are you ready?"

"Yes, Dad," I shouted back. "I'm ready."

14. My Sweet Lord

I ABSOLUTELY LOVED BEING A STUDENT. I HAD ESCAPED from Kilbrannan and really was hanging about with posh boys with names like Ewan and Fraser and Alistair. Every day when I got back to the hall of residence, there was a message pinned to the notice board saying that Joe had called and would I call back, but I never did. I had decided that I was not actually going to chuck Joe by telling him. I couldn't face it. He would get the message that he was chucked by me avoiding him for the rest of my life. Which could be quite awkward as my best pal was pregnant by his best pal.

I tried not to think about Carol, which was quite easy as my new roommate was fantastic. Anna was small and blonde and quite plumpish like me and we both wore our university sweatshirts and scarves every day. The other students thought we were sisters, which was quite believable until we opened our mouths—she had gone to a posh private girls' school in Edinburgh and I was from Kilbrannan. I knew that Carol would hate Anna instantly. She didn't like posh people and she would be jealous of me and her having such a laugh, but they would never meet. I would keep both lives completely separate. That would not be hard. There were people in Kilbrannan who had never been the twenty-five miles to

Glasgow and there were others who had only been to go to Ibrox or Parkhead or Hampden for the football, and some just came up at Christmas to see the lights.

Anna and I had skipped our psychology class to go to Metro, a vintage shop that sold very cool and cheap old clothes. We had realised that people were laughing at us with our matching scarves and sweatshirts, and after the bra debacle I could not face being mocked for my clothes again, so for five quid I bought a 1950s black velvet cocktail dress with a fitted top and a swirly skirt that made me look and feel like someone else, someone cool and arty—Anna had actually gasped when I walked out of the changing room. That's what I was wearing the first time I saw Jack.

I was standing outside the Students' Union while Anna was talking to some posh school pals of hers inside. I didn't like them. They said I was authentic working class and I thought they were a bunch of pretentious wankers.

There was a little group gathered around a low wall where someone was playing a guitar. I edged over to see what was going on, and sitting on the wall was a boy singing and playing his guitar, completely lost in his song. He had long wavy chestnut hair and despite the chill was wearing a black T-shirt that said "I Hate Maggie Thatcher."

His admirers, all girls apart from one boy in a long coat, clustered around him as he sang while looking down at his guitar. "My sweet lord..."

I pushed my way to the front and stared at him. I could not take my eyes off of him. He looked up and half smiled. I held my breath. He was gorgeous. It was unbelievable how gorgeous he was. I couldn't breathe. His nose was straight and beautiful, his eyes warm and hazel, his hair tangled and sexy.

He looked right at me.

Then he pointed right at me. And he sang that he really wanted to be with me. Me! Everyone looked as the gorgeous boy pointed right at me. It was the best moment of my life. My heart stopped as we looked at each other. A firm hand on my arm made me jump as the boy looked back down at his guitar.

"Fourth floor, room 432," hissed Anna.

"What?"

"He lives in our hall of residence. He's called Jack Logan, Jack the Lad. He's going out with half the girls on our floor."

"I've never seen him." My words were almost silent.

I have to tell Carol.

And I turned and ran, leaving Anna standing by herself.

I ran up the stairs, pushing my way through the crowds of students. I had to find a phone box. I had to tell Carol about the best moment of my life. I ran along Cathedral Street as the drizzle started and pushed an elderly lady out of the way to get to the phone box first. This was an emergency.

"Carol!" I shouted as I pushed in my 10p while the phone was still beeping. I looked away from the irate lady in the flowery headscarf tapping on the window with a 10p piece. "Carol, I have just seen the most gorgeous boy in the world. He was singing in the street and playing his guitar. He is gorgeous, Carol, and he looked at me and pointed at me—"

She was sobbing softly. "My mum knows, Karen. You have to come home."

I hung up the phone, pushed past the frowning tutting old lady again and sprinted along Cathedral Street, down Renfield Street and pushed and shoved my way through a crowded Central Station and onto the Kilbrannan train, which by some amazing luck was just leaving. As the old train wheezed its way slowly across the Jamaica Bridge, I caught my breath and knew that both of our lives had just changed.

I ran all the way in the driving rain from Kilbrannan Station to Carol's house. I couldn't risk the bus as I couldn't be seen. I didn't want my mum to know I was here, everyone would laugh at my dress, and I was soaking wet and frozen. I kicked open the gate then pushed past Jennifer, who pointed up the stairs, and in a final burst of energy, ran up the stairs two by two. My beautiful dress was heavy and soaking, clinging to my cold wet legs and leaving dark stains. My hair was wet and stringy and my kohl eyeliner was running down my face.

"My mum knows," sobbed Carol, bundled under a blanket on her bed.

"How?"

"You look ridiculous and you're soaking wet. Don't sit on my bed in that state. Put these pajamas on and I'll tell you."

I dropped the wet heavy dress onto the floor, pulled on the soft warm pajamas, then threw myself onto the bed, cuddling Carol as she sobbed—huge, heartrending tears, worse than when she thought Dan had kissed an Italian girl, worse than her frizzy perm debacle, worse than when her granny had died, worse than when she found out her dad was in prison. She was shaking and sobbing and wiping her face on the blanket, trying to form a sentence.

"I'll go and make us tea and cheese and toast, and then you can tell me."

She nodded as she wiped the snot with her sleeve. I placed the tray on the bed and offered not tea but Cadbury's hot chocolate, our traditional remedy for heartbreak. Carol had composed herself, the hot chocolate was lovely and warm and chocolatey and I was dry.

"I was making my bed this morning, and she just walked into my room and stood by the door, sucking on her cigarette. She didn't say anything and I knew she was building up to it. Then she said, very quietly and calmly: 'I know, hen. I know you're pregnant. And there's worse things in this life than a baby.' Then she turned around, went down the stairs, put on her coat, and walked out the door and up the street. She's gone to tell Mrs. Capaldi, I just know it."

"There's worse things in this life than a baby? Is that all she said?"

Carol nodded and started to sob again.

"Does Dan know?"

She shook her head.

"But he will now."

It was eleven o'clock at night by the time I got back to Glasgow Central Station on the last train, wearing Carol's jeans, sweatshirt and horrible yellow anorak and with my lovely dress sodden and dripping in a Fine Fare plastic bag. I had made cheese and toast for Jennifer too and got her into her pajamas and into bed, and then I sat with Carol until, exhausted and worn out, she fell asleep. I tucked her in too and slipped out, leaving the hall light on for when her mum came back.

I knew it was bad. Dan's mum hated Carol. She wasn't Italian, she wasn't Catholic, she had no dad, she lived in a council house, her wee brother was a hooligan, Jakey was her uncle and her mum worked in the factory. She also worshipped Dan, her only child, fussing over him and bringing nice Italian girls for dinner every Sunday. He had to sneak out to see Carol and she had never been to his house. This was going to be terrible. I was so relieved to be back in the halls and couldn't wait to get in a hot bath as I ran up the side stairs to avoid anyone seeing me in the yellow anorak.

There was a note pinned to my door. I thought it would be from Anna, telling me to come and smoke dope out the back with the three boys from Dundee.

It was from Jack the Lad.

Karen, I meant it. Jack.

This was the best day of my life.

15. Up the Junction

ANNA HAD WAITED UP FOR ME. I HAD COMPLETELY FORGOTTEN that I had run away from her at university in my beautiful black dress and had turned up eleven hours later with Carol's manky old jeans and yellow anorak on. I had actually forgotten all about Anna. She was sitting on her bed reading with her glasses on, and she looked tired and worried.

"Where have you been?" she asked quietly. "Are you okay?"

I needed more time to think of something to tell her, so I just nodded as I stood there frozen in the doorway, with my wet dress in the dripping plastic bag in one hand and Jack's note in the other. For the first time in my life, I really couldn't think of one thing to say—I didn't want to tell her anything yet about Carol or the baby or going to Kilbrannan or about Jack's note or my wet dress.

She took her glasses off and looked at me directly for a long time. I still couldn't think of what to say, so I just stood there looking like a right idiot. I knew that the situation was ridiculous but I just couldn't think of one relevant or sensible thing to say or do.

Anna finally sighed and said calmly, "Well, you obviously don't want to tell me anything, but you're okay, so I'm going to bed."

And at that she put her lamp off and saved us both from a very embarrassing and awkward encounter. In fact, in that moment, she saved our friendship. That was the first time I realised that posh people deal with things differently. She saved my embarrassment again by being gone when I got up the next morning. I still didn't know what to do. If Jack came to look for me to ask me out, I would have nothing to wear as my black dress was the only thing I had that I could be seen in at university, and that was still soaking wet under my bed in a bag that had turned black with the dye.

Carol would tell me to give myself a shake, hang my dress over the shower rail in the communal bathroom, and go for a bath, so that's what I did. When I was in the bath, starting to let myself think about Jack and the song he sang to me, I had the terrible realisation that maybe he didn't write the note at all. Loads of people had been there when he pointed at me, so maybe one of them was taking the pish. They were always doing that in the halls, leaving notes on each other's doors with messages that Hugh Jarse, or Mo Leicester, or Mike Hunt had called from the Academic Senate's office, or to go urgently to room 640, which was the cleaners' cupboard. Maybe Jack always pointed at first-year girls, and I was just the one he had pointed at that day, or that moment.

I was quite annoyed with myself by now, and had far too much to think about. I needed to gather my thoughts and decided to walk to class rather than get the bus, so I wore my old stretched nylon fake Adidas track suit that my mum had got me at the market for five quid, and trainers so I could walk fast. I didn't want to see anyone or talk to anyone—I was too tired and overwhelmed and unattractive—so I tied the hood around my face and ran the three floors down the fire exit, then I scurried along all the back lanes behind Bath Street so no one would see me. I would dart into the class after it had started, sit at the side with my hood up, dart out again at the end of the lecture and run home and go to bed. I really didn't want to go to the class, but the lecturer was giving out our first essay assignments and test dates so I had to. It would be over soon and I would feel better after another hot bubble bath and a good sleep. I would wryly laugh off the fake note, dry my dress, apologise to Anna, tidy the room, and all would be well. And I would buy some new clothes with my grant money, as my dress would be out of commission for a while.

I hid behind some lockers waiting for the class to go in—it was a huge class with hundreds of students so it was easy to hide myself. I waited until the last straggler ran in then I crept towards the door. Jack was standing there. Jack the Lad, my dream boy, who had pointed at me in public and had maybe left me the note, standing outside my psychology class looking for someone, maybe looking for me, and I looked like I lived in a caravan and had been picking tatties all day. I turned to run away, but it was too late; he was walking after me.

"Karen?"

So I did what any mature university student would do. I ran into the ladies' toilet. And he came after me. Jack the Lad followed me into the ladies' toilet.

"We can talk here, Karen, and I can get arrested, or we could go outside."

We went outside and sat on a wall.

Me sitting there sweating with no makeup and old tinky clothes from the market, the most uncool person in Glasgow, and Jack, gorgeous with his silky wavy hair and twinkly eyes, with his combat jacket covered in badges and his Doc Martens. He sat really close to me and I just wanted to lean on him and smell him.

"Did you get my note?"

I nodded. I didn't seem to be able to talk today. And he wasn't posh like Anna; he sounded like me.

I was overwhelmed with tiredness and relief and happiness that he'd been looking for me and it really was him who wrote the note. I took my hood down and shook out my hair, to make myself look nicer and to let him know that I liked him and was interested, as I had read in *The Jackie* magazine years ago. I still looked ridiculous but maybe slightly less so. Or more, as my hair was full of static with being in the nylon hood, and I could feel it standing in a circle around my head. I could tell that Jack was trying not to laugh.

"Well?" He was smiling right at me and I could feel my heart thumping. He really was gorgeous, and I could hardly believe he was sitting right next to me.

"Okay, you have obviously lost your power of speech today, although I have heard you talking and laughing loads of times at the halls, so I know you're not actually handicapped. You're actually funny and outgoing, and maybe not right now, but you're usually pretty and I really fancy you, and I know all that as I've been following you around."

He'd been following me around, this beautiful boy! And he fancied me? Where? When? How did I not know?

He continued slowly, as if he was talking to a really old person, or a two-year-old, or someone who'd just had a stroke.

"So I'm going to ask you a question, and you are going to shake your head for no, or nod for yes, then I'm going to go to my economics class. Will you go out with me?"

I nodded, and Jack said, "Good."

Then he got up and walked away. I sat on the wall for a long time, in my nylon track suit with my hair in a circle around my head, and I had never felt so happy in my life.

16. Life in a Day

November 1979

JACK AND I HAD BEEN GOING OUT FOR THREE WEEKS. I loved being his girlfriend—I loved kissing him and lying on his bed with him and I loved how he always waited for me after class to walk with me to my next class. He always had his arm around me or held my hand, and I loved how he looked at me. I understood now why Carol and Dan had slept together—some guys were just too delicious to resist. But I didn't like his friends, Stuart and Bree. They had all been friends since primary school, and Bree obviously fancied Jack even though she lived with Stuart and three horrible scratchy cats in a dingy damp basement bedsit in Kelvinbridge. Their room was covered in posters about Che Guevara, Fidel Castro and the Sandinistas, even though they'd never been further than Blackpool and lived on student grants and the broo as they'd never worked a day in their lives. And they were vegans.

Bree had hated me instantly. I thought I had looked quite nice in my Wrangler jeans, espadrilles, black T-shirt and love beads but she had actually snorted when she first saw me, which was in a pub up some trendy back street near Glasgow University.

I was still seventeen and had never tried alcohol before, and when I ordered a fresh orange juice and lemonade, Bree had laughed out loud. "Oh for God's sake, Karen, try some beer, you're not in your fishing village anymore."

I was outraged and looked to Jack for support, but he hadn't noticed. In fact, he hadn't noticed lots of things in the last three weeks. Like when Bree said that my espadrilles were "ironic" and my beautiful blue love beads a statement about western domination over the third world.

"They're just love beads," I had answered quietly.

"No, Karen," she said as if talking to a simpleton. "They're not just love beads. How much do you think the poor oppressed low-caste women in India get paid to make them just so you can swan around the disco in your fishing village?"

"They're from Saltcoats market. They're just 50p beads—"

"Yes, and that poor illiterate woman who made them got 1p and our corrupt government kept the rest. How can you even wear them?" She looked at me as if I was covered in cow dung while Jack sipped his pint and Stuart looked intently at his watch.

And when I thought that the monk guy in orange robes who stood outside the Students' Union really was called Harry Rama, Bree had laughed at me for hours.

This had been going on for three weeks. I had been to several horrible gigs in smoky pub basements with rubbish bands that Jack, Bree and Stuart thought were fantastic and had seen a really drunk stand-up comic who just stood on a box in a pub and shouted and swore while those three fell about laughing.

Some of the bands, like Positive Noise and The Alleged, were brilliant and I loved jumping about at the front with Jack, but in the pub afterwards, Bree always said that she had discovered those bands first before anyone else in Glasgow and that the Simple Minds had written a song about her as of course she knew them long before they were well known. And when she found out that I loved the Bee Gees and Rod Stewart, she had laughed for days.

I had asked Jack if we could go out by ourselves as he was so different with those two, he was a know-it-all arse like them. When we were on our own, he was easy-going and lovely and considerate but that changed every time we met Bree and Stuart, who I decided by now was the most pathetic guy I'd ever seen. Bree was always putting him down and laughing at him while he looked at his watch. Even when he wasn't wearing a watch, he looked at where it usually went on his wrist while she mocked and belittled him as Jack sipped his beer.

I even had moments when I missed Joe as he loved me the way I was, while Jack was always suggesting that I get Doc Martens and black tights and bleach my hair, and I thought about finishing with him, but then he would touch me or look at me and that electricity and the chemistry between us was so strong that I knew I had to be with him.

Until the night we went out to Koh-i-Noor for a curry. I hadn't seen Jack for two days as he was writing an essay. He was only a few months away from graduating with his economics degree and was determined to get a First Class Honors. I was so looking forward to seeing him and had had a long scented bath, painted my nails, flicked out my hair and wore my finally dry lovely black velvet dress. I looked like myself and I felt really nice from the top.

However, I wasn't sure about the bottom—I had bought myself thick black tights and a pair of Doc Marten boots from Oxfam, like the ones that Bobby Henderson and his punk pals always wore, in an attempt to look cooler and less like I just got off the bus from Kilbrannan. Anna had gone home for the weekend so I couldn't ask her what she thought of my new look, and Carol would have laughed, but I did need a new image. I needed to look like I was a cool person who had maybe gone to private school and knew about bands and pubs and beer, and could drive a car. The girls who hung about at the student bars we went to wore Docs. Not one person except me wore wedgies, and they probably never had. I was stuck in my disco image—I really hadn't noticed how uncool and frumpy I looked. I liked Jack and wanted to impress him, and he liked this look, but the boots were manly and horrible and made me look like I was going to work at the harbour or on the railway, and the tights made me look as if I fancied girls. I felt small too as I had been wearing high wedgies since I was fourteen and had never worn flat shoes except for P.E. at school. I had forgotten how small my real height was. I couldn't walk properly in the boots either, as they were heavy and clunky. I felt like I was wearing my dad's fireman boots but Jack would like me in them.

Jack did like me in them, and so did Bree and Stuart, as they were there too. The three of them were all sitting at a table in the Koh-i-Noor and had already ordered and were eating their curries, even though I was exactly on time. When Jack stood to kiss me, our fantastic chemistry was drowned out by my anger, which was boiling up inside my horrible tackety boots.

"You look gorgeous." Jack smiled.

"You really do!" agreed Stuart, with a bit of a pervy look on his face, while Bree scowled.

"Well, I must say, Karen." She sniffed. "Those Docs are a huge improvement on your usual disco efforts. Are they genuine Docs?"

Jack sipped his pint while Stuart looked at his nonexistent watch.

I had had enough. I fancied Jack beyond measure but I wasn't going to live like this. Jack could see by my face that something was about to happen and reached for my hand. I snatched it away and thumped my foot onto the chair that I was supposed to sit on, and I very deliberately unlaced the horrible old boot and took it off, then I thumped my other foot on the chair and unlaced that boot too. It took longer than I thought as the lacing system was quite elaborate but I couldn't really stop now that I was making a statement. Their faces were shocked as they all stared at me, and other people were turning to look too, including the waiter in traditional Moghul dress who was standing there with a jug of water and a huge grin on his face.

I dropped the boots onto Bree's lap, and although I was really small now and felt a bit stupid with all those people looking at me, it felt fantastic to stand up for myself and for all the uncool people like me, all the uncool people who were laughed at and who had seen that look of contempt when they walked into a cool place. All the people who were judged and sneered at for being themselves, all the people who had never heard of the latest band or been to the coolest pub, all the people who stood at the wrong rack in HMV Records and liked to do The Slosh. All the people who liked Kool and the Gang and Chic and Donna Summer and bought their clothes in British Home Stores and C & A and from catalogues, and even for the people worse than me, the ones who liked Cliff Richard and Barry Manilow and went to Butlins for their holidays. I was speaking for all of us.

"You know something, Bree?" I said with a voice that sounded more confident than I felt. "Or should I say Brenda, as that's your real name, isn't it? I saw it on your student card." Jack and Stuart obviously hadn't known that her name was Brenda as their heads swiveled to look at her red face. "You are the biggest, ugliest bitch that I have ever met in my life. And I come from Kilbrannan scheme, so that's saying something. You are spiteful and bitchy and you have never said one nice thing to me since you met me, and that's because you're a bitch! Your dad drives buses, your mum works in a supermarket and your brother is an electrician. They are good decent hard-working people and they must be ashamed of you, they must be black affronted for you and your horrible whiny vegan cats and your mung beans and your Fidel Castro posters. Do you know how many people he has executed? Do you know how many Cuban parents have put their children on planes to Miami? Do you even know where Cuba is? You're a pretentious lazy bitch! You've never worked a day in your life and you do nothing but laugh and sneer at people like me."

I was on a bit of a roll now. This felt fantastic. People were turning to look and that made me feel even more fantastic. "And you, Stuart, always looking at your invisible watch when Brenda is making an arse of you in public. Well I suggest you have a good rake in Brenda's vegan Fair Trade woven hessian handbag made by members of a collective organic farm in Nicaragua, who sing songs about comradeship while they weave, to find your tiny balls. I'm sure they're in there somewhere. And I know you're not a vegan. You're not even a vegetarian, I saw you coming out of Greg's the other day with a sausage roll."

I had made that up but his face went beetroot so I must have hit a nerve. Brenda's shocked face was all I could see as I continued. "And you keep cheddar cheese under your bed, real cheese from real cows. And you eat it on crackers with real butter when Brenda's in her weekly organic vegan mung bean bath."

Brenda looked like she was about to have heart failure.

"And all of you—" I dramatically swept my hand around the table. "All of you, laughing at me because I like the Bee Gees and ABBA and Rod Stewart, I like them because they're fantastic, and they make people happy and make them dance and have a laugh, and they've sold five hundred million records this year alone (I made that up) and they can sell out the biggest stadiums in the world in five minutes, while the bands you like, the Electric Eels and the Sad Cats (I made those names up too) are rubbish and can barely get sixteen people to come to a mingin' old pub in Glasgow on a Saturday night to see them and that includes their mums and grans, and do you know why? Because they're rubbish!"

(That wasn't true. Simple Minds were fantastic but I wasn't going to admit that right now.)

"Not one of those bands or comics will be famous, they'll all go home on the bus to their mum's house in the scheme, where they live, and they'll be on the broo or work in Fine Fare all their lives."

(That wasn't true either. One of the pub bands was U2.)

Then I turned to Jack, the love of my life who was definitely about to chuck me so I got in first. I had nothing to lose. I wouldn't be Jack's girlfriend after this, so I might as well say it. I couldn't look at him in case I crumbled. "And you, Jack—seriously, these two? Thirty thousand students at our university and you go about with these two rejects? And better not forget your guitar in case you feel the urge to break into song in public and point at another seventeen-year-old girl."

And at that I stomped away in my stocking feet.

"Gaun yerself, hen!" shouted the Moghul waiter.

Jack did not come after me.

17. I Just Want to Be Your Everything

I WISHED THAT ANNA WAS THERE. I JUST WANTED TO TALK to someone, and in the whole of Glasgow, I only knew Anna and Jack. Anna was still home in Edinburgh for the weekend, and Jack just lived upstairs but hadn't come to see me, or left a note, or anything. I knew I had gone too far last night but I didn't regret it. I just wished I had said it sooner and in a more sensible fashion so that Jack and I could maybe still be together. I felt quite heartbroken about not being Jack's girlfriend any more, but in a way, I knew I couldn't be with someone who didn't stand up for me and never had. Even Joe had stood up for me, one time in a pub when a guy said something pervy to me. I hadn't heard him but Joe did and had pushed the guy right out the pub door.

For the first time since I moved to Glasgow, I missed Joe. Even though I didn't really fancy him and never would feel for him what I felt for Jack, he was good to me and we liked being with each other. My mum and dad loved him too, and my dad always said that Joe's dad was the best roofer in Ayrshire. Joe worked with his dad so he had money and his own car, a red Capri, and he took me places like Loch Lomond and Largs and to the pictures. Every Saturday night, we went out with Carol and Dan for a Chinese meal then went to the Thistle, the pub that everyone in our school went to. I always saw Carol slip her hand into Dan's, and touch his arm and look at him like he was Andy Gibb, and I knew that I never did those things with Joe. There was always something missing for me, and I just wished I could feel that. I thought it would grow, but it didn't. I knew I had to finish with him one Saturday night in the pub, when I was ranting about Maggie Thatcher and Joe thought I was talking about a girl in my school.

The problem was that I hadn't actually told him we weren't going out any more. I just moved to Glasgow and avoided his calls, much to Carol's annoyance as he kept asking her about me and she was running out of excuses. So maybe Joe thought we were still going out. I missed his calm love for me and wanted to talk to him, just to talk and then we could be friends. His best pal and my best pal were having a baby so us being friends would certainly make life smoother. I rummaged through my bag and found fifty pence, then went down to the phone in the entry hall. I was still in my pajamas but didn't care. I just wanted to hear Joe's voice.

The sad girl from Lewis who was always crying on the phone was crying on the phone. She gave me an apologetic little smile and I waved back to let her know it was okay, even though it really wasn't. We were all fed up with her being on the only phone for hours every day, just whispering and crying. It was pathetic but I felt a bit sorry for her. She was obviously homesick and someone told me that her dad had just died, so no one ever asked her to get off the phone. We just lingered around waiting.

I sat on the stairs for a while with my fifty pence and forty-five minutes later went back to my room and lay on my bed. I was feeling really upset about Jack now and was desperate to talk to Joe. Someone knocked quietly on the door and I ran to open it—Jack!

It was the sad girl.

"I'm finished now, sorry," she whispered.

"It's okay." I said, grabbing my fifty pence and sprinting down the stairs before someone else got to the phone. I lunged for the receiver just in front of an English boy from Liverpool who had run down the other stairs. I knew I was rude but really didn't care anymore. My heart was racing as the phone in Joe's living room rang. His mum picked up.

"Hello, Mrs. MacDiarmid, it's me. Is Joe there?"

"Oh hello, is that you, Sheila?"

Sheila? Who's Sheila?

"It's me, Karen."

"Oh hello, Karen dear, how's your university in Edinburgh?"

"I'm in Glasgow, Mrs. MacDiarmid."

"Okay, all right. I'll get Joe, he's just upstairs getting ready to go out." She seemed distracted as if I had interrupted her telly viewing and she clearly couldn't wait to get off the phone.

Joe took a while to come downstairs. I tried to breathe deeply and stay calm. I hadn't talked to him for three weeks. I knew he was heartbroken.

"Hello?"

"Hi, Joe, it's Karen. I just wanted to say hello."

"Oh hello, Karen, nice to hear from you. How's uni?"

He didn't sound very heartbroken. He sounded breezy and normal.

"Well it's a bit … I'd like to … can we talk … could we meet up next weekend?"

"Sorry, this isn't a good time, Karen. I'm just about to go out."

"With Sheila?"

I knew who Sheila was. She was the very pretty, slim, dark-haired girl who worked in the chemist. She was always nice and always waved over to us in the Thistle. She was there every Saturday night with her sister, at the same time as us, and she always watched us and walked past a few times, with her ankle boots and short flippy dresses. I hadn't even realised.

"Yes, we're going for a Chinese and to the Thistle with Dan and …"

I knew who the fourth person was.

"Okay, bye."

I hung up and ran past the English boy and up the stairs to my bed, where I lay all afternoon. It was one of those bleak November days when it never really got light and I was crushed. Last night, Carol was my best pal, Jack was my boyfriend and Joe was waiting for me. Now I had nothing. I kept thinking about Jack, Brenda and Stuart sitting in a pub right now laughing at my outburst, and Joe, Sheila, Carol and Dan sitting in The Thistle pub laughing about me phoning Joe. It was the worst day of my life and Anna was still gone.

I woke up starving just as it was getting really dark, which in Scotland in November is about 3 PM.

I thought about running down to Sauchiehall Street in my pajamas to get a fish supper and a bar of Dairy Milk. That would not help my heartbreak but at least I wouldn't be starving anymore and would feel better.

The warm delicious fish supper, flooded with vinegar, did make me feel better. I decided to listen to the Radio 1 charts to see if Dr. Hook was still no. 1 or if it was The Police's "Walking on the Moon" or Queen's "Crazy Little Thing Called Love," which Joe loved. The one I loved and had bought was "My Simple Heart" by The Three Degrees. Carol and I always listened to the charts together in my room every Sunday, and we taped it, trying really hard to press stop before Tony Blackburn started to talk again, then we played the tape all week, rewinding to our favourite songs. Now it just felt sad to be listening to it on my own.

Tony Blackburn had just finished playing "Ladies Night" by Kool and the Gang when I heard a bit of a commotion in the hallway outside my room—people laughing, music, someone banging on the doors, obviously some drunk students who had friends and were cool, arriving home from an all-night party.

Someone banged on my door, and when I didn't answer, they banged again. I stomped over to tell them to shut the eff up, and when I opened my door, Jack was standing there. He had a small crowd around him and he was dressed like a Bee Gee. He had obviously borrowed some girl's curling tongs as his hair was flicked out dramatically, and he was wearing an extremely tight white shirt, unbuttoned to the waist to reveal a huge plastic gold medallion, white trousers which were very tight at the top and very wide at the bottom, a huge buckle belt and high white platform shoes. I covered my mouth with my hands in delight—this was the best thing I had ever seen in my life. Jack Logan was making a fool of himself for me. In public. For me. He was looking right at me, his eyes laughing, when he picked up his guitar and started singing "I just want to be your everything…" in a ridiculously high Andy Gibb voice.

It was the best moment of my life, even when people started shouting "Fanny!" and "Wanker!"

I pulled Jack into my room, locked the door and pushed him onto my bed.

18. Young Hearts Run Free

December 1979

CAROL'S MUM WAS STANDING IN THE MIDDLE OF THE LIVING room holding up the most hideous dress I had ever seen in my life.

"It's beautiful, hen, isn't it?" Her face was flushed and beaming. "Me and Julie went to Glasgow today to get these as a surprise for Carol! We went to Angelique's Bridal in St. Enoch's Square and hired them. Cost a fortune, so they did, but we got them on the Provvy checks. Then we went to see the Christmas lights in George Square, lovely wee manger scene with the baby Jesus, and we had a bar lunch in the station, chicken soup and a crusty roll, gammon, chips and peas and apple crumble and ice cream, then we had a wee sweet sherry each to toast this beautiful dress. It was a brilliant day! Carol's going to be so happy with this dress now that she's decided to marry that Italian boy. Did I tell you that he came round here the other day, telling me and Carol that he loved her and she didn't need to marry him now, she could go and be a nurse and he would look after the wean and then marry her whenever she wanted? Did I tell you?"

I shook my head. Mrs. Mackenzie definitely had not told me, and neither had Carol. When I had talked to her a few days ago, she told me that she and Dan were getting engaged at Christmas, but she wasn't getting married. Now there was a wedding and a horrible dress that I didn't know anything about. I had only been home for ten minutes and my life was upside down.

"Well, hen, that's what he said, and my Carol was delighted. You know how much she wants to be a nurse. But then when he left, I said, 'I don't think so, hen. Dante is a good boy and he'll be a good dad, but if you let him have your baby, you know that old Italian bitch will bring him up speaking Italian and you won't know a word your own son is saying. Yes, it's a boy. I just know it. And I'll never see him. I know she won't let me near my own grandson. She hardly lets that boy of hers out of the house and he's nineteen years old!' So at the end of the day, Karen, hen, Carol's getting married in three weeks, the Italians are paying for everything, it's in the chapel and the Kilbrannan Arms Hotel, very posh, and me and Julie have picked her wedding dress! And I'm going to help with the wean while she trains to be a nurse. But look!" She swished the dress around.

It truly was a horrific concoction of bright white shiny nylon lace, a satin pie crust collar, white plastic bead buttons all down the front and a skirt so hooped and wide that it was touching the walls of the tiny room. To add to the horror, it had a satin ruffled apron at the front, obviously designed to hide the baby bumps of many brides.

"Do you think it's really Carol's ... style?"

"Oh, hen, it's just beautiful, so it is. My Carol will be like a wee princess!"

I don't think I'd ever seen Mrs. Mackenzie so flushed and happy before.

I had just arrived back in Kilbrannan for Christmas. The halls of residence closed at the end of term so we all had to pack up our Glasgow lives and go back to where we came from. It was a wrench to leave my room, and Anna and Jack, and my life in Glasgow but it was only for a month. Mrs. Mackenzie had seen my dad and me arrive and had run across the road shouting for me to come with her. I hadn't even been in my own house yet, and I knew my mum was annoyed with her as she'd made my tea, and Mrs. Mackenzie hadn't invited her as she was so desperate to show me the dress while Carol was out.

"I don't know that it's the right size."

"Oh, it's the right size all right. I took that red velvet dress that she always wears to measure it—it's the exact right size, and, hen!" She carefully folded the hideous dress over the couch and smoothed it down, her face beaming. "We got one for you too!"

Out of a giant pink box, she tenderly lifted a dress the exact same as Carol's but without the ridiculous apron and in a bright candy floss pink. "It's for you, hen! Now go and try it on. I've been at that window all day waiting for you. I was just dying to see you in it! Now run upstairs and try it on!"

I was frozen to the couch. All I could think about was that Jack and Joe, and worse, Sheila would see me in that dress. Carol and I would be in the local paper in those dresses and everyone in our school would see them. Even after we were dead, our grandchildren and great-grandchildren would see us in the wedding album in those dresses...

"I know, hen, I know you're excited about being a bridesmaid and you can't believe that you'll get to wear that lovely dress. Now go and try it on!"

Mrs. Mackenzie was out the back having a smoke when I came downstairs in the dress—which was difficult as the sides were squashed against the walls of the narrow stairwell, and the front was sticking up with the stiff hoop.

I was standing in the middle of Carol's living room when she walked in the door. "*What* the eff is that!?"

"I know!" I hissed. "It's horrific, and yours is worse!"

"How could it be worse than that? Have you looked in a mirror? Where's my mum?"

"She's outside having a smoke."

"Seriously? She'll smoke in front of me and my growing baby but she won't smoke near that ugly bastard dress?"

Carol and I went to Glasgow the next day when her mum was at work, getting a taxi to the station so that no one on the bus would see us with the huge bright pink boxes.

Angelique's Bridal let us swap the horrible dresses for two beautiful elegant simple Regency style gowns, Carol's in ivory and mine in baby blue. They had ribbons around the high waist and a little frill at the bottom, and we had enough money left over from the return to hire a simple ivory veil for Carol and two lovely hoops of tiny delicate silk flowers to wear on our heads like hippies. Carol smoothed the soft material over her little bump to emphasize it as we admired ourselves in the huge salon mirror. I knew we looked taller and slimmer than we really were as we were standing on little silk covered pedestals, but these dresses were gorgeous.

I patted the bump for the first time and smiled at her, and she stuck it out even further. "None of the Italians know that I'm pregnant, not even Dan's dad. The old bitch told Dan that I had trapped him deliberately, because obviously I've always wanted to stay in Kilbrannan and work in a chip shop. She doesn't want anyone to know. Well, they'll all know when I walk down the aisle like this in three weeks."

19. Going to the Chapel

IT WAS CAROL'S WEDDING DAY, AND WE WERE STANDING AT the bottom of the stairs in our beautiful dresses, with our ears pressed against the living room door listening to an intense, whispered argument between Carol's mum and Grandpa Jimmy.

"You are *not* wearing *that* to walk my daughter up the aisle, Dad, so for the last time, take it off right now."

"Aw, hen, calm down, it's only a wee flower on my lapel." Grandpa Jimmy was clearly enjoying this.

"Take it off, and put in the flower I gave you. *Off*, Dad, I'm serious."

"All this fuss for a wee flower."

"It's not just a wee flower. You know fine well what it is. You are not walking my daughter down the aisle in a chapel wearing that. You're just taking the pish now. Take it *off*!"

"So who will walk her down the aisle if I don't? Your brother's been in the Thistle Bar all morning and can hardly walk the length of himself, and I don't see your Billy anywhere."

Carol winced.

"*Me*, that's who!" Carol's mum was raging now. "*I'll* walk her down the aisle, and you can walk yourself out the door right now. Turn left, walk up the street and get the bus home. And if my brother is wearing one of them too, then you can effing well take him with you."

We couldn't hear the rest until Grandpa Jimmy shouted, "Right, lassies. Anna, Agnes, the car's at the door, there's a crowd of thousands of your screaming fans out there, the paparazzi's waiting, it's time to go!"

We had to run frantically halfway up the stairs then walk serenely down again, to where Grandpa Jimmy was standing with Carol's mum. He had a little blue flower in his lapel, and squashed under Mrs. McKenzie's bright pink stiletto was an orange lily.

A small crowd had gathered at the door to see the bride, and if they didn't know she was pregnant before, they did now, as she had tied the ribbon on her dress tightly at the back to enhance and showcase her little bump.

"You look beautiful, hen!" shouted Mrs. McNamara, to nods and appreciative noises from the neighbours.

"Gorgeous, Carol, hen! And you too, Karen, hen!"

"Lovely bride!"

We really did look lovely and I was looking forward to Jack seeing me dressed like this. We had been going out for three months now and Carol had invited him to the whole wedding—the chapel, the dinner, the reception, even though she'd never met him. I liked to keep my two lives apart—my old Kilbrannan life with Carol, and my new fantastic life in Glasgow with Jack and Anna. I was quite nervous about these two lives coming together—I knew my mum and dad wouldn't like Jack because of his long hair and earring and his pointy boots, and they would think he was cocky, and he wasn't Joe. Carol had been desperately trying to meet Jack since she found out about the Andy Gibb night, but I had avoided it. My two lives just didn't fit together and I didn't quite fit into either of them. I loved going back home to see Carol and have a laugh with her and be myself, but she wasn't interested in any of my classes or the bands that Jack and I went to see or in coming to the Students' Union with me, and she definitely didn't want to hear about Anna. And Anna didn't get any of my funny stories about Grandpa Jimmy or Uncle Jakey, she just said, "Well, they sound a bit rough, Karen."

She hadn't even laughed when I told her about Uncle Jakey running away with Ally's Tartan Army. I still couldn't think about it without laughing, and when I told Anna about the *Evening Times* incident and the pal in jail in Spain, she just said, "Well, he's lucky he got his job back, as that was really irresponsible."

I hadn't even really told Jack much about my life in Kilbrannan at all, and I didn't know much about his old life that he had shed when he moved to Glasgow when he was seventeen, except that he was from Airdrie, his dad was a plumber who thought that Jack was a waste of space, his brother was a plumber too and was married to a hairdresser and had two young children, and his mum was a nippy woman who liked to moan and clean the house.

Jack hadn't actually told me any of that, I had just pieced it together as he had never really talked about them and had not gone home once in three months, even though his family only lived about fifteen miles away. I don't know if they even knew about me. We had our own world in Glasgow—going to most of our classes, late nights at the library, walks in Kelvingrove Park, going to see bands at the Students' Union, an Indian takeaway on a Friday night, and my heavenly bed—that was our wonderful perfect little world. And it was now on a collision course with my real world.

Grandpa Jimmy had dyed his hair jet black for the wedding and had got himself new bright white false teeth and a new black suit from the Empire catalogue. He was wearing a deep red lariat instead of a tie and burgundy cowboy boots, which had been another argument with Carol's mum, but one from which he wouldn't back down, saying, "If they're good enough for the Man in Black, then they're good enough for me."

He was annoyed that Carol's mum would not invite Mrs. Fleming to the wedding, not even to the reception, so he was making a nuisance of himself in as many little ways as he could. Carol and her grandpa stood in the doorway while the photographer, a pal of Uncle Jakey, took photos.

"You look beautiful, Carol, hen, and I've never been prouder in my life. Your granny would have loved to see you like this, hen." Grandpa Jimmy had tears in his eyes as he offered Carol his arm and they strutted to the waiting Jaguar which was festooned with white ribbons, and driven by another of Uncle Jakey's pals, who was wearing a ridiculous sea captain's hat.

Jennifer squashed in the back with them in her lovely little short dress, and I had to sit in the front. Grandpa Jimmy opened the car window and threw out a handful of coins to the crowd of jostling children who were waiting excitedly for the scramble. It looked like a lot of money but I knew that most of it was old pennies that were worthless since decimalisation years ago, pesetas, and tokens from the amusement arcade at the beach. One of the tokens hit the back of the Jaguar as we drove off.

As I walked up the aisle with Jennifer, behind Grandpa Jimmy and Carol, I was glad that I was wearing this beautiful gown and not the hideous pink one, as Sheila was there with Joe and she was glamourous and stunning in a scarlet coat and shoes, her dark hair piled high. I gave them both a little smile as I passed to let them know that there were no hard feelings, but Sheila's smile to me was thin. Joe looked handsome in his kilt and jacket and I felt a pang, until I realised that he was sitting right next to Jack, who was also wearing a kilt, and that the two of them had never met nor even heard of each other but were talking and laughing like old friends. Three hundred people in the chapel, and the only two boyfriends I had ever had were sitting next to each other. They both winked at me as I passed, and I really hoped that neither of them nor Sheila noticed that. Dan turned to watch Carol walk up the aisle and by the way they looked at each other every step of the way, I knew that my best pal would be happy with this boy.

Uncle Jakey had been warned severely for weeks by Carol's mum and Auntie Julie to behave like a normal person in the chapel and not to say a word about the pope or Catholics. Now here he was in the second pew in his ridiculous 1973 good suit, wide tie and platform boots with a pregnant and furious Auntie Julie. He was barely able to stand after his morning in the pub, but was crossing himself enthusiastically and genuflecting dramatically every few minutes and at completely the wrong times, standing up when everyone else kneeled, and kneeling when everyone stood up. Carol and I couldn't look at each other and I focused intently on the huge bronze statue of Jesus on the cross to keep myself composed.

The service was long but lovely, with incense and a choir, and then Carol was Mrs. Dante Capaldi and we were back in the cars, covered in confetti, and on our way to the Kilbrannan Arms.

The Italians had obviously paid a fortune for the reception as it was sumptuous—white starched tablecloths, huge white candles grouped together, ornate flower arrangements and a really delicious meal with an extravagant five-tiered wedding cake decorated with beautiful fresh flowers.

Carol and Dan's first dance was to Leo Sayer's "When I Need You," which had been their first ever dance at the Civic Centre Disco the night he had first plucked up the courage to ask her out. The night that Bobby Henderson had picked Kelly McNicol instead of me.

My mum and dad were polite to Jack when they met him, asking him the usual questions, but they wouldn't let Jack buy them a drink, and didn't offer him one, then my dad spent the next hour standing at the bar talking to Joe.

There was a peaceful and joyous mood in the room as Dan made his speech, while his mum, aunties and grannies listened adoringly.

Then it was Grandpa Jimmy's turn. He smiled smugly and looked around the room, slowly reaching into his boot to retrieve a piece of paper. I could feel the mood change to an anxious cringe and I really wanted to run to the ladies, but didn't want to miss it either.

Slowly, Grandpa Jimmy stood up and smoothed his dyed hair and his lariat. I could hear drumming coming from under the table close to me, and a faint whistling, which was getting louder. Then Uncle Jakey, who had not said a word all day, lifted two spoons and started drumming on the table and whistling a tune, his face like a smirking two-year-old who knew he was about to get in trouble but was going to do it anyway.

"He's whistling 'The Sash.' Get him out of here. Now!"

I had never seen anyone as angry as Auntie Julie was right now. Her face was crimson, her eyes narrow and furious, and I thought she might actually stab her husband with one of the fancy silver cake knives, but she just quietly and firmly grabbed his elbow and thrust him to his feet. Jack appeared from nowhere and the three of us quietly and efficiently hustled Uncle Jakey out of the room. The young waiter had already called a taxi as we got to the front door of the hotel, where the cold squall from the sea sprayed all over our lovely wedding clothes and the biting wind whipped my beautiful intricate hair and blew some of the little flowers away.

Julie's flowery dress was whipping around her legs and her hat blew away, but her wrath was keeping her warm as she gave her husband a good hard kick in the back with a sharp stiletto heel as Jack maneuvered him into the taxi. "Take him to his father's house, Eric. There's a key under the mat. I'm done with him now. Done."

"Right, Mrs. McMillan, will do."

The taxi sped away with Uncle Jakey sprawled in the back, then came to an abrupt stop by the hotel entrance. Uncle Jakey was sticking his hand out of the window, giving us the V sign and shouting "No surrender!"

I could hear Jack snorting under his breath and I knew that I couldn't look at him—Julie might have killed us right there in the posh hotel doorway if we had laughed. Auntie Julie and I went to the ladies' room to compose ourselves. She was surprisingly calm and unruffled as she fixed her hair and makeup then fixed mine. As we smoothed ourselves down, she lit up a cigarette. "I know I'm pregnant, hen, but after that ... and the baby's probably daft anyway, look at the poor thing's father. And, hen…"

She gestured towards the door, where I knew Jack was waiting. "That's a good boy you have there. You should marry him."

I knew in that moment that I would.

Jack accompanied us back into the reception, one on each arm. We smiled calmly and sat at the table as if nothing had happened, just in time to see Carol's Grandpa Jimmy raise his glass and say, "Let's all raise a glass to my beautiful granddaughter, Carol, and her handsome new husband, Dante. I am thrilled that my lovely lassie is joining such a good-looking family, especially you, hen. Would yous all look at that beautiful, stunning woman sitting there. Are you single, darling?"

He gestured towards Dan's ninety-five-year-old great-granny, an elegant and polished woman in an emerald green dress and diamante jewelry, with her thick white hair piled in a glamorous chignon, and winked at her. The old lady winked right back at Grandpa Jimmy and raised her glass, while her ninety-seven-year-old husband, in a cream linen suit and emerald green tie, stood up, leaning heavily on his walking stick, and raised his fist in a mock threat while the room erupted in laughter, most of it relief from the Scottish guests. Toasts were made, glasses were clinked, Dan kissed Carol and the fabulous wedding cake was wheeled in with sparklers to enhance the drama.

"I've booked a room upstairs," whispered Jack. "Want to see what a real Scotsman wears under his kilt?'

20. Sugar Baby Love

I WAS ABOUT TO START MY SECOND YEAR AT UNIVERSITY after miraculously passing my first year, and Jack had graduated with his First Class Honours degree in Economics and was working at the Bank of Scotland in George Square. Anna and I had a nice little cosy flat in Govanhill, with a view over the chimney tops and steeples of the Southside. Our flat was cosy because Uncle Jakey had come up one weekend when Anna was in Edinburgh and fixed the electricity meter so that we never ever got a bill. We had been there for four months now with free electricity and Anna had never noticed and never would. We had the warmest flat in Glasgow, with endless hot water and a growing collection of cannabis and spider plants on the south-facing windowsill. Jack lived on Byres Road with three messy drunk students and hated it, so he was always at our house, as was Anna's boyfriend, Justin, who was nice enough and very devoted to her, but I couldn't see why she fancied him, with his posh voice and mousy thin hair and glasses. Justin worked in a bank too and was always trying to engage Jack in long boring conversations about the economy and the interest rates, so Jack avoided Justin as much as possible and had devised a way of slithering in the front door and into my bedroom without Anna or Justin knowing he was there, then pretending to be asleep if Justin popped his head in, which he often did. Justin must have thought that Jack had narcolepsy or bilharzia, or else he just knew that Jack was avoiding him and was too posh to say anything. People who are not posh sometimes do take advantage of posh people's manners to amuse themselves, safe in the knowledge that the posh person will not be rude or fight back, and sometimes Jack would do that with Justin, until I stopped him with a prod. However, it was funny to see Justin squirm and try to be polite when Jack asked him ridiculous questions, like why the banks didn't give out spare cash to homeless people, or why the banks didn't have mobile tellers in ice-cream vans to go round Castlemilk and Easterhouse to give the working poor free services. They were good questions but Jack enjoyed seeing the sheltered, conventional unimaginative Justin get flustered as he tried to explain the ways of finance.

Anna and I liked living together. We were compatible and gave each other space when one or both of the boyfriends stayed over. So I had a great flat mate, a great boyfriend of a year, and I was quite slim as I had found a bike in Queens Park and cycled everywhere now. I had been walking in the park one day to think about an essay I had to write about criminology when I saw the bike. It was just lying there on the grass, a nice blue bike with a basket on the front. I hung around looking up and down to see if the owner was just doing a pee in the bush, or worse, but no one came, and after fifteen minutes I got on it and cycled home. I was always expecting someone in Victoria Road to shout that I was a bike thief and so I had put two Simple Minds stickers and an I Hate Maggie sticker on it to disguise it, but so far I hadn't been caught. I couldn't believe how great it was to have a bike, even someone else's bike, and I wondered why I had never thought of this before. I could get everywhere so fast and there were some great hills near the university that I loved to speed down on the way home. However, the best thing was that Carol was living in Glasgow too.

Dan's dad and uncle had given him an old-fashioned run-down family chip shop on George Street to manage, and Carol was about to start her nurse training at the Victoria Infirmary. Then there was baby Marco, four months old and the chubbiest, brownest, happiest, warmest, softest, curly haired baby I had ever seen. In fact, he was really the only baby I had ever seen and I loved him beyond reason and measure. Instantly. The first time I saw him at Irvine Central hospital in June, lying swaddled in blue in his plastic incubator, I had run up the ward to see him and had unwrapped him to look at his wee perfect toes. Then I picked him up and was smelling him when I remembered that I should probably say hello to my best pal who had just had a baby, and that I had left the huge bunch of flowers for her on the bus. I wasn't one of those girls who liked babies, I still didn't like ordinary babies and never wanted to look at one or hold one, and I never ever looked in prams. Babies just weren't appealing. But this one was perfect.

Carol, Dan and the baby lived on Bell Street in the Candleriggs in a huge top floor flat that had been untouched since the 1950s. The two families were helping them to do it up and renovate it, and like me, they had free electricity, heating and hot water. It still needed a lot of work but it was theirs, and even though Carol had to bump her pram up three flights of worn stone stairs several times a day, she liked being away from Kilbrannan.

The old Capaldi chip shop was as dilapidated as the flat, and Dan was there from eleven o'clock every morning until midnight, six days a week. I saw Carol and Marco almost every day as they lived close to the university, and we really did have an endless supply of free fish suppers, chocolate and ice cream. It was worth carrying my heavy bike up and down four flights of cold, worn stone stairs to see the baby and for the free Mars Bars and huge bars of Dairy Milk chocolate.

One evening, Carol and I had shared a fish supper, a black pudding supper and a family pack of Revels when she gave me the baby so I couldn't escape and she said, "You've been going with Jack for almost a year now, and I still haven't met him."

"You have met him."

"Yes, at my own effing wedding, for five seconds, with three hundred other people. I couldn't pick him out in a lineup at the police station, and he's been my child's godmother's boyfriend for a year."

"He's really busy, Carol. He works a lot, then he…"

"He works one mile from here, Karen, in a bank, and banks close at 3 PM every day and are closed all weekend and on all the Bank holidays. Why won't you let me meet him?"

"It's not that … it's just…"

I really had been avoiding letting Carol and Jack meet. Even though she lived in Glasgow now, Carol was my old Kilbrannan life, and Jack was my new Glasgow life, and I still couldn't see how the two lives could fit together without me looking like an impostor in both. I didn't want the exposure. Jack still wore an earring and a velvet jacket and pointy ankle boots when he wasn't at work, and he was always going to protests and demonstrations against Maggie Thatcher and apartheid and student loans and nuclear weapons, and Carol could be quite harsh about people like Jack. I knew that I would have to merge my lives at one point but not yet.

"Right, so tomorrow night, you and Jack will come here for a fish supper at 6 PM, end of story."

When Carol said "end of story" it really was the end of the story so I knew I had to do it. I told Jack that night after a lovely walk around Queen's Park, and we had our first argument since the Koh-i-Noor incident.

"Just don't go on about apartheid and British Steel and Zimbabwe."

"Karen, you're being ridiculous. Why would I talk about Zimbabwe to a baby? You obviously don't want me to meet your best pal or your godson. You keep me away from everyone, your mum and dad, the famous Uncle Jakey. We've been going out for almost a year now and you've introduced me to no one. I don't know if you're embarrassed for me or for them or for yourself."

"Right, so why have I not met your mum and dad? Or your brother? Or your nieces, I don't even know what ages they are, Jack! And why have I not met anyone from *your* life, eh, Jack? Well except pathetic Stuart and hairy Bree, and look how that turned out! You're obviously embarrassed for me! Is it the Bee Gees thing again? Do you still think I'm cool enough to shag but not cool enough to meet your school pals? Do they even know about me? You still think you're too cool for me, don't you?"

"Well, your best pal lives one mile from my work and you won't let me even see the baby, you keep me hidden away, you're just using me…"

"What am I using you for, Jack? You haven't even got a car and you live in a cold howf with three drunk rejects so you're here all the effing time. You're the one who's using me, just so you can get a free hot bath, a warm flat and a shag!"

And so it went on, loud, irrational and repetitive, while Anna and Justin pretended not to hear, until 2 AM, when the downstairs neighbour banged on his ceiling with a broom and Jack stomped out and got a taxi home.

21. You Are My Sunshine

I WAS SO ANNOYED THE NEXT DAY, BUT RELIEVED THAT THE argument had delayed the Fish Supper Summit. I knew I was in the wrong, but I was still irrationally angry with Jack, as he hadn't called nor come back. I wished that I could have stomped out but the argument was in my own house, so Jack had the upper hand.

When I cycled up Bell Street at 6 PM that evening, starving in anticipation of the fish supper and black pudding, Jack was standing outside Carol's close. I didn't even know that he knew where they lived.

"What are you doing here? How do you even know where they live?" I was out of breath from the final hill on Castle Street and didn't like how my voice sounded, and I was sweaty and disheveled, so Jack still had the upper hand.

"I was invited, so here I am." He had obviously gone home after work to change from his smart bank suit into his black velvet jacket, jeans and pointy boots, and he was carrying his guitar, which I must have been staring at as he said, "I'm going to Sean's later, to practice."

I couldn't face continuing the argument, so I banged my bike through the broken close door and locked it on the bannister, making a big point of not looking at Jack. I usually carried my bike up the stairs but didn't want Jack helping me.

"Come on in," shouted Carol. "Baby's sleeping in the living room, I'll be through in a minute. I'm pumping. My boobs are huge today. They're like volcanoes, just spilling out all over the place. I've been pumping all effing day…"

"What's she pumping?" whispered Jack.

"Oil. She's pumping for oil. Or milk for the baby, Jack."

"What milk? Oh." So Jack had his guitar and was dressed like he was in a band, and Carol was shouting about her boobs to my boyfriend—this was not going well. I just wished that Jack would go away and I could put the kettle on, pick up the baby and watch the news with Carol.

My bad mood disappeared when I looked in the pram and saw Marco, wrapped in his little blanket, his mop of black hair wild and sweaty. He was just adorable and I couldn't help but pick him up. He snuggled into me as I melted onto the couch with him.

"He is very cute for a baby," whispered Jack.

"You don't have to whisper. Just talk like a normal person, even though you're clearly not."

"Dan just left," Carol shouted from the bedroom. "The fish suppers are in the kitchen. Can you sort everything out? I'm like an Ayrshire cow today; it's just gushing out of both boobs. Seriously, I need a milkmaid and a milking pail. Is Jack the Lad coming?"

This was just getting worse.

"Jack the Lad? Am I Jack the Lad?" whispered Jack, indignantly. "Seriously, is that what you call me after a year together?"

"Hold the baby. I'll get everything."

I ran to the kitchen, wondering if I could scramble out the window and down the drainpipe. I took as long as I could, arranging the fish suppers, halving the black pudding, making a pot of tea, while there was silence from the living room and Carol's constant loud reporting from the bedroom about her boobs and overflowing breast milk.

Carol and I walked into the living room at the same time, me with the fish suppers and Carol with a bottle of warm breast milk.

Marco was rocking in his little chair on the floor, grinning at Jack, who was sitting on the couch with his guitar, singing softly to the baby and oblivious to the two of us. "You are my sunshine…"

Carol stopped dead, with tears streaming down her face. "That's what my dad used to sing to me when I was wee … that was our song."

When Jack and I were leaving at midnight, Carol roughly grabbed my arm.

"Marry him," she said quietly.

22. To Cut a Long Story Short

JACK AND I WERE LYING ON THE COLD GRASS IN KELVINGROVE Park, sweaty, exhilarated and exhausted after seeing Simple Minds at Tiffany's. It was the most exciting night of my life since the Andy Gibb occasion—the fantastic band, the hypnotic electrifying music, the crowd swaying as one, the vodka and coke in the hip flask that Jack had smuggled in. I had spent most of the show on Jack's shoulders, so when the drummer threw his drumstick into the crowd, I had lunged for it, fallen off Jack's shoulders and landed awkwardly on top of a large woman, while Jack jumped up and grabbed the drumstick at the exact same time as a tattooed man with a blue Mohawk. They had tussled over the drumstick and I thought it might erupt into a real fight, until the punk guy grabbed it from Jack, snapped it over his knee and gave Jack half.

We lay on our backs in the frozen cold darkness while Jack held the drumstick above our faces. "You know, I was ready to get into a fight with that punk guy for this drumstick, and now I don't even know what to do with it."

"Do you think he was there on the wrong night? Why would one punk Rocker go to a Simple Minds concert on his own with all those students dressed in Oxfam clothes? Or maybe he was at the wrong venue, maybe there was a Sham 69 concert in the pub next door, and he just wandered in, drawn by the music, then got himself stuck in the crowd. Anyway, I'm glad you got half a drumstick. We will treasure this forever."

It had been dark and cold all day on this bleak Glasgow January, and there were ice crystals forming on the grass underneath us as we lay side by side and held hands. I was starting to think about a warm bath and my bed.

"Karen, there's something I have to tell you. I've given in my notice at the bank. I finish next month."

I rolled over onto my elbow. "What?"

"I hate it. I've always hated it. I hate everything about it, except the pay and the chance of a low mortgage and finishing at 4 PM. I can't do it anymore. Last week I had to complete paperwork to repossess a house from a family in Mosspark. The dad lost his job, they couldn't afford the mortgage so the bank is taking the house back. I can't be part of it any more."

"But what are you going to do? How are you going to afford your rent and everything?"

Jack sat up and carefully placed the half a drumstick on the ground. "I'm going back to university. I've been accepted to Glasgow University in October to do Architecture. It's been my dream all my life."

"But isn't that about four years?"

"Six years."

"Six years?!"

"I've thought it all out, Karen, and I want to tell you everything all at the same time. I know it's hard for you, but I want to you stop talking for about three minutes while I tell you my plan. I'll give you the drumstick when it's your turn to talk."

I flopped back onto the freezing ground and covered my mouth with my hand. Jack's voice was firm and steady. "I hate the bank. I can't stay there for another fifty years, even though we'd be rich. I can't do it. I've always wanted to be an architect and I got accepted onto this course when I was seventeen, but my dad made me drop it and take economics. I know I'll be giving up my good wage but…"

"But what?" It just blurted out. Jack held up the drumstick to show that it wasn't my turn yet.

"I'm eligible for a student grant. But that grant would be a lot more if I was married. So I think we should get married."

I sat bolt upright as Jack lifted the drumstick again. "But I'm only eighteen!"

"I just have one question for you. Do you think you will marry me, or do you think you will marry some other guy?"

I pointed at Jack.

"You're the one, Karen. I've known that since the first time I saw you."

"When was that? When did you first see me?"

"I saw you the day you moved into the halls. I was in the hallway collecting my mail and I saw you get out of your dad's car. You wouldn't let him come in with you, and you just ran right in and didn't look back. Your dad sat there for a while, until a bus beeped at him, but you didn't look back. I followed you to the stairway and watched as you spun round and round, swinging your duffel bag and singing 'Dancing Queen' at the top of your voice. I knew then that you were the one."

"Well that's a bit stalky and pervy! And can't we just live together?"

"Can you imagine telling your mum and dad that? And we don't get any more grant money unless we're married.

Let's get married right away, Karen, and move into your flat. Anna is moving in with Justin next month."

"*What!*"

"He told me last week. You know how his granny in Perth died last year? Well she left him twenty-five thousand quid and he's bought a garden flat in Dowanhill. He's going to ask Anna to move in with him. He's trying to pluck up the courage tonight. He's got his granny's engagement ring in his pocket and he's going to ask her tonight. That's why we're staying at my flat. I think it's a bit creepy giving her his dead granny's ring, but it's a huge diamond and must be worth an absolute fortune."

"But she might say no. I don't know if she even fancies him that much." This was too much. A few minutes ago, I was lying in a park laughing at half a drumstick and now my flat mate was moving out, my boyfriend was unemployed and he seemed to be asking me to marry him.

"Karen, seriously, Anna could live in an attic flat above a kebab shop in Govanhill, with orange carpets, a calor gas fire, another couple, no privacy and one decrepit bathroom with a leaky roof and dodgy electricity, or she could live in a free huge posh garden flat in Dowanhill with a wally close, a dining room, a fitted kitchen, and a lounge with stained glass bay windows and a Rennie Mackintosh fireplace. What's the choice here? You're going to have to get a new flat mate anyway, or you could live with me, as your husband. And we can get a dog..."

23. I Will Follow

I TOLD MY MUM I NEEDED A COPY OF MY BIRTH CERTIFICATE to get a passport, and Jack told his mum the same thing. We posted our banns at Martha Street Registry Office the next week, just around the corner from where I had first seen Jack with his guitar. I felt terrible lying to my mum about my birth certificate—I told her I needed a passport to go to Benidorm with Anna. I couldn't really tell her that I was about to get married in secret in a registry office to a guy she had met once and hadn't even really liked. I had never wanted a big white wedding—the thought of wearing a puffy white dress and having a show of presents and cars and flowers was horrifying to me—but I never thought I would be getting married in secret at eighteen to a guy with long hair and an earring.

It was a delicious secret, though, and I had felt warm and excited since the night of the Simple Minds concert. Jack and I couldn't stop smiling at each other, and everything had a glow of happiness and excitement. I was going to marry the most gorgeous boy I had ever seen and he was going to be an architect. This time next month, I would be Mrs. Karen Logan, with a husband and a wedding ring and a dog. I told Anna that I was smiling and singing so much because I was excited that she was engaged to Justin, and that I couldn't wait to be her bridesmaid—one of three bridesmaids as it turned out—and she believed me. Her ring was stunning, a beautiful huge sparkling rectangular diamond in a 1930s Art Deco setting. She was delirious with it and kept walking around with her hand in the air.

I was a bit jealous of the ring as I didn't have one, and I did wonder if she loved the ring more than she loved Justin. And she had asked me to be her bridesmaid at her huge posh church wedding in Edinburgh in two years, and she already had a stack of bridal magazines that she wanted to endlessly look at with me. I felt guilty about that too as I was just having Carol as my bridesmaid. In fact, we were only having Carol, Dan, the baby, and Jack's pal Stuart at our wedding. Bree was living with a Welsh woman in a tent at a peace camp in Wiltshire, and Stuart had been trying to get back in with me by blaming her for everything, which just made him seem even more pathetic. I knew that after Jack and I got married, we would have to confess to our families and friends and everyone else who hadn't been invited, and I was dreading that but not enough to stop me.

Carol and Dan were delighted for me—they had loved Jack since he sang to their baby, and I think that Carol was happy to have me married so we could be the same again.

We went back to Angelique's Bridal and hired the exact same dresses that we had worn to Carol's wedding, only this time I wore the white one.

Carol was quiet the day we went to get the dress. "Are you sure, Karen? Are you sure about this? It's all so rushed."

"What are you talking about? You've been married for a year." I stood on the pedestal in front of the full-length mirror smoothing down the front of Carol's wedding dress, now my wedding dress.

She stood beside me in my baby blue bridesmaid's dress, as slim as she had been before she got pregnant. "I know, I know that, but I didn't have a choice, did I? I was seventeen and pregnant. I love Dan and Marco, but if I hadn't got pregnant, it would be me and you living together in that flat in Govanhill, and Jack and Dan would be our boyfriends. It happened one night at the beach, by the way, on the way home from the pictures, after we saw *The Life of Brian*. We were walking home along the beach, laughing so much that we lay on the sand, laughing hysterically, and next thing I know, we were doing it. I still think to this day that if I'd worn my Wrangler jeans that night and not my gypsy skirt, we wouldn't have done it, I wouldn't have got pregnant and I wouldn't be married."

I was always shocked when Carol told me things that I didn't know about her, but this was huge. I had to sit down on the fancy little enameled filigree chair to compose myself. "On the beach? *The Life of Brian*? Really? Really?"

"It was dark, no one saw us, and it really was a funny film, I laughed for weeks, and Dan kept saying 'He's not the Messiah, he's a very naughty boy!' But what I'm saying is—you don't have to do this too, Karen. You can live with Jack until he graduates. I love being married to Dan, and Marco really is the most handsome baby in Scotland, if not the world, but it's hard work. You and I should be living together in that flat you're in with Anna. It should be us going to see the Simple Minds and going out for curries and making chocolate cakes with cannabis, it should be us. Jack and Dan should be our boyfriends, not our husbands—we're eighteen years old! You don't have to do this."

I slipped out of my wedding dress, hung it back up on the rack and put my clothes back on, holding back the tears as Carol unzipped her dress, put her jeans and jumper back on and we slipped out of the dressing room and down the stairs into St. Enoch's Square.

24. Tainted Love

THE NEXT DAY, I TOLD JACK THAT I COULDN'T DO IT. WE were sitting on the windowsill watching a fight in Victoria Road when I said it. "I can't do it, Jack. I do want to marry you. I mean, when I get married, I want it to be with you, but maybe when I'm about twenty-one, not yet."

He just sat there looking out of the window and I saw that his eye was twitching.

"Right, fine," he said coldly and stood up and walked out of the flat, without even closing the door. I knew that I could make everything all right again by chasing after him and shouting, "I do want to marry you next week," but I couldn't say it as it wasn't true. I watched as the love of my life walked up Victoria Road and onto the 33 bus. He didn't even look up.

I pretended to Anna that I wasn't feeling well as I lay curled up in bed, feeling as if I was covered in lead. It was the worst ordeal of my life as she made me a cup of tea and sat on my bed all evening, chattering on and on about ribbons on chairs and hymns and wedding favours. I knew it wasn't her fault, as she didn't know anything at all about Jack and me and our failed wedding plans, but I really resented her happiness, her ring, her certainty about marrying Justin. I even hated her ribbons and cakes and hymns, and I really hated her other posh bridesmaids, Chloe and Pippa, even though I had never met them. If Jack had asked me to marry him in two years, as Justin had done with Anna, I would definitely have said yes. Getting engaged would have been fantastic, but now everything was going down the drain, and Anna and her ridiculous bridal magazines were making it worse.

I couldn't face going in to university the next day, as I'd have to pass the registry office where I wasn't getting married. I sat on the windowsill all day watching the normal people going about their normal lives. Despite my misery, I did laugh when a delivery truck almost crashed into a taxi, and both drivers got out and had a pathetic fist fight in the middle of the road, blocking the traffic up the entire length of Victoria Road while traffic beeped and people shouted at them to grow up. The fight, which was loud but quite halfhearted, consisted mainly of slapping and missed kicks and pulling each other around by the jackets, and it fizzled out when it started to rain and both drivers just got in their vehicles and went on their way.

It was a long and dreary morning for me but at least I got a respite from Anna's relentless wedding drivel.

The letterbox rattled just as I decided I was going to see Jack after he got home from work. I ran to the door in case it was him. I might have missed him because of the fight, but it was a postman that I had never seen before. "Hello," he said brightly. "I'm Samir Khan, your new postie. I just wanted to give you your mail." He handed me a small bundle of mail.

What a nice man. I was needing to see a friendly face today.

"So you'll be seeing my handsome face around, Miss Alexander. Oh, and I'll be taking my bike back." He pointed at my bike, which was chained to the banister.

"How is it your bike? That's my bike!"

"Oh, I don't think so, Miss Alexander. You stole that bike from outside John Menzies in Pollockshaws Road about a year ago. I had just popped in to get the *Evening Times*, a packet of cheese and onion crisps, and a bottle of Irn Bru after my shift, and when I came out, you had stolen my bike. So if you'll just unlock it, no more will be said and I won't report you to the polis."

"I did not steal that bike, Postie Khan. I found it in Queen's Park last summer."

"Aye, so ye did, hen, it's my bike. Look!"

He lifted and twisted the bike and pointed at some letters scratched under the seat. S.K. "In case you can't read as well as being a thief, that there says S.K. and that's me. Samir Khan."

He pointed to his Royal Mail badge, which clearly stated Samir Khan. "If it was your bike, it would say K.A, for Karen Alexander, wouldn't it? But it doesn't say K.A., does it? It says S.K., Samir Khan, and that's me. So get me the key for the padlock and I'll be on my way."

He stood with his hand out, looking smug and full of himself in his postman uniform, as I fumbled around in the many pockets of my bleached denim jacket, which was hanging by the door, for the tiny little padlock key.

Samir Khan sighed theatrically as I untangled the key from all my other keys and put it in his hand.

I watched from the window as he cycled up the street on my bike, with his Royal Mail bag swaying behind him.

It was only 11 AM, and my day was ruined so I decided to make the bleak journey to Martha Street, disguised in Justin's green snorkel parka, which was also hanging by the door, with the hood protruding about ten inches in front of my face, to cancel my wedding.

When I got there, Jack had already canceled it, and the registrar was looking at me as if I was three years old, simpering and patting me on the back. "I see this all the time, dear. They just run a mile, they get cold feet and they just run, but at least yours had the decency to cancel, saved you the embarrassment of him not showing up on the day! You're young, love, and you're quite nice-looking, there's plenty time for you, plenty fish in the sea, pet."

It was a nightmare day and getting worse.

I had to see him, so I ran to Queen Street Station, got the subway to Hillhead Station and skulked along the street and up the filthy close to Jack's front door.

His stoned flatmate peered out of the peephole then opened the door halfway, with a lit joint is his hand.

"I'd like to see Jack."

"He's not in, sorry," and at that he went to close the door in my face.

I stuck my foot in the doorway and kicked the door open. "I can see him, Tony. I can see Jack sitting in the kitchen smoking a joint."

And if I could see Jack, then he could see me, but he just sat there smoking his joint.

"Let me in, Tony. I need to talk to Jack, and I can see him right there."

"That's not Jack. That guy looks like Jack and he wears the same kind of clothes as Jack, but that's my pal Zack, from my maths class. We're always getting them mixed up."

I was seriously done with smug men today and was feeling angry and humiliated as I could hear Jack and his infantile flatmates sniggering and laughing. I knew I should gather up my dignity and walk away while I still had some, but I didn't.

"Right." I said, like an idiot lured into a ridiculous argument with a two-year-old. "So that guy I can see sitting in the kitchen wearing Jack's velvet jacket, Jack's jeans and Jack's *I Hate Maggie Thatcher* T-shirt, sitting in Jack's kitchen, that guy is not Jack—is that what you're saying?"

Tony blew a cloud of cannabis smoke onto my face, smirked, and said, "That's right, sweetheart, that guy in there is Zack, from my maths class. Isn't that right, guys?"

"Hey, Zack!" chorused the stoned arseholes in the kitchen.

I had never in my life hated anyone as much as I hated Tony and his stupid stoned pals right now, including Jack— or Zack—who sat there smugly and let them all humiliate me. I knew I should just walk away but I had let this go on for far too long now and was making a fool of myself. Tony won by casually swinging the door closed in my face.

25. The Tide Is High

I WAS SITTING IN THE WINDOW SILL HOLDING THE ENDS OF my hair up to my face, unable to decide if it looked sexy and edgy like Debbie Harry or cheap and bleached like Kelly McNicol. Anna had come home last night with a bottle of Sun-In, excited for us to try it. We both had the kind of hair that had been very light when we were younger and was now still blonde but not as bright and could look mousy if we left it too long to wash it.

"Look at this, Karen!" she had declared, holding the bottle in the air like the Olympic torch. "A girl in my English Lit class came in today and she looked fantastic! Her hair was the same as ours, mousy and dull, but then she used this and now she looks like Kim Wilde or Debbie Harry. She's sexy and all the guys were staring at her. Let's do it!"

I didn't think my hair was mousy and dull, but maybe it was. "What is it?"

"What is it? It's a miracle, that's what it is! Fifteen minutes from now, you and I will be sexy blonde bombshells! You just spray it in your hair, blast in with your hairdryer and voila— Marilyn Monroe!"

"You do it first."

135

Fifteen minutes later, Anna really did look fantastic. Her hair was lighter and brighter and blonder, and she was beside herself.

"Look at me. I love it!" She was dancing around the room, thrilled with herself.

"Give me that bottle!" I grabbed it from her and sprayed it all over my mousy hair.

"Not so much, Karen, just a little bit."

"If I'm going blonde, I'm going *blonde*!"

I couldn't wait to see myself as I put the hairdryer on full blast and held it as close to my hair as possible, while Anna put on a red dress I'd never seen before, and scarlet lipstick. "We're going out tonight, me and you. I'm moving in with Justin in a few weeks, and he's nice enough, but not exactly exciting, so these two blonde bombshells are going out! We'll go to Hoops Bar and see how many thousands of men chat us up!"

She put "The Tide Is High" on the record player as she tied a little black ribbon in the side of her hair.

My eyes were stinging with the Sun-In and my hair felt dry and rough as I tousled it in front of the hairdryer, excited to see the new sexy blonde me.

I could see the panic in Anna's eyes as I switched off the hairdryer, and I ran to the mirror on my dressing table. I looked like I had a bale of newly harvested straw on my head.

"What happened?" I could barely hear myself. "Switch the music off, Anna. What happened?"

We stayed home that night as Anna smoothed thick layers of conditioner on my hair and combed it through, then she washed it and dried it on a low heat which did make me look less ridiculous, but still like Kelly McNicol. This was now officially the worst week of my life.

I took one more day off from university, as the girl in Salon Shari across the road said she could "tame" it with a few lowlights, and thankfully she did. It still looked terrible compared to my real hair and was still too light and frizzy, but I could resume my life after my terrible few days in which I'd lost my boyfriend, my bike and my lovely hair.

I was trying to work out how long it would take to grow out at half an inch a month, which was what Shari had said was the rate that the average person's hair grew at, and the answer was twenty years. So at least it would be nice again for Marco's wedding. It was getting dark outside, a time of day I usually liked as I loved watching the lights go on inside the houses and shops, and I was waiting for the neighbour across the road to put his kitchen light on when I saw a man wobble along the pavement on a purple bike that was far too small for him.

It was Jack. Jack was cycling along my street on a small purple bike. By the time I got halfway down the four flights of stairs, Jack was halfway up, with the bike on his shoulder.

I threw my arms around him as he struggled not to fall down the stairs with the bike.

"I heard the postman took his bike back, so I got you a new one."

It was a beautiful bike, shiny and purple, with a wicker basket on the front, a zipped bag on the back and a shiny silver bell.

"How did you know?"

"I met Stuart at my leaving do, he couldn't wait to tell me. What happened … you look … what happened to your hair?"

26. Romeo and Juliet

CAROL AND I WENT BACK TO ANGELIQUE'S BRIDAL THE next day, taking the baby with us in a cute blue teddy bear coat as we knew that Angelique would be annoyed with us for running away and we thought the baby might distract her. Angelique was standing behind the counter, and when Carol and I pushed each other in the door, she lowered her 1950s tortoiseshell glasses to glare at us.

"Can I help you?" she asked, frostily.

"I really am getting married this time, Angelique."

"It's Jody." She pulled her beige cashmere sweater down and adjusted her silk scarf. "And you girls are wasting my time. So just trot on down the stairs and along the street to What Every Woman Wants, where you belong. I'm sure you'll find what you're looking for there. Mind how you go now. Goodbye."

I could tell that her posh accent was fake, but was in no position to argue. "I'm really sorry, Jody, but I really am getting married this time, so if we could just hire those two Regency dresses..."

"The ones that you tried on last week before you ran away?"

"Yes, those ones."

"The plain ones that you swapped last year for the beautiful dresses that your mum and I carefully selected for you?"

"Yes, those ones."

"And why did you run away? That was very inconvenient for me, not to mention extremely rude of you."

"I'm sorry, Jody." It was really hard not to call her Angelique. "I just panicked. I thought my boyfriend was going to work in a bank, but now he wants to be an architect, and then the postie took my bike, as it was actually his bike, but I didn't steal it, I found it in Queen's Park. Then my boyfriend bought me a new bike, and that made me realise that I really did want to marry him after all, as he was so thoughtful and he really loves me, even though I bleached my hair and that was what he liked best about me, my real hair, and now it will take twenty years to grow out, unless I dye it or get it cut. And it will obviously be harder to get another boyfriend now, you know, with my hair like this. So Jack must really love me, even though he pretended to be Zack."

Jody nodded. "All excellent reasons to get married at eighteen years old."

She looked at Carol. "Is this your baby?" Carol nodded. "Is that why you got married?"

She nodded again. Jody looked at me. "And are you expecting too?"

I shook my head. She looked at the baby again.

"Well, he's very handsome." There was a hint of a smile. "Is his dad Indian? Or Pakistani?"

"Italian."

"Well, he's very cute. What's his name?"

Jody let us have the dresses but didn't let us try them on again. As she folded them into the huge pink boxes in layers of tissue, she asked, reasonably, "How are you going to pay today, my dear? Cash or cheque?"

It really hadn't occurred to me that I would have to pay, as Carol's mum had paid last time.

"Oh, cheque!" I replied breezily, relieved that I still had some of my student grant left after paying Shari for fixing my hair. I flipped my Bank of Scotland chequebook open. "How much altogether, Jody?"

"One hundred and twenty pounds, please."

"Oh, Jody!" I laughed fondly. "We're just hiring the dresses, not buying them!"

"One hundred and twenty pounds, please. And I'll need them back three days after your wedding, at the latest."

Jack and I got married two weeks later in Martha Street Registry Office. We told no one except Dan and Carol and Jack's pathetic pal Stuart. I didn't even tell Anna although I knew she'd be upset. I would think of a good excuse, but it would have to be something dramatic, like Jack was terminally ill or joining the army and going to Belfast next week. I decided on the army story. It would be easier to live that lie.

I was standing in the hallway of the Registry Office in Martha Street, feeling beautiful and deliriously happy. Jack and I were getting married, in the same street where I had first seen him, and I thought I might burst with joy.

"Are you ready?" Carol whispered.

Jack and Dan were standing in front of the registrar, in their hired kilts, in the adjacent room, waiting for us.

"I'm ready, Carol. I'm ready to marry Jack Logan."

She took my hand and led me to the doorway.

"*Stop!*" The door to the street burst open, and a cold blast of air hit us as Grandpa Jimmy burst in, wearing his black suit, red lariat and cowboy boots. "Looks like I got here just in time!"

"Grandpa! What the eff are YOU doing here?"

"What am I doing here? I'm here to give the bride away, that's what! The bride needs a man to give her away, and that's me. And don't worry yourself, hen, I haven't told anyone, not a living soul, well, hardly anyone. Come on, hen." He offered me his elbow. "Let's go and get you married to this fine young man."

"Grandpa, you're not invited! How did you even know?"

"I know everything, hen." He tapped the side of his nose. "Don't forget, hen, your old grandpa was a spy in Berlin and Moscow during the war, a double agent. Nothing gets past Grandpa Jimmy."

The registrar appeared in the doorway.

"Is everything all right?"

"Yes." I smiled. "Yes, it is."

I took Grandpa Jimmy's arm and walked with him through the heavy double doors to the registrar's table, and I was happy that he was there.

Jack held my hands tightly as we said our vows. When it came to obey I just mouthed it and Jack tried not to laugh. He really knew me and I knew that we would be married forever.

We took two taxis to the Koh-i-Noor for our wedding dinner, and had so many people come by the table, congratulating us and admiring Marco, it was like being bathed in a halo of love. I never ever thought that my wedding would be in an Indian restaurant in Sauchiehall Street in Glasgow with three invited guests, Grandpa Jimmy, and a baby, with no cake, no speeches, and no confetti, but it was a perfect, wonderful day, especially when Jack's guitar appeared from the restaurant kitchen and he sang Dire Straits' "Romeo and Juliet" to me, and the Moghul waiter brought over a bottle of champagne and said that the entire bill was on the house. That was the first time in my life that I cried with happiness.

That night, our wedding night, Jack spent his last pay from the bank on a lovely corner suite, champagne and room service in the posh Grosvenor Park Hotel overlooking Kelvingrove Park. My life was complete.

Now we just had to tell our mums and dads.

27. Up Where We Belong

December 1984

"Rewind it, Karen, just one more time!" Carol and I had been sitting on my couch, rewinding and watching the final scene of *An Officer and a Gentleman* for over two hours. Between us lay a soggy pile of wet hankies, a half-empty tin of Roses chocolates and my little Jack Russell dog, Frankie.

"One more time, then let's put the quiche in the oven." Carol sighed, exhausted with crying. "In fact, arse the quiche. I'm running downstairs to get us kebabs."

We had been planning this week for months. It was finally the school Christmas holidays. I had a two-week break from my class of funny, demanding and exhausting six-year-olds in one of the most deprived areas of Glasgow, and Carol had a week off after two grueling months of early shifts on her nursing job. Jack was on his way home from a two-month student exchange trip to UC Berkeley in California to study architecture in an earthquake zone, Dan was in Italy with his dad as his great-grandpa slowly faded in a hospice, and Marco was in Kilbrannan for the week in the middle of a power struggle between his two grannies, who were desperately vying to become the favourite granny. Dan's mum was winning, and Marco spoke Italian more than English.

Carol and I had imagined, planned, longed for and saved up for this week for months. We were going to go Christmas shopping in Next, Lewis's and Marks and Spencer's, get new sparkly dresses in Principals, see the Christmas display in Fraser's, go out for curries at the Koh-i-Noor and pizza at Di Maggio's, go dancing in clubs, and have tea and scones at Kelvingrove Art Gallery, but in reality we were both so exhausted that we had hardly left my flat. It was so cold and dark and windy outside, and so warm and cosy and inviting inside, thanks to Uncle Jakey, and we had filled the fridge with luxurious and delicious Marks and Spencer's treats that we couldn't afford. And there was my beloved cheeky, chubby and handsome wee Frankie, formerly a flea-ridden skinny stray in Nitshill and now the most spoiled dog in the Southside, who just wanted to run downstairs to the overgrown back garden several times a day, then race back to curl on my knee on the couch. And there was Richard Gere in his white officer's uniform.

"So," Carol asked. "Richard Gere in that white navy uniform or Nick Santiago in his tight jeans in the Band Aid video?"

We had recorded the Band Aid video of "Do They Know It's Christmas?" from *Top of the Pops* and had been playing it nonstop when we weren't watching Officer Zach Mayo saving Paula from her life of drudgery in the factory.

"Probably Nick, but then there's Bono ... tough choice ... I've seen Bono live and he is very sexy indeed, but at the end of the day, it's Nick. Now if he could just slip into a wee tight white navy uniform."

We both sighed.

"I wish Richard Gere had turned up in the playground of Craigbank Primary School last week when the janitor and I were breaking up a fight between two twenty-two-year-old mums, one the mother of Versace McLatchie, and the other the mother of Tyson Thompson, who were fighting over a Transformer that one of their lovely little darlings had stolen from Woolworths. I hate my job sometimes."

"Me too." Carol sighed. "We had three methadone-addicted babies born last week, and one, a wee boy, didn't make it. I would have gone with Richard in his white uniform that day."

We sat in a sad silence for a few minutes. Working was hard, and we didn't get paid that much. Carol pulled herself together first. "We should wrap our Christmas presents tonight. What have you bought so far?"

"Those Roses chocolates for you, which we just ate, a blue Swatch watch for Jack, and the wee guitar for Marco. That's it. I'll need to go to What Every's on Saturday and get everything else. What about you?"

"You can't get posh Anna something out of What Every's! They don't allow that stuff in Dowanhill. You'll need to at least go to Marks and Spencer's for her, or even Fraser's."

"She'll never know."

"Yes, she'll know. The stuff is actual crap."

"Hmm, there are drawbacks to having a posh pal. Okay, I'll get her and Justin a tin of Roses chocolates from the newsagents' downstairs. Who doesn't like Roses? What about you? Have you got all of Marco's Santa stuff?"

"Not a thing. My mum and Dan's mum are trying to outdo each other with the Santa presents. It's ridiculous. My mum's opened a new Provident account to get him Optimus Prime figures that she can't afford and that he's not interested in, and Dan's mum has imported the entire unbelievably expensive wooden Brio train set from Sweden, including every Thomas the Tank character ever created and a revolving bridge. It's ridiculous. He's three years old. He just wants to play with a stick, watch Thomas the Tank, sing Winnie the Pooh nonstop and pick his nose. So far I've got a black Swatch watch for Dan, and you've nearly finished the Marks and Spencer's peach bubble bath I got you, with your endless free baths. That's it."

"Right, so we don't need to wrap anything, because we haven't bought anything, and we are going to Argyle Street tomorrow."

"You put the kettle on and I'll run downstairs for the kebabs. So are you a vegetarian this week, or do you want one of Mehmet's delicious spicy chicken kebabs?"

"I told you when we had the Marks and Spencer's chicken pie this afternoon."

I had told her that. What I hadn't told her was that Jack had been offered a scholarship to finish his architecture degree at UC Berkeley.

28. Two Tribes

"Support the miners! Coal, not dole!" shouted Jack, jangling a plastic bucket heavy with coins. "Every penny goes straight to Polkemmet."

"*Socialist Worker*!" yelled the beardy guy in the combat jacket who was standing at the opposite entrance of St. Enoch's Underground station.

"Hey, pal," Jack retorted. "What are you doing here? We agreed that you'd go to Buchanan Street Underground! This has been my spot for a year now!"

"Naw, it hisnae," shouted the *Socialist Worker* guy. "You've no been here for months. This is ma spot now, and I'm raking it in, so piss off."

The bold Frankie was growling in my arms, building up to a bark. "Quiet, Frankie! Leave it!"

"I've not been here right enough. I've been away, but my wife's been at this spot every single Saturday without fail. Isn't that right, Karen? So you piss off. We're supporting the miners here. Go back to Buchanan Street!"

"Yer wife's no been here, pal. Just me, and the miners are at Buchanan Street too, so piss off."

"What's he saying, Karen? You've been here collecting for the miners every week, haven't you?"

"What? I didn't hear you for that bus." I was caught. Jack assumed that I had continued collecting for the miners while he'd been in California, and I may have let him think that I had, but the *Socialist Worker* guy was right. I hadn't been once since Jack had left for California in October, not once. On Saturdays, I had a long lie, a hot bubble bath, read *Woman's Own* and the *Glasgow Herald*, walked Frankie in Queen's Park and did all my lesson plans for the week. I still supported the miners in principle and wore the badges, and I still put money in other people's buckets. But I had not once stood outside an Underground station with a bucket. It was too cold.

Today I was wearing a thermal vest, two T-shirts, a wooly polo neck jumper, Stuart's parka that he left on the peg by our door, a wooly hat, thermal tights, insulated ski pants, two pairs of socks, boots, gloves and a scarf but I was still chilled to the bone and just wanted to go home for a bath. Even Frankie was wearing a thick coat that said FRANKIE SAYS RELAX. And I was too tired after a week of thirty-two rambunctious six-year-olds and their twenty-two-year-old parents at my classroom door complaining about each other and fighting with each other every single day.

Jack and the *Socialist Worker* guy were both looking at me intently, each waiting for me to confirm that they were right, when by some stroke of great fortune, a Strathclyde Police officer sauntered into view and the *Socialist Worker* guy grabbed his bag of newspapers and ran down the stairs into the Underground station and onto a train bound for Govan.

"Chancing bastard!" said Jack.

"Yes, chancing bastard!" I agreed.

We collected a full bucket that day, even though it was just after Christmas and everyone was skint. A large bucket full of support, generosity and sacrifice.

Here you go pal.

Good luck, son.

Good for you, here you go.

I don't have much, son, but here.

Eff Maggie, son, eff her, we have to win this, for Scotland, for the working man.

Support the miners, every one of them.

We're fighting for dignity here, son.

Eff Maggie, eff that bitch.

We had only had one lecture that day, when two well-heeled elderly ladies in expensive raincoats and plastic rain hats tied under their chins stopped to talk to us. They were so old that we had to be polite.

The taller lady, who must have been in her nineties, peered at Jack's face, removing her glasses to do so. I tried not to laugh when, like a schoolboy, he called her Miss.

"How old are you, young man?"

"Twenty-seven, Miss."

"And do you work?"

"I'm a student, miss."

They both tutted. "Did you hear that, Dorothy? This young man is still a student at twenty-seven years old!"

Dorothy was clearly outraged. "That's ridiculous, Elspeth!"

"It certainly is, Dorothy. And is this young lady your girlfriend?"

"My wife."

"Well!" Dorothy and Elspeth shook their heads in disgust.

"And do you have a job, dear?"

"I do. I'm a teacher at Craigbank Primary School."

"Did you hear that, Elspeth? A married man of almost thirty years old and still not working, and his poor wife out every day working with these rough unemployed people in Craigbank, trying to teach them to read. And why are you collecting money for grown men who are on strike, who have perfectly good jobs to go to? Not only that, they are forcibly stopping all the decent miners who just want to go to work to feed their families. And they call them scabs! Now why would a clearly intelligent married man like yourself collect money for these sorts?"

Dorothy and Elspeth were too old for Jack to get really angry with, as he did with all the others. Normally he got into a heated argument every Saturday with the few Maggie supports that lived in Glasgow. We had this same argument with someone every single Saturday.

"The miners are fighting to keep the livelihood and economy of an entire country, Miss, they are fighting for the chance to work and feed their families, and they are fighting for dignity and respect, and to keep an established industry alive. We have to support them. We can't let Thatcher win." Jack was struggling to keep calm, and a small supportive crowd had gathered, nodding in agreement with him.

Dorothy leaned in and spoke quietly in Jack's face, her old lined and powdered face scarlet with outrage, "I'll tell you something, young man. Mrs. Thatcher is going to crush the miners."

That night we had our usual Saturday Chinese takeaway of Lemon Chicken and Chow Mein, paid for from the bucket, but Dorothy's hostile words were hanging over us.

"These are dark days for our country, Karen. Britain is so divided. There's so much violence and bitterness. Thatcher has ruined our country."

"We'll be in California in eight months. Away from the rain and the sleet and Maggie Thatcher."

"Reagan's no better."

"Well at least it's sunny there, and I know I've been saying this for weeks now, but I really am going to tell Carol tomorrow."

29. Wake Me Up When September Ends

"Okay, Eilish, you first. Are you ready?"

"I'm ready, Mum!"

"Give me an E."

"E!"

"Give me an I."

"I!"

"Give me an L."

"L!"

"Give me an I."

"I!"

"Give me an S."

"S!"

"Give me an H."

"H!"

"Whadda ya get?"

"*Eilish*!" we both shouted as we did our little cheerleader routine around the kitchen table.

"Okay, Miss High School Sophomore, now get in the car. Lunch box?"

"Check!"

"P.E. kit?"

"Check!"

"Pencil case?"

"Check!"

"Shoes on?"

"Check!"

"Knickers on?"

"Check!"

"Okay, now get in the car!"

"Shotgun!" shouted Eilish, as she ran to the minivan to get the front seat before her brother.

"Okay, Finn, your turn, are you ready? Give me an F! Hello, Finn? Give me an F! Finn?"

Finn sauntered into the kitchen in his pajama bottoms and a wrinkled T-shirt, his fair hair flopping all over his face.

"Finn! We're leaving right now. You're not even dressed."

"Yeah, Mum. The thing is, I'm like … dressed … yeah?"

"Finn—are you stoned?"

I was getting angry with him—his hair, his pajamas, the way he talked, and how, since Marco had been here for a month, they both said yeah? at the end of every sentence, like Cockney TV-AM presenters, except they'd never been to London, apart from Heathrow Airport, and it was really annoying. And now he was going to make Eilish late on the first day back at school.

"Course I'm not stoned, Mum. It's … like … 7 AM … yeah?"

"Finn, I'm not waiting for you. I'm going to drop Eilish off at school, and you better be dressed and ready when I get back in fifteen minutes."

"Take a chill pill, dude, the thing is, like, I won't be going in the minivan with you any more, like … ever … yeah? I'll be going to school in that thing, whatsit called again … that thing that Dad got me … the thing you go places in … oh yeah, my car!"

"Oh, don't be ridiculous! What's the point of you going to school in your own car and having to get a parking permit and then find a space and then wait for forty-five minutes to get out of the car park this afternoon, when I could just drop you off and pick you up? I'm going anyway! And don't call me dude."

"Yeah, Mum, a high school senior getting dropped off by his mum, right? In a minivan, right? No way. And I keep my guitar and my stuff in my car anyway, so it's just easier."

"Is that right? Well at least get yourself dressed. Yeah?"

"I am, like, dressed … yeah? Oh and Mum, I'll be giving you plenty of F's this year. In my grades!"

When I got back from dropping Eilish off and having a conversation from my minivan window with some PTA moms about the school dress code not including pajamas, Finn was gone. His school backpack was still lying by the door, and his packed lunch on the kitchen countertop. And Eilish had just told me that she would be going to school on her bike from now on.

It was time for me to go back to work.

30. *Teenage Kicks*

SEPTEMBER 6, 2006—NEW YEAR'S DAY FOR MUMS everywhere, as that was the day that the California schools went back after a ridiculously long summer of almost three months. Three furnace-hot, air-conditioned months of Finn and his posse of extremely loud, funny, annoying, hungry and exhausting pals, newly graduated from high school and celebrating their last summer together before they scattered to their colleges and universities around the country, with one boy, Daniel, whom I'd loved since he was a chubby funny four-year-old, joining the military and about to leave for basic training in Virginia. I couldn't look at him without tearing up, and when I'd bumped into his mum in the supermarket and given her an impromptu hug by the organic fruit stand, she had burst into tears and clung onto me while we both sobbed. I just couldn't shake the feeling of dread that overcame me when I thought of him, and that day in the supermarket I knew that his mum felt it too.

The boys' days were spent working at their summer jobs—in fast food restaurants, pizza delivery, garden work, and one on his under-the-bed mushroom-growing enterprise that he thought the mums didn't know about, then every evening they gathered at someone's house, usually mine, to empty the fridge, soak all the towels, dive into the pool and ruin the tranquility of the street with their loud rap music, Dr. Dre and Too $hort, and their overexcited yelling, singing and laughing. Sometimes there was a girl in the group, but most evenings it was just these noisy young men, then the next morning the odd empty beer bottle or little piles of burned cannabis stuffed into and under plant pots.

Then there was Eilish and Rosa, best friends since they were five years old, who spent their days watching *Lord of the Rings*, reading *Twilight* and *Harry Potter*, going on their bikes for frozen yoghurt, volunteering in the animal shelter, and being disgusted with Finn and the boys.

Now Finn was at summer school at UCLA, living in a dorm with a boy from Iowa, Eilish was back at school, and I had three wonderful, beautiful tranquil days of solitude before I started back at my teaching job in the local community college. My lesson plans were ready, my print-outs printed, my online lessons prepared, thanks to Eilish.

Now I had a big decision to make—yoga class or a chapter of *The Da Vinci Code*, or walk the dog before it got too hot, or just read the paper.

I put the kettle on, lifted the *San Francisco Chronicle*, and ignored the phone ringing in my bag. The house was quiet and tidy, there was food in the fridge, the towels were clean and folded, the laundry was done, and I was sitting on the sofa with the patio doors open, enjoying the quiet bubbling from the pool. The air was warm, the jasmine was sweet, and two doves were cooing in the tree by the door.

The ringing persisted.

If someone in Scotland's dead, they'll still be dead when I finish my tea...

When the house phone stated to ring and didn't stop, I knew I had to answer it.

"Mrs. Logan?"

"Yes, hello?"

"Hello, Mrs. Logan, this is Elizabeth Sanchez in the school office. Your daughter, Eye-lash Logan, has been suspended. Can you come here as quickly as possible, please?"

I sat outside the assistant principals' office on the Seat of Shame, texting Jack and telling him to call me as soon as possible. I had seen parents sit here before, on this utilitarian plastic seat in full view of the office, the ladies' toilets and the maths corridor, but now I was the one receiving the sympathetic glances from passing staff and student workers.

On the door was a sign that stated "Morten Andersen, Ph.D." I could hear the lacrosse team clattering across the sports field and downstairs, the choir was practicing "America the Beautiful" for the Back-to School event this very evening, an event I would no longer be going to. Oh, the shame. Eventually I was summoned in.

Dr. Andersen was clicking a pen on his polished desk, and he smiled and offered his hand as I scuttled in the door, wishing I had changed out of my yoga clothes as Dr. Andersen was wearing a tailored three-piece suit.

Dr. Morten Andersen, the Big Viking Principal, the Nordic God, Mighty Morten, the most fancied man in the town, and I had the great fortune not to find him at all attractive—too tall and too blond. I was the only mum I knew who could have a sensible conversation with him, and he knew that and had sought out my counsel on school issues over the years.

"Good morning, Mrs. Logan. I see that Mr. Logan is not here?"

I still hated how, after over twenty years in California, I often couldn't tell if an American was asking me a question or telling me something. "No, he's not here."

"Well, Mrs. Logan, I am very surprised and disappointed to tell you that I have suspended Eilish."

At least he could say her name properly.

"She's only been back at school for three hours, Dr. Andersen. What did she do in that time?"

He stopped clicking his pen and laid it down at the end of a neat row of expensive pens. He sighed. "We have a new calculus teacher, Mrs. Rosenblum. Very experienced, came highly recommended from Sacramento. Eilish is in her class, the advanced class, as you know."

I nodded.

"Well, this morning, Mrs. Rosenblum asked the students to introduce themselves, and Eilish told her that she was a new student from Kazakhstan and didn't speak English, and that her name was Miss Borat. Now, you're a teacher yourself, and as you know, we all have students giving us silly names on the first day of class, There's always a Soon Mi Bang, a Phil McCrotch and a Vye Agra."

I stifled a snort, I'd never heard that one.

"Every class, every semester. But this went on for a while, with Eilish blurting out ridiculous rude questions in a ridiculous accent. However, it went too far and was causing hilarity and disruption in the class, and so Miss Rosenblum asked Eilish to stand outside the class to let things calm down."

I nodded again.

"And now, Mrs. Logan, you are well aware of my political affiliations. Our paths have often crossed at local Democratic Party fundraising events, and as you know, I do not allow military recruiters on campus, but when a student at my school, who has already been removed from class for disruptive behavior on the first day of a new semester, takes a black permanent marker and writes AMERICAN IDIOT across the portrait of the elected US president that I am required to display in the hallway, well, I'm afraid that a two day suspension is the absolute minimum that I can impose. Eilish can go home immediately and must remain with you at all times. Please sign this."

He slid a piece of paper and a pen across the table. "And Eilish can return to school on Monday the 11th, after she apologizes to Mrs. Rosenblum."

As Eilish and I walked to the car, I grew increasingly annoyed about her suspension and even more annoyed at missing my day to myself. "What were you thinking, Eilish? You now have a suspension on your record, and that's going to affect your college applications. And it's ridiculous. This is the very first day of your junior year."

She jumped into the front seat of the minivan.

"Sit in the back, I don't want to see you."

"Oh Mum, don't be ridiculous!"

"Back."

She sat in the back. "I am quite sorry, Mum, but not really. Everyone was making up names. Rosa was Anita Lay and Ethan was Dick Long, and the new teacher believed them, so I just joined in, and mine was the funniest, and everyone laughed, especially when the teacher said, 'Thank you, Miss Borat.' How could you teach in a high school and not know? Where's she been teaching? Utah?"

"Okay, but you took it too far, didn't you?"

"I did, Mum, sorry."

She didn't sound sorry.

"And what about 'American Idiot'? You shouldn't have done that, Eilish."

"Mum." Eilish sighed. "George Bush is the biggest idiot in America. I actually heard you say those exact words last week, at your book club, and all your pals agreed. I got really annoyed when I saw his stupid smug face on the wall, and then I saw the marker on the table, and I just couldn't help myself. Half the school agrees with me. My inbox is full already and my phone's going nonstop. I'm going back there a hero, Mum. I'm like Rosa Parks."

"And what about the other half?"

"The other half? I don't give an arse, and let's face it, neither do you, and neither does Dad. In fact, I know that Dad used to do stuff like that, and so did you. Dad was on the news once because he defaced a Maggie Thatcher poster, and you were with him when he did it!"

I stifled a grin. The BBC Scotland News cameras showing Jack, with a balaclava over his face, climbing up a drainpipe to spray *Eff Thatcher* and draw a Hitler mustache on a poster of her face in Shawlands. Except he wrote the actual word. And there was me at the bottom of the billboard with Frankie, and with no balaclava, so everyone watching *The Six O'clock News* saw me as I picked up the dog and ran away.

"But that was different, Eilish, you can get away with that more in Scotland. We had the whole country behind us. It's more serious here. Not everyone agrees with us, and this will be on your record."

"Mum, Caroline Lee got suspended four times and she's at Stanford. On a scholarship. I know that Dad will be annoyed about the Borat thing and me getting suspended, but admit it, you can't wait to tell him and Auntie Carol about 'American Idiot,' can you?"

"That's not the point, Eilish." Although I knew that it kind of was. "We're not from here, Eilish. We're newcomers, guests;, we're ex-pats, immigrants; we have to walk a line; we can't offend people. You have to be sensitive to…"

"I was born in Oakland, California, Mum. I was Born in the USA. I'm a Free Born Man of the USA. Keep on Rockin' in the Free World."

I decided there and then that my daughter would spend the next three days cleaning out the garage, and that she was her father's daughter in every way. And that Jack needed to help me sort her out.

31. Rebel, Rebel

EILISH WAS CLATTERING AND BANGING AROUND THE kitchen, followed by Buster, the ever-hopeful Boxer, as she made herself a smoothie with dozens of ingredients that I'd never heard of until her smoothie craze started two weeks ago, the very day that she did not go to her high school Senior Homecoming Dance as a protest. I still didn't know what the protest was against. My giant fridge was now full of expensive organic ingredients and unidentifiable foodstuffs such as acai, almond milk, chia seeds, wakame, and astragalus. I had to delve through the disorganized chaos every time I wanted a wee bit of cheese and my patience was wearing thin. In fact, my patience had been wearing thin since the first week of school last year when my lovely, funny, clever and sweet-natured seventeen-year-old daughter with the exact same wavy hair as her dad got suspended, then came home after a weekend at her new friend Mara's house smelling like she had been in a small enclosed space with Bob Marley, Willie Nelson and Snoop Dogg. That was the same day that she had acquired scarlet hair, black lipstick to match her thick black eyeliner, a piercing in her nose, and a sarcastic sullen attitude.

The next day she had told her dad that he had to stop flying on business as he was encouraging the government to use chemtrails.

"What's a chemtrail, Eilish? I don't think I've ever see one of those, and I'm a Platinum Status Frequent Flyer with two different airlines."

"Dad, you know those trails in the sky behind planes?"

"Yes, contrails, vapour trails."

"That's what they want you to think. That it's just vapour. But it's actually chemicals."

"Oh for goodness sake, Eilish, and what would these chemicals be for?"

"To modify and control the climate."

"Oh, I see, those trails of condensation that appear in certain atmospheric conditions? They're actually chemicals released by the government?"

"Yes, Dad." Eilish sighed. "And you're part of the problem."

"Not any more I'm not! Not now that I know about this! Why did you not tell me sooner? I'm just going to my office right now to cancel all my flights, then I'll call my team and tell them that I may be late to Atlanta next week as I'll be going on my mountain bike. The following week, I'll hitchhike to Philadelphia. And can you call the Greyhound Bus terminal in Oakland and get me a ticket to Houston next month, on the bus with America's Most Wanted? Sydney might be a problem, but I'm sure there are boats that go there. Problem solved! And with all the money we save, I'll get you a nice tin foil hat!"

That was the first time that she had stomped out of the room.

It had been funny at first. Jack, Finn and I had walked around the house shouting, "Eilish, hello, hello? Missing person report, has anyone seen Eilish Logan? Calling Eilish

Logan? Excuse me, Miss Angry Punk, have you seen Eilish Logan?"

Now I was completely out of patience with the constant complaining, sulky silences, endless conspiracy theories, and angry loud punk music from her pigsty of a room. I was waiting for the day that this unpleasant ungrateful girl would go home and my lovely wee happy Eilish, with her shiny hair and lacrosse uniform and Judy Moody books would dance back in the door.

"I see that Finn and his tribe of white privileged generic California college boys are here," she stated, indicating the garden where there was indeed the usual daily gathering of noisy, ravenous twenty-year-old boys.

"Yes, they are." I tried to keep my voice neutral. "Yes, Benyamin, Salim, Josh, Brendan, Miguel, Shah and Kevin Yu are here. And there's a new one here, Brett. Have you met him? He's at UCSD with Shah."

Eilish snorted and stomped out of the kitchen, followed by Buster. The dog was the only one who wanted to be with her any more. We all avoided her and her constant complaining. I was exhausted with it.

I was sitting at the kitchen table preparing for my first lesson for my English learners' class when she reappeared, with the dog trailing behind her.

"What you doing, Mum?"

My heart leaped with joy and hope at hearing that word, Mum.

"It's my first lesson this semester for my ESL class. We are working on words with three syllables. So far I've come up with: a/ni/mal; fa/mi/ly; cho/co/late; ba/na/na."

"Oh, I've got some!"

Eilish pulled a chair to the other side of the table, facing me, and looked me in the eye. "Gov/ern/ment; co/rrup/tion;

cli/mate/change; hu/rri/cane; Ka/tri/na; New/Jim/Crow; Mon/san/to..."

"Okay, thank you, Eilish."

"You can't close your eyes to reality forever, Mum."

"Eilish, why don't you put a load of laundry on and walk the dog?"

"You see all those college boys in our pool right now, Mum?"

"I do indeed, I've been seeing and hearing them all day. In fact, the whole street can hear them."

"Well, do you know why college is so expensive in the USA?"

"I could take a guess. Professors, teaching assistants, libraries, books, research, disabled students' programs and services, digital media, assistive technology, equity programs, ..."

"No, Mum, how can you not know this when you're part of the system?"

I braced myself. I had about 2 percent of my lifetime patience reserve left and today might be the day I ran out.

"It's the military, isn't it? They keep boys like Finn and Kevin Yu in college with their parents' money, and they keep the minorities out so that they can have a pool of poor young men for the military. Men whose families can't afford college—they're cannon fodder, Mum. And people like you and Dad keep Finn out with your money."

This was a new one and my patience was now officially gone.

"Eilish, I am sick fed up with your theories. The US military is voluntary. We've not had a draft since Vietnam. Every single male in the USA up to the age of twenty-six has to register for Selective Service. That's a nationwide list of young men of military age if we ever do a draft again. Finn has signed up and so have all of those boys out there. And you know that Daniel has been in Iraq for over a year."

I gathered my strength and continued, my anger with Eilish growing by the second. "Over half of all college students in California pay nothing. They get their fees paid because their families have a low income, and they get financial aid. Over half. Yes, I am part of the system, Eilish, the system of education."

There was a loud burst of laughter from the pool as someone was thrown in. Eilish looked out of the window in disgust and stomped back up to her hovel. I finished my lesson plan and decided to do a towel-gathering raid in the garden. At least if the towels were hung across the back of the chairs, they would dry in minutes. There was a polite chorus of "Hello, Mrs. Logan," and "Thank you for having us, Mrs. Logan."

"You're welcome!" I waved, too. They were welcome, but how I would cheer when they all returned to college.

As I turned to go back into the kitchen, I heard a loud guffaw, and one by one, the boys fell onto the patio laughing, really honking, slapping each other on the back in hysterics. Eilish came to her window to glare.

"What did I miss?"

"Nothing, Mum!" Finn could hardly breathe as he lay draped over a lounger, laughing helplessly.

After several minutes of this, I called Finn into the kitchen. "What did I miss, Finn? What's so funny?"

"Oh, Mum!" He was struggling to speak and trying to compose himself through decreasing bursts of laughter. "The new guy, Brett, he said you were hot!"

"Right, and that's what you're all laughing at? Because I'm not?"

"Oh, Mum, you're a mum, and you're old!" He was hysterical again.

By the time Jack got home, I was desperate to tell him about the latest Eilish confrontation and the fact that a twenty-year-old had thought I was hot, even though a large group of other twenty-year-olds obviously could not see it.

Buster ran to the door when he heard Jack's car roar up the street, top down despite the ninety-five-degree heat, and his music blaring The Stereophonics. He was on the phone when he walked in the door, ignoring Buster and giving me an absentminded glance. He disappeared into his office while his goat cheese and heirloom tomato pasta bake shriveled and crusted in the oven, then he reappeared, still on the phone.

"Jack, we need to talk."

He motioned for me to be quiet as he took his burned dinner from the oven, looked at it in disdain, poured himself a glass of red wine and sat at the breakfast bar, still on the phone and reading the paper. Eilish had not budged from her room, but I knew she was alive and well as I could hear her having loud outraged conversations on her phone. I emptied and filled the dishwasher, packed my bag for my class tomorrow, cleaned up the second pile of wet towels and empty soda cans and plates with baked-on food that Finn and his pals had left lying around the garden, put the washing machine on, and came back through to the living room. There was a man sitting on the couch watching the news. I didn't know who he was. He looked like Jack and had Jack's hair but greyer, and this man was boring and overweight and self-absorbed and completely uninterested in me or anyone in this house.

"Hello?" I turned the volume down on the TV and sat beside the man. "I'm looking for my lovely, handsome, sexy, attentive boyfriend, Jack Logan. Have you seen him?"

I thought I looked quite cute in my yoga clothes, and I had new highlights, but the man didn't even look at me.

"Oh, for goodness sake, Karen." He grabbed the remote, still not looking at me. "It's been a long day. Just let me watch the news in peace."

"Want me to walk the dog with you, Mum?"

Finn was standing in the doorway in his pajama bottoms and a T-shirt. I felt my eyes fill with tears. My lovely boy.

"Oh, never mind, Shah's car just pulled into the drive. We're going to Jamba Juice. Later, Mum."

32. Leaving on Your Mind

KHALIL, WHO AT SIXTY-EIGHT YEARS OLD WAS THE OLDEST student in the college, was standing in front of the class reading aloud his scholarship-winning essay. As this gentlemanly, scholarly, qualified engineer read slowly and deliberately about his struggle to learn English while driving taxis in Fremont, I felt the pride in my heart that teachers live for. Every student was silent and focused, with not a phone in sight. The magic was broken by an insistent tapping on the door and the appearance of my co-worker, Magda, flustered and out of breath.

Khalil looked at me hesitantly and I gestured for him to continue, while the class murmured and shuffled in their seats and I stepped outside with Magda.

"It's your son, Finn. He keeps calling the office. He says that no one's dead but you need to call him urgently. Your daughter has been arrested and is at Bryant Street Police Department in the city. I'll take care of the class, you go."

By the time I was on the Bay Bridge, I was beyond livid. My hands were white as I clutched the steering wheel and I could hear my own angry breath. I had called Jack's assistant right away and told her that he had to immediately go to

Bryant Street Police Station, which was several blocks from his office, and I would meet him there.

Finn was waiting outside the police station, pacing up and down looking for me as I parked right next to a sign that said "San Francisco Police Department Vehicles Only— Violators Will Be Towed."

He was with a girl that I did not know. "Mum, this is Courtney. She drove me here."

Was he really introducing me to his new girlfriend right now?

By then, I knew that Jack was on his way and that Eilish and Rosa, neither of whom had a full driving license, had skipped school, taken Finn's old Honda, driven into the city along the six-lane freeways, over one of the busiest bridges in the world, through the congested city streets to the Westfield Center and been arrested for shoplifting.

By the time Finn and I and the girl I did not know had got through the metal detectors and security, I knew that Eilish and Rosa had gone into the changing room in Hot Topic with an armful of the horrible ripped punky clothes that they liked and instead of doing what normal shoplifters do and removing the tags and slipping the stolen clothes into their bags, they had put all the clothes on, layers and layers of ripped leggings and tiny red tartan skirts and printed tights and black hoodies with skulls, and had tried to nonchalantly stroll out of the shop looking like two Michelin men, setting off the alarms. When the security guard had asked them to stop, they ran, which was not very effective with multiple layers of clothing on, getting as far as Macy's cosmetics department where they were trying to hide behind the Lancôme counter when they were arrested. A sizable crowd had gathered, many of them filming it on their cellphones, so I knew it would be all over YouTube and Facebook by now.

We sat in the waiting room—me, Finn and this new girl who held Finn's hand as he silently fumed. We were the only people in the room with full sets of teeth and no tattoos, and that made me even more angry—that I was here and Jack was not, and that in the eyes of the staff behind the strengthened glass, I was the same as everyone else in the room.

Rosa's mum swept into the room crying her eyes out, followed by her entire extended family, all talking at the same time in Spanish. I didn't know whether to hug her or not, but she saw me and ran over, weeping onto my shoulder.

"Logan and Gonzalez." An officer appeared, reading the names from a piece of paper in his hand. No one moved.

"*Logan* and *Gonzalez*!"

We all rushed towards the officer, all twenty of us—me, Finn, the girl, and Rosa's family.

"Finn," I hissed. "Go outside and wait for your dad, bring him in here as quickly as possible."

"Parents only. Come this way." The officer motioned for us to follow him.

I stepped forward with Rosa's mum and dad, and her tiny little immaculately dressed grandma.

"Parents only, ma'am."

"I am *abuela*. I am coming too."

The four of us were led along bleak green corridors, through multiple reinforced locked doors and into a small airless room where Rosa and Eilish sat huddled on a bench.

"I am the arresting officer, Officer Belardes, and I would like to speak to the parents only, please."

"I will leave," stated Rosa's grandma, then she stepped forward and slapped Rosa hard on the face.

"Is Eilish Logan's father here?"

"No, he is not." I spat out the words. Jack was still not here.

Eilish and Rosa were released on the condition that the parents sign multiple documents and report to our local police station within a week, as the shop was pressing charges. It was worse than I thought, as they were also being charged with resisting arrest, truancy, driving without a license, and evading a police officer. Macy's was possibly charging them too with something.

Courtney drove us home in silence as Finn's car was impounded and mine was towed. It was the worst day of my life, and when Jack arrived home at 8 PM as usual, delighted with himself that he had arranged for the return of the cars, I was the angriest I had ever been. Finn saw my face and scuttled out with Courtney.

"Where the eff have you been, Jack? I called you nine hours ago." My voice was quiet and controlled.

"I've been at two different pounds, one by the airport, one in Bayview, getting the cars back. You're welcome. Finn and I will BART in and pick them up tomorrow."

I was shaking with rage. "Where were you, Jack? Your daughter got arrested today and was handcuffed and put in a police car and in a cell and I had to go and get her. In the police station which is three blocks from your office. It was humiliating, and do you know who took charge of this family? Not you. Our nineteen-year-old son. Finn took charge because you weren't there. And some girl I don't know. Look at you, Jack, turning up to a crisis nine hours after it's over. We could have got the cars back any time. Where were you? Why didn't you show up?"

"You obviously handled it. Eilish is home, isn't she? You've sorted it all out."

My rage increased as my heart thumped and my fists balled. "We needed you, Jack. Rosa had her entire family there, and I was there by myself. It was humiliating. You didn't leave your meeting, did you? This didn't affect your day. You didn't call me or Finn; you didn't even care. You didn't show up, Jack."

"No, but I got your car back, the one you parked illegally, and you handled everything else."

"Yes, I did handle it, by myself. What's the point of you, Jack? What's the point of you being in this family when you let us down in a time of crisis?"

"Well, it was hardly a crisis, was it? Shoplifting? You didn't pay for makeup until you were about twenty-five years old, and you've never bought a record in your life. You and Carol were compulsive shoplifters back in the day, weren't you?"

"This isn't about two girls nicking 50p lip gloss from Woolworths to go to the local disco, Jack. They tried to steal hundreds of dollars of merchandise, and there are multiple other charges. This is serious. We have to go to Juvenile Court. You know what this is like, Jack? This is like when hairy Bree used to laugh at me and belittle me when I was seventeen years old, and you pretended you couldn't see it, and you didn't stick up for me. And it's like when your mum used to criticize everything I did and said with the children, and again you pretended you didn't notice."

"Oh for goodness sake, Karen, that was almost thirty years ago!"

"And that makes it worse, because you're still doing it. You've learned nothing. You're selfish and you don't stick up for me. You've never stood up for me, now that I come to think of it. You just wait until I've calmed down, then you do a little performance to get me back—sing a song, buy me a bike, get me a dog—a big gesture that means nothing as nothing changes, but you never actually show up when I need you. I had to leave my class today when one of my students was reading out an award-winning essay that I had coached him on. I had to walk out and leave my class, Jack."

"We've been over this before, Karen. I bought you a bike after you left me, remember, and I had to cancel our wedding? And there's no need for you to work at all. Couldn't you just go back to your voluntary work? None of the other partners' wives work. It seems like an indulgence, and it's really inconvenient for me and the kids. Why don't you give up your job if you're so stressed?"

Then he glanced at his watch. Naked rage boiled in me. For the first time in my life, I understood why wives sometimes kill their husbands.

"That's a great idea, Jack. That's what I'll do. I'll give up the job that I love, and I'll fanny about all day, getting my nails done and my lip fillers and Botox like your coworkers' twenty-five-year-old wives, then we'll all go to Nieman Marcus for lunch and talk about Britney Spears and Paris Hilton. That sounds fantastic and very fulfilling, and I could be standing at the door every night waiting for you to come home from work, holding your slippers and pipe and wearing my best frock and lipstick. You know what, you're right. I'm resigning tomorrow. Why waste my time with a silly little job like teaching English to people who don't speak it, when I could fanny about and iron your effing shirts and hoover. You've known me since I was seventeen years old—how can you even say that?"

"You're being ridiculous, Karen. Just calm down and I'll get us all a Chinese takeaway."

"A Chinese takeaway? You haven't even asked about Eilish, you haven't asked about Finn, you haven't asked about anything and do you know why? Because you're a fat pompous selfish arsehole and I can't stand you!"

I looked at my husband, and he really was exactly that, and I decided that I was going to leave him.

Twenty minutes later, as I was opening Jack's suit closet with a pair of scissors in my hand, Marco called me to tell me that Grandpa Jimmy had died.

33. Let Me Go

I HAD ALWAYS LOVED CAROL AND DAN'S COLOURFUL, warm, welcoming flat. The light pouring in from the huge windows, the red and orange walls, the big squashy couch and chairs, the faint scent of honeysuckle candles, the warm wooden floors and bright rugs—I even loved the little yellow kettle she had had for twenty years. As newlywed teenagers, she and Dan had bought the flat for eight thousand pounds, just weeks before Marco was born, when Dan's dad gave them the old family chip shop on George Street as a wedding present. Just off Glasgow High Street, near the old fruit market, in a run-down, almost derelict street in a soot-stained old tenement with leaky rickety windows and a litter-strewn back court, Carol's new home had been full of aggressive pigeons that came in and out at their leisure through the broken windows. We had spent an entire week scrubbing and bleaching—me, Carol's mum, Auntie Julie and the two Mrs. Capaldis, Dan's mum and gran, still pretending they didn't speak English—while Carol's Uncle Jakey and Grandpa Jimmy fixed the windows, doors and plumbing and rewired every room and Carol sat on a deck chair, crying her eyes out and nursing her new cousin Christopher. Jakey's creative wiring ensured that the flat was always roasting hot with endless free hot water and no electric bill ever. Carol and Dan had spent years sanding and varnishing floorboards, painting vibrant reds and oranges on the smoothed walls and sweeping the communal close clear of drunks, beer cans, smashed bottles and chip papers. The evicted pigeons had screeched and pecked at the windows for months but had eventually found a new home.

The first sign of change had been when Café Gandolfi had opened around the corner. Carol and I had loved it instantly: the warmth, the sophisticated atmosphere, the heavy wooden tables and chairs carved into wonderful art deco patterns, the big stained glass window lined with dozens of spider plants, the creamy hot chocolate, the caramel shortcake, the rich wooden floors, the lack of bingo women, and no whinging babies in buggies, apart from Marco. The music was soft, European and jazzy, unlike the tinny juke box in the West End Café, and the clientele a mix of well-heeled business people and artsy indie students from my nearby university in their carefully put together scruffy Oxfam clothes. We could never afford a meal there and would sit for hours with our hot chocolate, except for the time Carol's Uncle Jakey gave us fifty quid after he won several thousand on the horses, and we blew it on fabulous goat cheese salads, delicious fish in a creamy sauce with scalloped potatoes, warm apple crumble with thick Scottish cream, two pieces of caramel shortcake each and a pot of tea. We sat there for four hours that night, savouring every morsel and every minute.

The following year, a tiny sweet-smelling flower shop opened, run by the gayest guy I had ever seen in Scotland, then another bistro, and next door to that a warm pub with leather sofas and a fireplace, dark red walls and live music. Next came an authentic Mexican restaurant and a clean little newsagent shop that sold the *Financial Times* and the *Glasgow Herald*, Swiss chocolate and ready-made sandwiches on ciabatta with fillings like smoked salmon and chicken tikka. Then the builders arrived, singing crudely, whistling and cat-calling in orange jackets and hard hats, with acres of tarpaulin, sandblasters and scaffolding. When they finished, Carol was living in the new, expensive, trendy Merchant City.

I lay on the old soft red velvet sofa, watching the grey skies and greedy seagulls sail past on the gale-force winds which in Glasgow pass for a wee breeze. The bay window was the biggest I had ever seen, overlooking the old steep tiled roofs, the dozens and dozens of chimneys going up the hill towards the Cathedral. It was my favourite view in the world.

"Remember the day you bought this couch from Habitat? I was so jealous. It was so red, so squashy, so expensive, and the delivery men cursing and swearing as they tried to carry it up four flights of stairs! Then a gang of wee boys tried to nick their van and they shouted out the window at them, told them to eff off, the polis were coming."

Carol laughed and handed me a cup of tea. "Dan and I spent all of our wedding money on this couch, every penny we got from his family in Parma. We slept on a mattress on the floor, me pregnant and him working all hours in the chippie, but this couch was my pride and joy. I was a married woman and I had a gorgeous couch from Habitat. Me! Mrs. Capaldi. After my mum's old yellow plastic couch, I wanted the best couch in the world, and I got it. Remember before we moved in, us scrubbing this flat, with Dan's mum pretending she didn't speak English and shouting at the pigeons and my Uncle Jakey in broad Glasgow when she forgot?"

"Carol! You never touched a brush or got your hands wet. You just sat there sniffling and snottering, with your huge belly and giant boobs. Pity they shrank back down."

She ignored me. "Can you believe that old bitch wrote to the pope after I got pregnant, asking forgiveness from the Holy Father, telling him that it was entirely my fault, that her poor devout boy had been led astray by a Protestant? And can you believe that the pope wrote back granting his blessing? Then six months later and she thought the sun shone out of my Marco's arse and he was the most wonderful baby in the history of the world! She still worships him. It's ridiculous, he is her whole world and the old bitch still can't stand me!"

"Can you believe your mum still has that stinky old couch? The fake leather is so cracked now it looks like Mrs. McNamara's face."

Carol sank into the big brown velvet chair, balancing the huge white cup on her knee. She was going to ask me about Jack. I could tell by the way she was looking at me, her head to the side, her eyes narrowed. "So what's this shite about you leaving Jack?"

I wished I hadn't told her, but I had just landed at Glasgow Airport, jet-lagged, exhausted and drained after crying about Grandpa Jimmy for the entire twenty-hour journey from San Francisco. "I don't want to talk about it, Carol, not today. I am planning to leave him, though. He's a fat, boring arsehole, with no interest in me, Eilish or Finn. I just don't like him anymore. I actually can't stand him. He didn't turn up at the police station; he let us all down on the worst day of our lives. I can't forgive him. And he said something terrible."

"What?"

I shook my head.

"Oh, come on, Karen. I've got two pieces of Café Gandolfi caramel shortcake in the fridge, I'm going to put the kettle on, and you're going to tell me."

I sat in silence, working out how best to say it, and then I blurted it out. "He said that Maggie Thatcher was right to crush the miners."

Carol ran through from the kitchen with the teapot in her hands. "Why? What were the circumstances?"

"We were watching a BBC TV show a few months ago, about the miners' strike, and that's what he said."

"What? Those exact words?"

"Not exactly. He said that British coal mining had become uneconomical and that Thatcher had to win."

Carol gasped and sat on the arm of the sofa. "That was a terrible thing to say, but you can't leave your husband of twenty-six years because he likes Maggie Thatcher now. Isn't she dead anyway? I don't think it's legally grounds for divorce, Karen. Move him into the spare room and don't give him any for a while until he comes to his senses, but that's a bit much to divorce him."

As she refilled my cup with jasmine tea, I told her about how Jack had promised to work from home while I was in Scotland for Grandpa Jimmy's funeral but instead had flown his moaning, grey-faced, narrow-minded parents to look after everything as he couldn't inconvenience himself for one day. His mum and dad, who didn't drive in America, wouldn't go on a bus in case an "immigrant" robbed them and wouldn't sit on my lovely sunny patio in case they were bitten by a snake or a deadly mosquito, neither of which had ever been seen in our well-heeled San Francisco suburb. They were also deadly afraid of being robbed at gunpoint in our sedate manicured neighbourhood where no one locked their doors or cars, dogs had massage therapists, and expensive bicycles lay on lawns all summer, so they had to stay in the house all day. They had their daily mince and potatoes at 4:45 PM without fail, just about the time that Finn and Eilish were having their weekend breakfast. Then they had a cup of sugary milky tea at 8 PM, with the teabags and biscuits they had brought from Asda in Coatbridge as you couldn't get decent teabags or biscuits in America, then went to bed at 9 PM every night, she in her wincyette nightgown, he in his flannel pajamas, their teeth in a cup in the bathroom, moaning because it was too hot but they wouldn't put the air conditioning on as it gave you cancer—they saw it on Esther Rantzen—and they wouldn't open their bedroom window in case the nonexistent snakes and mosquitoes got in.

Like his father, Finn ignored them, laughing to himself and playing his drums in the garage with his college pals, keeping out of their way. But Eilish loved to entertain herself. Every day, she had a ridiculous story to tell them, and every day they called Jack at work, outraged. Then when he didn't pick up, which he never did, they called me in Scotland. So far, she had told her grandparents that our neighbours, both professors at Stanford, were Korean spies, that a teacher had asked her out on a date, that she was a lesbian and the mail lady was her girlfriend, and best of all, that Finn was selling cocaine outside the local Baptist church. And every day, Jack's parents blustered about, outraged, believing every ridiculous word.

I told Carol about Jack falling asleep and snoring on the couch every evening, how he never wanted to go for a walk with the dog or for a swim, or have anyone round, or go anywhere, or talk about anything apart from house prices and the economy and the banking crisis. My husband was an overweight selfish corporate bore who loved Maggie Thatcher. And he let his family down on a day when we really needed him. He was everything I hated. Jack had never been to Finn's college or to Eilish's high school. She had been suspended three times in the past year: first for the Borat/American Idiot incident; then for picketing the school cafeteria because they didn't employ anyone from the LGBT community; and the third time for cheating on her English exam and telling the teacher that she had found the answer sheet inside her locker that very morning and had taken it as a gift from Jesus. Every time, Jack had said he would be at the Meeting of Shame with the Viking Principal, and every time, it was me, by myself, with the empty chair and the usual withering, "I see Eilish's father couldn't make it."

"So have you told him?"

Outside the sky was greyer, the seagulls gone, and I was hungry. Maybe I would take Carol out to the little Thai restaurant downstairs, where they had good noodles. Or we could go to Café Gandolfi. That would be delicious—they had cauliflower gratin and we could get garlic bread and more caramel shortcake.

"Karen, have you told Jack?"

It was almost dark now. No wonder I was starving.

"No, not yet." My eyes were fixed on the window of the building opposite, where a young woman was pulling the curtains closed against the drab evening.

"He knows I'm angry with him. I don't remember the last time we shagged and he sleeps in the spare room, but he really doesn't have a clue how serious this is. Do you know, the day Eilish got arrested, he came home from work at his usual time? I was absolutely fuming by then. I was like Tam O'Shanter's wife, nursing my wrath to keep it warm. Well, he just walked in the door, picked up his mail and his *Financial Times*, read the headlines, ignored the dog, and poured himself a glass of wine. He thought he was great as he had got Finn's car back from the pound and mine from wherever it was. I can't stand him, Carol. I can hardly stand the sight of him. No, I haven't told him. He is flying through Glasgow on Monday, on his way to a meeting in Frankfurt, and we are going to meet up for a quick coffee in the airport. I was going to gently introduce the idea to him then, but now he tells me he is traveling with a colleague, Sam, and has invited him to join us. So I can't even tell him then, but I will as soon as I get back and his parents leave. The thought of never seeing the two old moans again is an added bonus. Can you take me to the airport at two o'clock on Monday?"

Carol was clearly horrified. She and Dan had been together for almost thirty years and she still lit up when he came home late at night smelling of chips and black pudding. And every night he brought her a little treat, a quarter of Italian Creams or fudge or a tub of ice cream. "What are you going to tell him?"

"Trial separation. I'm going to say that I need space, then get him out of the house, see a lawyer and start to make it final. I can't stand him, Carol, seriously."

She narrowed her eyes at me. "I can't take you to the airport. I'm working a late shift on Monday. And it's not that simple. You have children together, a whole life behind you and ahead of you. You need to talk to him, sort it out. You couldn't get enough of Jack. You used to sit and look at him when he was reading and tell me how you couldn't believe how handsome he was. No, Karen, it's not time to walk away. I'm not having it, you and Jack…"

I was squirming and cringing and was so relieved when Marco burst in the door, all jeans and black biker jacket and his handsome face and floppy dark hair. Carol and I had adored him from the day he was born. He was the first new baby I had ever seen and I had loved him instantly and beyond reason. His fat little brown feet and body, his dark unruly hair, how he squealed with delight every time he saw me. Before I had Finn I used to think I could never love my own children like I loved this beautiful boy. In fact, I didn't even think I needed to have children as I had Marco.

"Auntie Karen!"

I ran over to him and pretended to pick him up, a little joke we had continued since he was eight years old and too big for me to carry.

"Sorry I never got to talk to you yesterday, at the funeral, you know ... I had to carry the coffin and it was creepy with dead Grandpa Jimmy inside and I just went home after the church. I hear I missed a fabulous performance from my Uncle Jakey, though."

"Marco, it was fantastic and horrific and so inappropriate, your mum and I almost died trying not to laugh, and the guild ladies were scandalized. They'll be talking about it for years!"

"He's the biggest brass neck I have ever met. I can't believe I'm related to him! By the way, he's having one of his parties at his house on Saturday, for his birthday. Who has a party for their own birthday? I can't go, I'm doing this really important thing very far away, but I said you two would go. He's going to get your favourite biscuits, Auntie Karen. I wish I'd seen him in the church hall; it sounds like a right laugh. Anyway, Mum, Auntie Karen, wait till you hear this! You know I play at Murphy's on a Friday night. Well, this old guy came in last week, watched my set, said he was from BBC Scotland and wanted to meet with me. Then Grandpa died, but I met the guy today, and he wants me to audition for an acoustic session for a show on young Scottish musicians—me! I nearly did a big pee in ma boxers!"

"Marco, that is fantastic, but don't be crude!" Carol was on her feet, thrusting her hands in the air. "Our boy is going to be famous! This is fantastic! Did you call your dad? What time is it in Italy?"

"I'll call Dad tonight. Oh and listen, you two old bags, there's more. The agent told me that there was a live acoustic session today in the BBC studio, that old fanny that you two fancy. Old fat guy from London. Used to be in a boy band. Spanish name. Always in the paper for not paying tax and getting drunk ... used to be married to that fit telly presenter, now he's married to a man."

"*Nick Santiago!*" We both shrieked at the same time. "Nick Santiago! Here in Glasgow! When! Where? Where is he staying, Marco? Where is he right now?"

"You two are pathetic! You're nearly fifty, you know. He was at the studio today and is going back to London tomorrow after an interview with the *Daily Record.*"

"Go and call the agent, find out where he is staying. Where is he, Marco? You need to find out!" Carol frantically handed her phone to her son.

"Mum, don't be pathetic. I'm not going to call my new agent and ask him where an old fanny is staying. But these people, they usually stay in that posh hotel on Great Western Road, One Devonshire Gardens."

"Get your coat, Karen. This is it. And Marco, stop calling our darling beautiful handsome Nick an old fanny! He is the most beautiful, talented, gorgeous, sensitive, handsome, wonderful man who ever lived and I love him. Now you can make your own tea. You might see us on the news tonight."

We ran down the four flights of stairs, screeching and shrieking. It was too much—our idol, our hero was in this very city, just a few miles away. And I was off the hook.

34. A Different Corner

"Nick Santiago? The big fat boy band wanker who married a man last year? Aye, he's in Glasgow right enough. Big Tam picked up his musicians at the airport yesterday. Probably One Devonshire Gardens, lassies. The posh folk and celebrities always stay there. Him from *The Generation Game* and the dancing show was here last week, whatsisname, Bruce Forsyth, dead funny he is—nice to see you, to see you nice."

The taxi driver laughed uproariously at himself as he drove along Great Western Road, one hand on the wheel, the other trailing out of the open window holding his cigarette.

"Nice to see you, to see you nice!" he shouted at two teenage girls in school uniform crossing the road.

They replied by giving him the two fingers and shouting, "Wanker!"

The wet roads were reflecting the colours of the shops, the busy pubs and cafes, the traffic lights, the car headlights—it was magical. Nick was here.

"Aye, looks like you're at the right place, lassies."

At least fifty women our age were huddled at the bottom of the grand stone staircase of a handsome but unassuming sandstone terraced building, and sitting on the low wall were three chunky fifty-something men in leathers, probably the entire middle-aged gay biker population of Scotland. They all turned to look as we got out of the taxi.

"He's inside!" called out one of the men, waving to us frantically. "Nick is inside!"

We ran over as the crowd of women enveloped us, their voices tripping over each other in excitement.

"He's been in there for an hour now, ran in out of a taxi."

"He's pure gorgeous, so he is."

"He says he'll see us later so he must be coming back out."

"He was wearing lovely jeans and a nice patterned shirt underneath his suede jacket."

"He has a lovely accent, very posh … He smiled right at me."

"Marion, he did not. He smiled at all of us."

"He's lovely. Just lovely."

"I saw him at the window."

"But we can't get in. That big Phil Mitchell arsehole at the door is not letting us in."

We all looked up. At the top of the stairs stood a massive man with a bald head, sunglasses although it was already dark, a black bomber jacket, a phone in his ear, his arms folded menacingly in front of his giant chest.

"Step aside, ladies! We have inside information," I trilled, grabbing Carol's hand and marching confidently to the door.

"Good luck, hen!" shouted Marion.

"If ye get in, open the back door and let us all in!"

The big man didn't even look at us as we approached, didn't acknowledge us as we stood beside him.

"Good evening, Sir."

His head turned towards me. He was not happy.

"We are from the *Daily Record* and have an interview with a Mr. N. Santiago scheduled for 8 PM." I stepped towards the door and banged into him. He wasn't moving. His face didn't change. Carol looked nervous.

He stuck out his hand. "Press pass."

I fumbled in my bag, glad that I had brought my nice Coach fabric satchel. I handed him a card.

"Contra Costa Public Libraries," he read in his flat London accent and handed me it back.

I handed him another one.

"City of San Francisco Transit pass." He handed me that back too.

My laugh was breezy and casual. "Sorry, Sir! I must have misplaced it. It must be in this pile. Now if you will just step aside…"

He did not step aside. He did not laugh or sneer or register any reaction whatsoever as he read through my cards as the women shuffled closer to hear.

"City of Martinez Juvenile Criminal Court. No. Mr. Jacob Rosenblum. Family Lawyer. Specializing in Juvenile Crime. Nope. Warrior Goddess Yoga Studio. Definitely not."

Carol shot me a mocking look at that one, and one of the women laughed out loud.

"Fab at Fifty Weight Loss Management. Don't think so."

One of the leather men shouted something disparaging that I couldn't quite hear, but it must have been funny as the fellow Nick fans laughed.

I grabbed my cards back and turned to Carol. "Carolina, I seem to have misplaced my press pass. Did I hand it to you in the limo earlier?"

"Let me have a look, Karenina." With a flourish, she unzipped her little black bag and waved a handful of cards in front of his ridiculous mirrored sunglasses. "I think you'll find they are in here. Now if you'll step aside, Mr. Santiago is waiting for us and will be getting annoyed by now."

"Glasgow Association of Midwives. No. Madame Minty Morgan, Tarot Reader and Clairvoyant. Nope. Capaldi Chippy, Best in Scotland 2006. Very good but no. Sassy Seaweed body wraps. Don't think so." He handed the cards back and stood a bit taller than his already six foot five inches. "I'm not going to let you in, ladies. Now leave these premises. And take your pals with you. You are causing a public nuisance."

"Public nuisance my arse!" shouted a wee woman in an anorak.

"It's you that's the public nuisance! We're the public and you're a nuisance! Stop being a fanny and let us see Nick Santiago!"

The crowd muttered in agreement as Carol and I scuttled up the cobblestone street and out of sight around the corner.

We stood against a wall in the darkness. We weren't giving up. Nick Santiago was behind those thick cream linen curtains and we were going to see him.

"There's a back door, Karen. I was at a conference here once. There's a wee garden at the back with a gate from the lane. Let's go. This is what we'll do…"

A woman appeared beside us, sidling around the corner, slightly older than us and immaculate in black linen wide-legged trousers, black high pointy boots and a dusky pink short wool jacket, her blonde hair in a beautifully coloured and styled bob. She was struggling for breath and laughing, holding herself up against the wall.

"I'm Judy," she laboured. "I am a respectable grandmother, assistant head teacher of a large and prestigious primary school in the Southside and the wife of a doctor. And I have loved Nick since he was in Boytown. I know what you're doing and I am coming with you. And Boytown? How did we not know that he was gay?"

"Karen," I offered. "Mother of two, PTA member, college teacher, food bank volunteer, Obama 2008 campaign local manager and I have loved Nick Santiago since Summer Girls. I know, I know, I'm sorry but I was too cool in the boy band days."

She laughed warmly as Carol offered her hand. "I'm Carol. People trust me to deliver their new babies, my husband runs the best chip shop in Scotland, I have a twenty-seven-year-old son who is the next James Blunt and I have loved Nick Santiago since he wore those tight white jeans for Ti Amo."

The three of us tiptoed silently along the dark, wet, narrow cobblestone back lane, past the rows of bins and parked cars, our nervous clammy hands linked together.

"This is it. This is the back gate of the hotel. Give me a punty up and I'll check." Carol and I bent ourselves at the knees, crossed our arms at the wrists and grabbed each other's hands, forming a secure little basket for Judy's pointy boot. She was surprisingly light and nimble.

"Taebo," she explained.

She was over the wall in a second. It was amazing, all those women, the three burly bikers, and the big scary guy at the front and just a wooden gate here at the back. She quickly opened the latch for us, and we sneaked inside grinning at each other, joyous in our achievement, laughing quietly. The security light went on, illuminating the tidy little slabbed terrace with one wrought-iron garden table, two fancy little chairs and a rain-soaked umbrella. We were frantic, grabbing each other's hands in a complete panic, then darting down behind a manicured bush in a huge terra cotta tub, the three of us kneeling on the cold hard tiles, trying not to laugh, trying not to cry, our hearts thumping. Discovery now would mean humiliation, maybe even the police. I could be deported. We had to stay quiet. We peered through the bush, trying not to hyperventilate. A heavy wooden door creaked open, and a little white fluffy dog ran out, wagging its tail frantically, snarling and sniffing the wet flagstones that were revealed by the light from the open door.

"Josephine! Go potty, Josephine. Good girl, go potty." The voice was deep, American, Texan. The door opened a bit more.

A figure appeared from the shadows. We all recognized him instantly. It was Nick Santiago's husband. We gasped and gripped each other's hands. The dog was growling and snarling now, heading straight for us, its stubby little legs scurrying determinedly. I held my breath. Judy squeaked. Carol closed her eyes. The horrible little Josephine had found us and was barking and yelping, high-pitched and incessant. The husband was striding towards us.

"Josephine! Come here now, what is it? A cat?" He was standing looking at us, his hands on his hips, dapper in his white fitted shirt and flared jeans. He was laughing. Thank God he was laughing. "Nick honey, you better come out here! I think there are some ladies here to see you."

Nick Santiago was standing there, just ten feet from us, the light from the porch illuminating his body like a halo, truly gorgeous in his fitted Pucci shirt and jeans. He was unbelievably handsome. Carol and Judy squirmed into each other but I stood up. I stood up, I dusted down my nice little jacket, I smoothed my hair, I smiled hugely and I strode towards Nick Santiago, confident and thrilled. The little dog was in his arms, wagging and panting, and as I stretched my hand towards Nick, Josephine, whom I will love eternally, licked the back of my hand, frantically and joyously, and just kept on licking. Nick and his husband laughed quietly as I locked eyes with Nick Santiago, his big beautiful smile for me only. Nick Santiago and Karen Alexander, eyes locked and smiling at each other. Then Nick Santiago put his warm, soft, beautiful hand on mine and rubbed the back of my hand with his thumb, drying off the dog saliva. It was the most magical moment of my life and was completely ruined by Judy and Carol grabbing me by the arms and pulling me out the gate as the big ugly bouncer thudded out of the door towards us, his face in a complete rage, his fist shaking in the air like in a cartoon.

We ran along the wet slippery cobblestones, and even though we were in heels and at least twenty years older than him, we easily outran the lardy Londoner, jumped into a taxi and escaped into the magical night.

35. Your Cheating Heart

I WAS STILL SMILING, GLOWING, COCOONED IN THE WARM glow of Nick Santiago as I sat in the ripped passenger seat of Marco's rattling old van on my way to Glasgow Airport.

"Look at your face. You look like a stroke victim. Seriously, Auntie Karen, you look handicapped. They'll probably bring a wheelchair for you when we get to the airport."

"Marco, he was gorgeous. You should have seen his face. He's so handsome, it's unbelievable, and the way he looked at me … if only we'd had a few more moments together."

"Yeah, he was probably about to ask for your number. Rich millionaire superstar gays are very attracted to wrinkly overweight middle-aged married women; it's a well-known fact. He definitely fancied you. What you and my mum did last night was ridiculous. You're nearly fifty years old! And by the way, you're not my godmother any more, and I'm looking for a new mother. Seriously, Uncle Jakey has always been the official brass neck of the family, but now it's you! What were you thinking?"

"It was fabulous, Marco! Best moment of my life, he is *so* handsome close up. He touched my hand, this one, looked me right in the eye and was about to talk to me when the big bouncer threw us out."

"Can't think why you got thrown out. Famous people love stalkers who climb over fences in back alleys on dark nights in Glasgow. And you did mention the hand. I'll drop you at the front of the airport so that your hair doesn't get wet and frizzy. You look bad enough already with that stupid grin. Say hi to Uncle Jack. And please, just try to act like a normal person."

He sidled the old van around orange traffic cones and a sign that said "NO DROP OFF."

"I'm not supposed to be here, so I'll just pull up to the door behind the taxis and you jump out."

I reached into my purse and handed him a five-pound note, which he put firmly back into my bag. "Auntie Karen, you have to stop giving me money. I loved it when I was a wee boy and you would slip me fifty pence for the ice-cream van, but I'm almost thirty years old now. I have a girlfriend, a job, a flat and I'm going to be on the telly. Take it back."

I opened the door and jumped out of the van, throwing the money back in the window at him. "Keep the money. It's for petrol. Marco, I really appreciate you dropping me off like this." I slammed the rickety door to make sure it shut, and waved.

"Take it back! Buy yourself some of that new anti-aging cream from Boots; you really need it! Or some heavy-duty Spanx," he shouted as he laughed and threw the money out of the window as he drove off.

I grabbed it, ran after the van and threw it back in the window. Victory was mine! That age-old Scottish tradition where people, even the most poverty-stricken and debt-laden, loudly insist on paying for each other, throwing coins and notes across tables, rooms, cafes, shop counters, and bars, thrusting money into the other person's bag or pocket—it was ridiculous but this is what we do. And I had won.

Or not. A few yards away, the rusty Astra van screeched to a halt, beeping noisily as the blue five-pound note came floating out of the window and onto the windscreen of the taxi behind, causing it to screech to a halt, followed by the Holiday Inn shuttle bus and two cars behind that. The taxi driver beeped angrily on his horn, shouting out of his window. The shuttle bus driver got out onto the road as his anxious passengers craned their necks and stood up to see what was happening. Two huge policemen, both heavily armed and wearing fluorescent bullet-proof vests, ran over, one to retrieve the forlorn fiver from a puddle in the middle of the road, the other to stand in front of the van, hand on his gun belt, and order Marco to get out.

A small crowd started to form, including a group of excited Japanese tourists with cameras, a dozen or so pensioners bound for Malaga, and a teenage boy recording the whole thing with his phone. We had started a full-scale security alert at Scotland's major airport. Marco was going to be arrested, we would be on the news, the bouncer might recognize me and call the police, and within twenty minutes the whole thing would be on YouTube. I could slip into the terminal, pretend I hadn't noticed—that was my overwhelming urge—but Marco was standing forlornly in the middle of the road, his hands in the air, looking right at me. He looked about six years old.

"Officer, Sir! Constable!" I ran over.

"Stay where you are." His voice was loud and firm. I stayed where I was.

"It's only a fiver, Malky."

The other officer was waving the wet fiver in the air, trying not to laugh. His partner was not amused. "Let me see." They inspected the note.

"Right, you." He pointed at Marco. "Pull your van over and stand at that sign. And you." He pointed at me. "Stand beside him. We need a little word. Right everyone, show's over, move along. It was nothing. Move along now, goodbye."

"Move along!" he shouted at the crowd, who all scuttled off.

"Wanker!" yelled the taxi driver as he passed Marco's van.

The lecture was humiliating. It was in public, just outside a large busy revolving door into the arrivals hall. It was loud, it was watched by many people, and it covered the themes of national security, public safety, terrorist alerts, responsibility, stupidity, idiocy, and the fact that I was old enough to know better.

Marco and I swore never to tell anyone and I ran after the teenager, who turned out to be a young goalkeeper on his way to a football tournament in Holland, and gave him twenty quid to delete the recording there and then, while his team mates rolled about laughing.

It would be a relief to get this over with. I had been hoping that the flight would be late and Jack and I wouldn't be able to meet, but it was on time. It was landing right now. I had to face him sometime, start the unraveling and my path to freedom. It was sad. I had really loved Jack, but I no longer recognized this middle-aged, overweight, dull, disinterested man who lived in my house.

I knew he wasn't always the way he was with me. I heard his car come up the street every night, the hood down, the music louder than Finn's, playing U2 or the Stereophonics, the joy disappearing and the cloud descending when he walked in the door of his own house. His colleagues thought he was a great laugh—good old Jack, funny Jack, a great co-worker, dedicated, one of the team, supportive. I had seen him at functions, charming his way around the room, chatting, laughing, listening, telling funny stories, gathering an admiring crowd. It was just with me and our children that he was unhappy and detached. I could see that. He would be relieved to be away from us too, that was obvious. His real life, his happy life, was in the blue glass tower of P. B. Associates in San Francisco. It would be like lancing a boil. We would smile wryly and a little sadly, hug awkwardly, wish each other well and move on, both relieved that someone had had the courage to say it. The moments when I caught a glimpse of the old Jack were powerful, like when our eyes had met over his laptop last week and he just stared at me intently but said nothing. What was he going to say? I love you? I miss you? I can't stand you? I want out?

I always liked to watch flights from Britain arriving in America and flights from America arriving in Britain, trying to guess the nationality of the passengers as they appeared on the little television screen just before they came through the wide automatic door into arrivals. First and Business Class passengers were always first through. Nick always travels First Class, I thought to myself and smiled again. I just couldn't stop it. The small round couple in their late sixties in matching beige windcheaters—he in brown slacks, she in beige trousers, both in comfortable slip-on shoes, definitely Scottish—probably had a successful little business and had been visiting their family somewhere like Baltimore or Philadelphia.

The next small round couple in their sixties—perfect teeth, he in a baseball hat, sweatshirt, light blue jeans and white training shoes, she the exact same without the hat—were definitely American, probably here to play golf, see Edin-bro Castle and explore their heritage. So many Americans I met every day in the supermarket, at work, on the train, in the dog park, at the farmers' market, at Finn's college and

Eilish's school told me they were Scottish that it was amazing there was anyone left here.

All the Business Class men in their forties and fifties in smart navy blazers, open-necked pressed shirts, jeans and dark leather shoes to match their briefcases, definitely British, probably from London and still thinking they looked good in the jeans/suit jacket combination that had peaked in 1982. The skinny, very worn decrepit-looking man in his late fifties in a black T-shirt straining over his paunch, ridiculously tight black jeans, high black lace-up boots, his arms completely covered in tattoos, his thinning hair long and dyed jet black— an old rocker, maybe the drummer or bass player in a hugely successful 1970s heavy metal band, definitely British, as the old American rockers keep their faces surgically unlined. Rich old rockers always travel First Class, I thought, just like Nick does, booking two seats for themselves as they don't want to be bothered by middle-aged women slipping them their phone number or middle-aged men wanting to show them an air guitar rendition of their greatest hits.

The young woman behind him took my attention— she was so like me thirty years ago, or at least how I could have looked if I had had confidence, poise and been pretty and slim. Small, with shoulder-length blonde hair swinging underneath a navy newsboy hat, she was wearing a dark fitted 1950s coat with huge buttons and a fake fur collar, just like the one I had bought in Victoria Road Oxfam for two quid and had worn through those harsh Glasgow winters when I was a student. I couldn't help but smile to myself. I missed me. She looked so happy and young and carefree as she strode along wheeling her bright blue case behind her, smiling up at her companion, who had his arm lightly around her shoulders. He was an older distinguished-looking man in a long navy wool coat with thick charcoal hair. They must be Californian as they were wearing coats in summer and had that personable self-confidence that they seem to teach in schools there. I watched as they walked along the corridor, their heads close together, smiling into each other's faces. He was looking at her with delight and amusement.

The man was my husband.

The jealousy hit me like a cannon ball in my stomach, and I had to grip the railing to hold myself up.

It was a horrible half hour. My husband and Sam, for this girl was Sam, sat with me at the little table in Costa Coffee. He helped her take her coat off and carefully placed it on the back of her chair, smiling at her. Smiling at Sam as she crossed her long slim brown young legs and swished her shiny hair. He hardly looked at me and, apart from the perfunctory kiss on his arrival, did not touch me. She talked to me kindly, as if I were her elderly auntie, while my husband couldn't take his eyes off her bright blue eyes, her toned arms, her sleeveless dress, her perfect young face and full lips. When they went through the gate on their way to the second flight, he did not even wave or turn around. He just carried her bag and gently helped her take off her expensive coat to go through security as he adjusted her perfect hair. Jack had never looked so handsome and I had never felt so old or useless or stupid in my life.

36. Two Cigarettes in an Ashtray

I LAY ON THE BOTTOM BUNK BED UNDER THE GLASGOW Rangers Football Club 1872–1972 scratchy itchy nylon quilt. Every time Carol moved, the bunk above me squeaked and groaned, the whole house smelled of cigarette smoke and I had never been so depressed in my life. We were staying at her mum's house for one night, as we always did when I was home. Mrs. Mackenzie loved having "her lassies" back and always stocked up on our favourite scones and biscuits.

I wished it hadn't been tonight. I knew that Carol was fed up listening to me but I couldn't stop. "It was horrible, Carol. The three of us sat in Costa Coffee, her all young and brilliant and successful and sexy, him all businesslike and important and handsome. I don't think they even noticed me. They couldn't take their eyes off each other. They sat together, facing me, like they were the couple, can you believe that?"

"Yes, you said." The voice from the top bunk was impatient and edgy.

"They laughed about a colleague, talked about the project in Frankfurt, joked about the other passengers in the cabin with them, so they must have been sitting together on the plane, for six hours to New York, then seven hours to Glasgow, sitting together for thirteen hours, plus two hours in the posh lounge in Newark Airport laughing, chatting, flirting, her perfume, oh and did I tell you that Jack had obviously been drinking? He always gets frisky after a few glasses of wine, and it's free in the lounge and on board. He was laughing at everything she said. It was pathetic, I was embarrassed for him. It was ridiculous. Oh, and did I tell you that he was wearing his good Tom Ford aftershave, the one I bought him, the one he only wears for me?"

"Well, he was meeting you."

"Uh-huh, after fifteen hours with her!"

"Karen, it is three o'clock in the morning. I was on an early shift, I've been up for twenty-three hours and I need to go to sleep. Jack is not having an affair. Yes, he probably fancies her, feels flattered because you haven't been arsed with him for months, but they are on business, on a project, professional colleagues. You have been telling me all this for nine hours now, nine hours. I need to go to sleep."

I ignored her. "I know they're probably not having an affair yet, but you know what posh hotels are like, you know what Business Class is like."

Carol had had enough. "*No*, Karen! *No*, I do not know what posh hotels are like. I do not know what Business Class is like. I am a midwife in the Princess Royal Maternity Hospital in the East End of Glasgow and my husband owns chip shops. I deal with belligerent drunken new fathers and anxious undernourished teenage mothers every day. New babies addicted to methadone. Stillbirths. Prematures. Understaffing. Every day. I have been a mother since I was seventeen years old. I am fed up listening to you. You come over here and tell me that you're fed up with Jack, want him to move out, want your own life, and now you've been whinging and moaning for nine hours because he sat beside a pretty girl on a plane. Nine effing hours! I am fed up with you. And you might as well know: I've been fed up with you since 1978 when you made that sanctimonious speech in Modern Studies about apartheid. Everyone was laughing at you, Karen, you in Kilbrannan scheme with fourteen-year-old glue sniffers down the beach and drunks fighting in the street on a Friday night, and women counting the pennies as the men were laid off from the harbour, and you're going on and on about Soweto? At least it's sunny there and they get a good summer and don't get frozen pipes. Then you pissed off to university to live with posh Anna, left me here pregnant, and started going on about Maggie Thatcher, you trying to save the Scottish steel industry all by yourself, then it was Support the Miners, then Maggie Thatcher again during the nurses' strike. I actually was a trainee nurse then, with a baby, breaking the strike, crossing the picket line, on fifty quid a week. Remember? Trying to get through my shift with you standing at the hospital gate with your posh pals and your banners, shouting and trying to get on the telly. I was black affronted for you! Any of you ever think about getting a wee job? And that snobby Anna, your best pal, I always hated her, still do. She always turned up whenever you and I met, looking down her nose at me, with her stupid black eyeliner and that stupid long velvet coat saying, ooh Karen and I this, Karen and I that, and you laughing at every stupid thing she said. I hated her guts! Then it was Nelson Mandela, CND, the Greenham Common lesbians, Tibet, Nicaragua, the rain forest, whales. Then you went to America and tried to teach every single illegal immigrant to speak English. Meanwhile, I was here with my long shifts and my chip shop and my boy at school, you fannying about with illegal Mexicans. Then, going round the doors of every black person in Oakland, telling them to vote for Obama. You are *so* effing pious, Karen. No wonder poor Jack fancies that sexy wee thing."

Fury, rage, naked anger coursed through me. I jumped up, stood on the bottom mattress and put my face next to hers. "Say that to my face, bitch!" My heart was pounding with rage.

She burst out laughing. "Oh for eff's sake, Karen, go back to your bed. You haven't told me to say something to your face since we were sixteen, when I suggested that you might want to try on a size twelve or fourteen jeans rather than lying on the floor and squeezing your huge massive arse into a size ten."

Blind fury. "Right, that's *it*!"

I pulled her orange and blue Rangers quilt and threw it violently onto the brown nylon carpet. She laughed again, a condescending evil little snort. Livid, in a red mist, I grabbed her hair and pulled her onto the floor with a thump at the exact moment that Mrs. Mackenzie opened the bedroom door and put on the light.

Carol was lying on top of the Rangers quilt on the floor, screeching with laughter. I was standing on the bottom bunk blindly and ineffectively kicking at her.

"*What* the *eff* is going on, lassies?"

I burst out crying. "Mrs. Mackenzie, my husband is having an affair with a sexy young thing and Carol thinks I'm pious." Tears and snot ran down my face quicker than I could wipe them with the Rangers quilt.

"Well, I don't know about pies, but I do know about husbands and affairs. Now Carol, go to bed, this is ridiculous, you were on an early shift today. And you, hen, come downstairs with me and have a cup of tea."

I sat on the yellow couch as Mrs. Mackenzie lit the gas fire to take the chill off the room, then she handed me a huge mug of hot milky sugary tea. Scottish tea. The kind I had hated since I discovered orange pekoe and jasmine tea, but I drank it gratefully and it tasted good.

Her shiny dressing gown was quilted and pale pink, her slippers fluffy and with a little heel. She reached into her pocket, took out a packet of cigarettes and a box of matches, lit the cigarette without even looking at it and took a few long puffs before she spoke. "Now, Karen, hen, you've always been clever. You did the right thing, did well at school, had a wee job, went to university, married a clever man. You read books and papers and you watch the news and *Reporting Scotland*, you vote and you don't watch *Big Brother*. I'm not clever, hen. I left school at fifteen, went to work in the factory. I wanted money for cigarettes and makeup and to go to the dancing. I had Carol when I was sixteen—aye, hen, sixteen. Look at your face! You and her ..."

She gestured upstairs. "You and my Carol always thought I was an old bag. You thought me and Julie was past it, over the hill, but, hen, when you and my Carol were runnin' aboot the discos with your gipsy skirts, I was only thirty years old, same as our Marco is now. I'm only sixty-three, hen. You probably go to yoga and Starbucks with wummin who are my age. In fact, hen..."

She cackled and spluttered on her cigarette. "We're practically the same age now, you and me!"

I couldn't speak. I was horrified. It was true.

"I was only twenty-eight when my husband Billy went to work in Corby, and so was he. Twenty-eight with a lassie at the big school and two other weans, he couldnae get away quick enough, hen. I was here with Carol, our William and wee Jennifer and I was that happy when he left. I was like you, wanted my freedom, the bed to myself. I couldn't be bothered making his tea every night and him coming home drunk from the pub, wasting the rent money on the horses and the dogs. I was well rid of him. And he earned good money in Corby, at the steelworks. I paid off the debts, paid off the provvy wummin, paid off my catalogue and had the house to myself. I loved it, so I did. I had ma wee job, the weans. I saw Julie every day, and then Jakey moved in when Julie chucked him oot. Aye, hen, I was happy. Billy came home every few months and I was glad to see him but glad to see the back of him. I never ever went down to England to see him, hen, never. No wonder he started seeing that wummin. Then he was in the jail in Glasgow—did you know that, hen?"

"I guessed, Mrs. Mackenzie. What did he do?"

"Armed robbery, hen, at the Royal Bank in Kilmarnock. They were drunk, him and his daft pal Shug. They took copper pipes as their weapons, put my American Tan tights over their heads and robbed the bank. They got ten thousand pounds, hen. That was a fortune in they days. Then the daft bastards went into the pub two doors along from the bank to count the money and get a pie and a pint. You couldn't make that up, hen. He was a laughingstock, and so was I. I never ever went to see him in jail, but she did, the wummin from Corby. I was black affronted. It was all over the papers. Carol was too wrapped up in her boyfriends and discos to know anything about it. I just told them their dad was working down in England. When he got out, he came here for his tools and donkey jacket, never even waited until the weans got home from school, then he went to Northampton on the bus and I never saw him again. We're still married, hen, and he's still with that wummin. I heard they had a lassie of their own. She must be in her thirties now. Maybe he even has grandchildren there. He still sends me a tenner in an envelope every week. I always thought I would wait until the weans grew up and then I would go out to the dancing and meet someone else, a nice man to go to the pictures with, a wee walk, someone to walk along the prom with or to go a wee holiday to Blackpool. But I never did. Let me tell you this, hen, and this is important. Your man Jack, he's a good man, hen, a good husband, a good faither. I've never seen him drunk, he never lifts his hand to you, he has a good job, and he's handsome. Do you think he would go away and cry and live in a wee flat by himself if you ditched him? Aye, hen, he would. He would do that for about six months, and then he would replace you. That's what he would do, hen. He would replace you. And let me tell you this, hen, and you listen, because I'm sixty-three and I've seen it all hundreds of times. Jack would replace you, it would be within six months and it would be with someone younger than you. That's what men do."

I felt as though she'd slapped me. My cheeks burned and my eyes nipped with tears.

"I'm sorry, hen, but it's true and someone has to tell you these things. You think you'll love it on your own, your own house, plenty money, your weans and dog, but, hen, how long do you think that dog of yours will live? That old boxer must be on his last legs by now. How much longer do you think Finn and Eilish will keep coming home? That lassie of yours will be off in a cloud of dust the minute she gets out of school. She's just like you. Your Finn, he loves his mammy, he's your wee boy, but the minute he meets a lassie he loves, you'll be lucky to see him at Christmas. When our William was in the Falklands, then in Belfast, I used to sit here all night, hen, worried sick, smoking and listening to radio for news. I was ill with worry and had no one to talk to. Oh, I had Julie, but she had Christopher and Jakey, and I was sitting here myself, worried sick about William away to war at seventeen, and Jennifer getting in with the bad crowd, and Carol getting pregnant by that Italian boy with his overbearing mammy, still pretending she can't speak English after fifty years. Well, I heard her, at the back of the chip shop, blethering away in broad Scots. Do you know she's only ever talked to our Marco in Italian and the two of them laugh and blether away together and me and Carol don't know a word they're saying, hen, not a word? Aye, it's lonely, hen. And you think maybe you'll meet another man, a better man. Well, let me tell you something, hen. Men in their late forties and their fifties, they're no looking for someone your age, they're looking for a younger wee thing, someone thirty-five at the most, preferably with no weans. Sorry, hen, but it's true. And you can stop snottering and sniveling because there's more. When your husband that you don't want does settle down with this younger lassie, well, she's going to want a family, isn't she? And how long do you think he'll bother with your weans when he has a new one with his young girlfriend? That's exactly what my Billy did, never saw him again. I'm sorry, hen, but that's how it is. Aye, you will have men come around, hen, looking to give you one. Your friend's husbands and your husband's friends, men you never thought were that sleazy. Aye, that's just how it is, hen, and someone had to tell you." She handed me a lit cigarette and I had the first and last smoke of my life.

37. Older

THE WEST END CAFÉ HAD ALWAYS BEEN OUR WARM delicious haven and lookout point. We had spent many rainy 1970s Saturday afternoons in this warm booth by the window overlooking Kilbrannan High Street and the bus stop, Carol and I facing each other on these red vinyl squashy bench seats, huge mugs of foamy hot chocolate on our hands, the yellow sparkly Formica table strewn with our clutch bags, Pick & Mix sweeties we had stolen from Woolworths, and Mrs. Macari's delicious cheese and bean toasties and homemade fudge. Her nephew, Dan Capaldi, whom Carol had fancied madly even then, sometimes worked here on a Saturday and from our vantage point she could watch him make frothy drinks, smiling over at him while I scanned the street for Bobby Henderson, who with his entourage swaggered noisily up and down the High Street every Saturday afternoon, buying their punk records and bags of five pence chips.

I bundled myself against the window, wrapping my cold hands around the hot chunky mug. It was a wet Tuesday afternoon—dreary, dreich and miserable like me. After the airport incident and the bunk bed debacle I was feeling foolish and fragile. I sighed dramatically, nostalgia and wistfulness making me tired.

"The café still smells the same—coffee, chocolate, hot toast, and Mrs. Macari still looks the same—I think that's even the same stripy apron she's wearing and it's definitely the same pink lipstick. Remember she used to make Dan wear an apron? I wish we were still fifteen, Carol. The discos, the makeup, the homework were all we had to worry about. We had a laugh then, didn't we, sitting right here looking for Dan and Bobby and any other nice-looking boy who passed? It was so simple then."

"Simple, my arse! My dad was in jail, your dad was out looking for us if we weren't home by eight o'clock, my uncle was drunk and singing sectarian songs on our couch for months, the spots, the periods, waiting for the phone to ring, Kelly McNicol, God rest her soul, shouting and spitting at us, the fights at school, your mum making you eat pies and sausages, the overboiled potatoes every night, the swirly carpets, not having boyfriends."

I laughed despite myself. "The drunk men on the bus, everyone smoking, what was that about? No one was allowed to be gay or clever or different. The disgusting boil in the bag gammon on a Sunday, I had forgotten about that! The horrible racist sexist *Benny Hill Show*, Sid James and the moronic *Carry-On* films, everyone laughing their heads off at *Are You Being Served*, trifle from a box, school dinners, weighing ourselves every day, getting the belt, it was horrible!"

She laughed, I laughed, the hot chocolate was thick, creamy and delicious and my soul was warming up.

"Remember that ridiculous game we used to play for hours sitting here, when we could discuss for hours if we'd rather go out with Andy Gibb or John Travolta?" Carol asked. "Well, how about an updated version. Jon Bon Jovi or Richie Sambora?"

"Richie." I answered, smiling at the thought.

"Me too." She agreed.

"Bruce Springsteen or Hugh Jackman?" I asked.

"Hugh."

"Bruce for me. Still the sexiest man in the world. Antonio Banderas or George Clooney?"

"Antonio. I like dark men, obviously."

"I would pick George for a date and Antonio for a shag. Denzel Washington or Daniel Craig?"

"Denzel. But only just. Depends if Daniel was wearing those blue trunks. Then it would be him."

"Colin Firth or Hugh Grant?"

"Both. Bridget Jones had both but she's younger than us. David Beckham or Johnny Depp?"

"David." We chorused.

"John Travolta in *Saturday Night Fever* or Richard Gere in *An Officer and a Gentleman*?"

"John Travolta. Still love him," I said.

"Nick Santiago or Jude Law?"

We both sighed.

"I can't believe we actually met him," Carol added.

We sighed again, smiling contentedly as Carol stirred her spoon round and round the cup, lost in her thoughts of the three seconds we had had with Nick Santiago before the big ugly bouncer ruined it. We had sat in a café in Byres Road with Judy, delirious and hysterical, reliving every second of the short but wonderful encounter. It was the most exciting thing that had ever happened to us, and we still couldn't believe it. Judy had been emailing us constantly. We just needed to believe it was really true.

Carol was still dreaming aloud. "He's still so handsome. A bit chubbier and a bit older than I had imagined, but that smile!"

"He is completely gorgeous, Carol. His face is beautiful, and when he touched my hand, his was so warm and soft. Even his voice was lovely. I wish I'd had his baby."

"I would leave Dan for him, I really would, and he's the only man in the world I would leave for. And maybe that Polish porter at the hospital … Nick's husband is so lucky. Every night he goes to bed with Nick Santiago. Every night…"

"I go to bed on my own every night, in the spare room. Jack snores so much. I hope he snored on the plane and she heard it and was disgusted. She was so pretty, Carol, and so young." The despondency took over.

"Who?"

"Sam. My husband's girlfriend."

"He's not having an affair, Karen. She's just a colleague."

"Colleague, my arse. He has talked about her nonstop for months now, about Sam, this new hotshot architect from Yale. I just assumed it was a man!"

Carol put her mug of hot chocolate firmly down, spilling some onto the table. Ever the nurse, she wiped the tiny drip up with a hanky. "Karen, listen to me."

I put my cup down. Tears stung my eyes.

"Sam is not Jack's girlfriend. I googled her. She's twenty-nine years old and is engaged to a multimillionaire thirty-five-year-old Yahoo executive called Vikram, who looks like a Bollywood superstar. She's not interested in a middle-aged man with grey hair, a house in the suburbs, and children her own age. He is enjoying the attention but they're not having an affair." She looked directly at me.

"Maybe not yet, Carol, but they're in Frankfurt together. Nice hotel, dinners, wine, we've not shagged for months, and she's so gorgeous…"

"We're gorgeous too. Look at us!"

We both turned to look at our reflections on the window, wiping the condensation with our sleeves first. It was true, for two women approaching fifty, we didn't look bad. Her shoulder-length hair was dark and glossy, mine three artificial shades of blonde and well cut in nice soft layers. We were a little plumper than when we squeezed into those size ten Wranglers but we were still reasonably trim. We walked, did yoga, wore jeans and not the high-waisted ones. Ours were from GAP, and we wore them with belts with big buckles. No Hush Puppy slip-on shoes for us. We had boots with heels and nice short little cardigans in bright colours, always wore earrings and lipstick with some tasteful, hardly-there but expensive makeup.

But at the end of the day, we were nearly fifty. When my gran was fifty, she had snow-white hair in a bun and wore long shapeless dresses, thick support tights and sensible lace-up shoes. She was old at fifty. When my mum was fifty, she had her long graying hair in the same bun fastened with a clip and always wore slip-on elasticated trousers from C & A and comfy slip-on shoes or wooden Scholl's in the summer. Now I was nearly fifty and until last night truly believed that I could have passed for thirty-five. Carol and I had always complimented each other on how great we looked. But were we stuck in 1978? Were we truly the only ones who saw it? We were middle-aged. We just hadn't seen it. What age did we think we were? Our children were almost middle-aged.

I sipped on the thick creamy foam of my delicious hot chocolate and, despite myself, laughed. "Can you imagine if we had to go for three months, just three months and we weren't allowed to do anything to ourselves, nothing at all, what we would look like? No Boots the Chemist, no Walgreens, no hairdresser, no hairdryer or straighteners, no tweezers, no makeup. If we had absolutely no money and couldn't buy anything, or there was an earthquake and we were in tents in a refugee camp on Glasgow Green for three months. What would we really look like, Carol? I mean, that Sam, she would look good after a month in a soggy tent in Barra, but what about us, what do we really look like? Remember we went to that fantastic pop festival on Arran and camped in a soggy field for a week with all those Danish bikers and the students from Ireland? We look great in those photos: no makeup, no shampoo, just shorts, T-shirts and a tan and we look gorgeous. Well, that's what she looks like, but a million times better. And look at us. The real us."

"That is the most depressing thing I have ever heard, Karen. Three months. Well, let's start at the top." She did look old as she studied herself in the window, the lines around her mouth marked and deep. I truly had never seen it before. "I would have grey hair, like my mum. I mean, almost completely grey. I have it coloured every three weeks, every three weeks! It grows in grey, has done for years. I haven't been naturally dark since Madonna was a virgin."

"And my lovely blonde hair." I sighed. "Fake now. And Jack doesn't even know. Every six weeks I go to the lovely Loretta and she makes me blonde again. I really was this colour, round about the time that Michael Jackson, God bless his soul, was black. I wouldn't be grey all over, more a depressing mousy brown with grey streaks at the side, and it would be quite frizzy without my straighteners. Like that fat old biddy that used to work in the Co-op, the one who couldn't work out the new decimal money and always gave us loads of change because I told her that the coin with the corners was five pence."

Carol laughed, spraying hot chocolate foam onto her bag.

"And my eyebrows," I continued. "Formerly known as lush and shapely, are sparse and pathetic, and now they have grey in them. Who knew you could have grey hair in your eyebrows?" I ran my fingers along my beautifully shaped arch. "I draw them on every morning with a fantastic wee brush and brown wax from Urban Decay."

"I have the opposite problem. Mine still meet in the middle. Thirty-five years of plucking, cutting, threading, shaving, electrolysis, waxing and laser, and I still have the unibrow like Frieda Kahlo. I pluck it away every single day, Karen, every single day! It would be one big long eyebrow from here to here after less than a week!"

"Well, talking of waxing, you know what I have to do now?" We both pointed to our chins and sighed loudly, causing the two wee bingo women at the next table to look over and tut. "We would look like them, Carol, that's what we really look like!"

We looked over to the next table to the two wee women in their belted beige raincoats and patterned plastic headscarves over their tight white perms, their faces taut and lined, their lips thin and beige.

"They're probably our age and just out without their makeup," I hissed. "In fact, one of them was in my French class at school."

Carol sprayed more hot chocolate. I had always loved how easily I could make her laugh. She genuinely thought I was young, pretty and funny, and that was why we were still best pals.

"And this too." I pointed to my upper lip. "I get a wee mustache now, a mustache, like my Uncle Tom. Okay, it's fair and slight, but a definite mustache."

"Fair and slight? Mine is dark and thick, it's an Iraqi mustache. I have to wax it myself every Sunday, and sometimes I even have to shave it." She whispered the S word and leaned forward over the table. "And you know where else I get grey hairs?"

"No! Not there!"

She nodded towards her jeans. "Yes, there."

We sat in respectful silence for a few seconds.

"So back up to the face," I said. "My wee Cindy Crawford mole grows a black hair now. Just one, but it's as thick and springy as fishing wire. I feel for it a few times a day and pluck it out right away. After three months it would be two feet long."

"I've seen you run your hand over your mole, so that's what you're doing? Back to me, my arms … like the Bee Gees chests but dark. I do the S thing every shower. Can you imagine having stubble on your arms?"

I shuddered. Being fair-haired meant pale freckly white skin all year round while Carol had her golden tan after a day in Saltcoats, but it did have its benefits.

"Okay, moving down. My boobs. Used to be here…" She showed me where they used to be. Quite high.

"Now here." Quite low.

"You should see my face in the morning," I countered. "I look grey and all around my nose and mouth is red and pink, I look great with my makeup on but without it—pasty and ill. I ran out to get the paper one morning and the delivery boy asked me if I was okay—he just hadn't seen me without makeup before! But the worst thing…"

I spread my hands on the table, palms down. "Look."

"What?"

Bless her, she really couldn't see it.

"Huge brown freckles on the backs of my hands. I have been wearing factor 50 sunscreen on my face every single day since I moved to California twenty-two years ago, but forgot about my hands. Look. Old Lady Hands."

Carol gasped in horror and whispered, "Liver spots."

"Yes, liver spots. I have liver spots on my hands. And you want to hear something worse than that? One time, Finn brought some pals back for a swim. There they were, all these tanned fit bronzed California college boys in their board shorts, throwing each other in the pool, slapping each other with towels, playing rap music, having a great laugh. I took them out some cold drinks, thought I looked quite good in my yoga trousers and T-shirt. When I came back into the kitchen, I could hear them all screaming and laughing, I mean, really honking. Finn was lying on the ground kicking his legs in the air, and two others had collapsed over the loungers, slapping each other's backs, actually crying with laughter. Another one was lying on the ground on his tummy, screaming and guffawing into his phone. I was dying to see what was so funny, and eventually Finn gathered himself for a second to tell me that one of the boys they hung out with had said that I was a hot mom. That's what they were laughing hysterically about! They thought it was hilarious that their pal said I was hot."

Carol finished her drink, sighed, and picked up her bag. "You know what we need? Half a pound of Mrs. Macari's homemade vanilla fudge and a raisin and biscuit Yorkie."

"Yes," I agreed. "Each."

38. How You Broke My Heart

UNCLE JAKEY KEPT CALLING ME TO TELL ME THAT HIS birthday party was on Saturday at six o'clock at his house and he had bought three packets of Cadbury's Chocolate Mini Rolls just for me, and that he had a surprise, also just for me, which I imagined was a packet of Jaffa Cakes. He said he was going to be fifty and Julie had ordered balloons and a cake that said so, but as Carol and I were almost fifty, he must have been at least sixty. We went along with it, getting him a fiftieth birthday card and his favourite Brut aftershave.

It was just as fantastically bad as we had imagined—the exact same as the ridiculous birthday party of thirty something years ago and every year since then. The same food—soft floppy sandwiches with thin slices of tinned ham and overripe soggy sliced tomatoes, plates piled high with Custard Creams and Jammy Dodgers, bowls of cheese and onion and tomato sauce crisps, and beside the ancient record player, a pyramid of warm cans of Tennent's lager. The same people—a dozen or so neighbours and pals of Jakey, all now in their late fifties and early sixties wearing the same ridiculously dated clothes and hairstyles of their youth and all in various states of loud drunkenness. Same music—Showaddywaddy, Rod Stewart, Elvis and Shakin' Stevens blaring tinnily from the same record player in the corner, the lid open, the record going round and round and lurching from song to song as Jakey and his pals danced and stomped around singing "This Old House." Auntie Julie and Carol's mum were fussing around in the kitchen, piling egg sandwiches high on chipped plates and squeezing fifty brightly coloured candles onto a child's SpongeBob cake from Tesco. We didn't know whether to laugh or cry as we were enveloped in drunken bear hugs and showered with the floppy triangular sandwiches and cigarettes.

"Karen, hen!" shouted one vaguely familiar drunken face who was splayed on the couch in his faded T-shirt and flared jeans, now strangely back in fashion on the college campuses of California. "Ah huvnae seen you for ages! You're looking weel, hen!"

I smiled, nodded and waved back through the thick smog of cigarette smoke. He hadn't seen me for thirty years.

Jakey saw us and lurched across the room. "Karen! Carol! Ma favourite lassies."

He waved a plate of Chocolate Mini Rolls in front of me, and I happily took two, tearing open the purple and silver foil wrapper. "Ma faither bought these for you, hen, God rest his soul. He wanted you to have them, so wire in, hen."

He opened my Coach bag and poured them in, choking back a tear. I was touched by him keeping Grandpa Jimmy's gift for me and had to gulp down a little sob.

"So, Uncle Jakey, what's my other surprise?" I was hoping it was Jaffa Cakes.

He learned towards me, unsteady on his platform boots, and put his hand to his mouth to whisper in my ear. A loud voice from the couch interrupted the moment. "Hey, Jakey, come over here a minute. Shug wants to play Sydney Devine. How do you change the record? Your music is pure shite, so it is. We want Sydney!"

The chorus started on the couch and was accompanied by the rhythmic stomping of their Gary Glitter platform shoes.

"Sydney! Sydney! Sydney!"

"Aye, aye." Jakey dismissed them with a wave. "I'll be over in a minute. I'm just telling Karen here about her surprise. You lads all know Bobby Henderson that I work with, right? Army Boab who lives in the bought houses up the Seamill Farm? Radio operator. Wee nice-looking black-haired Irish wife who works in Asda. His lassie works at the doctor's. His boy's an electrician. Big black dug. Well Karen here…"

I was mortified. They all stared at me. The music stopped. Auntie Julie and Carol's mum came through from the kitchen. Carol was actually crying with laughter, her mouth twisting to keep it in. Jakey turned to address the crowd. "Karen here, our wee Yankee, well, Karen pure fancied him for years, so she did. She loved Bobby Henderson, pure loved him. She followed him around in that ice-cream van of hers, went to the discos he was at, phoned his house and hung up, walked by his door, followed him home from school…"

How does he know all this?

I tried to laugh sportily and nodded my head, giving Jakey a good-natured but hard thump on the shoulder. My face was burning.

Please stop, please stop, dear God stop!

The women saved me. Carol was at the record player and had put on the Sydney Devine record. The chorus on the yellow couch joined in, singing about tiny bubbles. Julie and Mrs. Mackenzie ran through with the egg sandwiches. They were all singing and chatting again, drinking and dancing, and Julie was by my side. "Sorry about that, hen, you know what he's like when he's steaming. He works with that Bobby Henderson that you used to like when you were a wee lassie and has invited him here as a surprise. In fact, there he is right now."

Bobby Henderson was standing in the doorway. I would have known him anywhere. Same smile, dark brown leather jacket, blue shirt, jeans, boots, thick graying hair in a crew cut. He looked just like Jack.

"Jesus, he looks just like Jack!" hissed Carol.

He looked exactly like my husband. Bobby's hair was darker and he was fitter, but he looked just like Jack. I had married a man who looked like Bobby Henderson. For almost thirty years I had been with a man who looked just like Bobby Henderson. How did I not know? He looked at me. I looked at him. He winked. He was coming over.

"He's coming over!" hissed Carol.

Thankfully, the drunks hadn't noticed. "Tiny bubble." They rocked and swayed on the yellow couch. "Make me warm all over."

"Stay!" I grabbed Carol's arm.

He was standing right in front of me. Bobby Henderson. I could smell his musky aftershave and the leather of his jacket. I couldn't speak or breathe.

Carol nudged me.

"Hi, Bobby, sorry about this, we really didn't know that Jakey …"

"It's okay." He smiled nervously.

His voice was rough, Kilbrannan, deep.

"Jakey made me promise I would come for five minutes, so here I am."

"I'll get you a drink," said Carol, then she was gone.

We stood in the corner, me with two Mini Rolls and a glass of warm sugary Coke in my sweaty hands, him fumbling his hands in his pocket, both of us looking at the swirly orange and brown carpet.

You're forty-five years old, I told myself. You're a successful, mature, confident attractive woman. And suddenly I was.

"Bobby." I offered my hand. "What a nice surprise and, I must say, brass neck!"

He laughed and took my hand. His was big and warm and strong. I was fifteen years old again. Forty-five, I told myself.

"How are you, Karen? I hear you live in San Francisco. Did you become a teacher like you wanted to?"

How did he know?

"I did. I teach English as a second language. I love it. What about you?"

"I work with Jakey, offshore. It's a bit smoky in here, and noisy. Want to go out the back?"

Watched by Carol, Julie, and Mrs. Mackenzie, we made our way through the tiny kitchen and out to the back garden.

Forty-five, forty-five, I kept telling myself as he followed me.

He sat on the back step. I did too. I knew that the three pairs of eyes searching through the blinds on the kitchen window wouldn't be able to see me here.

"Don't you smoke?" What a stupid question.

"Not for twenty-five years."

"And you work with Jakey?"

Why couldn't I say anything intelligent or funny?

"It's nice to see you, Karen. How can we be this age?"

"I know!" I laughed.

Our shoulders were touching. He was perfect, he was Bobby Henderson, and I might as well have been wearing my old overall from the ice-cream van instead of my jeans and lilac cardigan. Thank God I had put on makeup and straightened my hair, and it was dark out here.

"You haven't changed a bit, Karen, since Kilbrannan Academy. I would have known you anywhere. I heard you went to university. I've worked with Jakey for twelve years now, and last month he realized that I was the famous Bobby Henderson and has been telling me about you ever since. He says your husband designs airports and built that big tower in Dubai."

"He really didn't." I laughed, relieved to have something to laugh about as my voice sounded ridiculously high. "Jakey made that up. He is an architect. Jack…" The name caught in my throat and came out a bit quieter than I had planned. "Jack does work on airport projects all over the world. He's away a lot."

"You must miss him."

"Not really."

I closed my eyes and smelled Bobby Henderson's aftershave.

This was terrible. I was forty-five years old and I still fancied Bobby Henderson. It was pathetic.

"Karen." His voice was quiet. "I did like you at school."

He did like me at school!

"I thought you were gorgeous. I still do. But I was a young lad, I was into the Jam and the Clash and the Sex Pistols, and you were into ABBA and the Bee Gees and wedgie shoes. You wanted to get your Highers and become a teacher, and I wanted to get steaming and fight and shag girls."

"So, Kelly McNicol, did you…"

"Yes, I'm afraid I did, several times, God rest her soul."

"So did you know that I fancied you?"

"Karen, the whole school knew!"

I leaned against him as we laughed. I was glad it was dark.

"Remember that old English teacher Wiggy? With the toupee and brown cord jacket? Well, Wiggy lives next door to me and had his sixtieth birthday party last week. He still has a lot of hair. It wasn't a wig after all, just a really bad cut. Wiggy must have only been in his late twenties when he was at Kilbrannan Academy, but we thought he was ancient. I couldn't believe it when I saw him cutting his grass just after I moved in. I thought he would have been dead decades ago. He hated me, gave me the belt loads of times and now we stand at the fence and talk about the roses and hydrangeas. Isn't life funny?"

"What did you do, Bobby, after school?"

The funny thing was, I had never thought of Bobby Henderson after I left Kilbrannan, not once. I had been obsessed with him for probably three years, then it was all lost in my new cool wonderful student life. Then I met Jack—he was the student pub debating champion, clever, witty, funny, sexy, wore a combat jacket from Oxfam with a big U2 logo on the back, played rugby and sang and played his guitar, hated Maggie Thatcher, noisily supported Nelson Mandela, the miners, cheap beer and huge student grants, and my crush was instantly transferred. When he asked me out in my first week at university, I never thought of Bobby Henderson for one second ever again. Until now. He was wearing sturdy boots. Jack never wore boots any more, just shiny old man shoes to work and old smelly leather flip flops to lie in front of the TV.

The sides of our feet were touching. He crossed his foot over mine and now our calves were touching, entwined. Mine was shaking a bit. He truly was still gorgeous. This was ridiculous.

Forty-five, forty-five...

He turned and looked right at me, intense and direct. I couldn't breathe.

Almost fifty, almost fifty.

"I left school on my sixteenth birthday, couldn't get away quick enough and worked on a building site with my Uncle Rab. I loved it. I got twenty-five quid a week, gave my mum five and spent the rest on beer, cigarettes, pie suppers and going to see punk bands in Glasgow. Shagging, steaming, fighting, got arrested a few times, got sacked from the building site, then one day my dad dragged me out of my bed at two o'clock in the afternoon and took me on the train to the army recruiting office in Queen Street in Glasgow. They told me to come back when I was sober, so I did, signed up for fifteen years, got a good signing-on bonus and went to Germany. I loved it, Karen. It turns out I wasn't daft, just dyslexic..."

Fate. Karma. Destiny. I could shag him, then teach him to read.

"Well, that was me. I'm still not great at reading, my pals in the army were fantastic, they covered for me and taught me what I needed to know for the job. I still couldn't read a book, even now, but I get a newspaper every day and fill out all the forms at my work. After the army I went to the Community College in Greenock and did a class for new readers."

"Bobby, I never knew you couldn't... "

"No one did, not even my mum. Not Wiggy, not my best pal Derek, no one."

He put his arm around me. I closed my eyes and leaned against his shoulder, smelling him. So delicious. My head was swimming. Me and Bobby Henderson.

Forty-five, forty-five...

"I served in Germany, the Falklands, Northern Ireland, twice, that's where I met ... and then Kosovo. That was the worst, worse than Belfast. The hatred, the violence, it sickened me. I couldn't take it any more. I was glad to get out."

He unwrapped his arm from me and went to stand up.

No, don't go.

"I need to go, Karen. How long are you here for? I'd like to meet up for coffee. You know, years ago I met your dad at the bowling club, and gave him my BFPO address in Germany, asked him to give it to you. He didn't, did he?"

I shook my head.

"Meet me before I go."

I nodded.

I could smell the Charlie perfume and the Hai Karate aftershave. I could taste the Orange Woolworths lip gloss. I could hear Rod Stewart singing. I actually could hear Rod Stewart from the record player in the living room: "I don't want to talk about it."

Bobby Henderson turned to face me, our knees touching, his hands on my arms as he looked into my eyes and sang, "How you broke my heart." And at that he put his two hands on his heart and leaned over and kissed me. Then he jumped over the fence and was gone.

I sat on the cold step, my eyes closed, trying to hold on to the smell, the feeling. I was tingling and trying to breath. I had finally kissed Bobby Henderson and it was the best moment of my life.

"He's married, hen, and so are you." Julie was standing there, her cigarette an orange glow in the darkness, her voice cold and accusing.

"I know, Auntie Julie, we were just…"

She threw her head back and laughed heartily. "Karen, hen, how old are you?"

"Forty-five, Auntie Julie."

"And I'm fifty-five, so how about you just call me Julie?"

She sat beside me on the step. It was ridiculous. We were the same age. I had never noticed before. She had bright blue eyes and smooth dark shoulder-length hair. Small silver earrings. Nice makeup. Despite the thick cigarette lines around her mouth, she was pretty. She looked like the sort of woman I would chat to at the bookshop or in the dog park. I had never seen her before.

"Okay, Julie."

We both laughed. She softened and sat beside me. "Look, hen, he's a good-looking man is Bobby Henderson, and he's a good man. He was the first boy you ever fancied, but he's married. This isn't right. I work with his wife, Sinead, and she would kick your arse up and down the street if she saw what I just did. He has children, a wee granddaughter that he dotes on, and you have your own husband and children. He's another woman's husband, hen, it's not right."

But it felt right.

39. How Deep Is Your Love?

LYING ON CAROL'S OLD BUNK BED I SQUEEZED MY EYES SHUT and pretended to be asleep.

"This is ridiculous, Karen. I saw you sneak into bed thirty seconds ago, and you still have all your clothes on. I know you're not sleeping. Get up right now."

I faked a little snore and some drool as Carol slammed the door in exasperation.

I couldn't face her. I couldn't face Julie ever again, or Mrs. McKenzie. I could hear them all whispering urgently outside the bedroom door and prayed that they would go away. After a final effort by Carol, during which she threatened to remove me from the position of Marco's godmother, they did go away and I had to stay there on the tiny hard squeaky top bunk all night, afraid to even go to the toilet in case of an ambush.

I had kissed Bobby Henderson and it was just as thrilling as I had imagined it would be all those years ago. It was warm and sexy and meaningful and I just wanted to relive every second of the most romantic moment of my life.

Carol made as much noise as possible getting herself to bed, kicking the bottom of my bed with her feet as she lay on the bottom bunk, but I could not face her. I could not think of one thing I could possibly say. It was so hard to ignore her. I desperately wanted to tell her everything, every detail—the singing, Rod Stewart, the heart, the kiss—but she already knew and her disapproval was heavy and disconcerting and was ruining the magic. I hated her coldness and judgment and just wanted to wallow in the warm glow of going over and over every second of this evening. Tomorrow I would face Carol, face them all, face myself and deal with this ridiculous situation. Unravel the stupidity, claim a drunken indiscretion even though I'd just had Pepsi, pretend I couldn't remember, beg for their discretion, have a hot bubble bath, get my makeup on and become a forty-five-year-old mother, wife and teacher again. But tonight I wanted to be fifteen and think about Bobby Henderson.

I felt an increasing sense of relief as each taxi arrived, then left with more of the drunken crowd. When I heard Mrs. McKenzie lock the door and puff her way up the stairs, I fell into a dreamy sleep until Carol started banging and huffing around the room a few hours later as she prepared to leave for an early shift. I had never been more relieved to see the back of someone and fell into a deep sleep as her car spluttered away.

It was eleven o'clock and bright sunshine when I woke to an empty house. I knew that Mrs. McKenzie had gone out to allow me to leave with some dignity. She knew that Carol would deal with me.

I lay in the hot jasmine-scented bath with my tea and tried to hold onto the magic of last night, but I was starting to feel a bit foolish. I didn't regret what happened, I just wished that no one had seen me. I don't know why I still cared so much about what Mrs. McKenzie thought of me but I did, and I knew that I had just dropped dramatically in her estimation.

I would sort this out, I was famed as a problem solver, good in a crisis, and I could do this, I thought as I applied my lipstick and pulled on Carol's cute little ankle boots. I made myself look decent and respectable again. I was always more productive when I looked pulled together. On the train back to Glasgow, I would think up my damage-limitation plan and this would go away. One more cup of tea, then I would sneak off before Mrs. McKenzie came back.

The front door rattled quietly as I filled the kettle, and my heart lurched—Carol's mum was back. If I had my bag I could run out the back door, but it was upstairs. No one came in. I walked quietly through the living room and looked out from behind the net curtains. Bobby Henderson was standing on the step. He saw me and smiled.

I grinned back. Uninvited, he opened the front door and walked right into the living room and stood in the doorway as he had last night, with his hands behind his back.

My smile was out of control. I must have looked manic, but I was unbelievably pleased to see him and felt a warm glow around me. I knew I should have told him that I was just leaving but I didn't.

"I have something for you, Karen." He grinned, thrusting his hands towards me. In one hand was the *Rod Stewart's Greatest Hits* LP, the pink one, and in the other hand was a huge bar of Dairy Milk chocolate.

He was still gorgeous. He was wearing a pale blue shirt and his jeans and boots, and he was still unbelievably gorgeous. And he was standing two feet in front of me in Mrs. McKenzie's living room offering me my favourite LP ever and my favourite chocolate.

"Bobby." I tried to sound in control and composed. "I'll be back in a minute—just sit for a minute, the kettle's on."

Then I pushed past him and ran up the stairs.

I sat on Carol's old bottom bunk bed, my heart racing in case Mrs. McKenzie came back. This would look terrible. I had to take control. This was ridiculous, I had to be mature and composed here, get him out of Mrs. Mackenzie's house. I took a deep breath to prepare myself to go back downstairs when the bedroom door opened. Bobby Henderson was standing in the doorway looking at me with an intensity that took my breath away. He didn't say a word as I walked across the room and into his arms.

Being with Bobby Henderson was as wonderful and magical as I had always imagined, but I had never for a minute thought it would happen in Carol's old bunk bed.

40. More Than a Woman

THE WIND WHIPPED MY HAIR AGAINST MY COLD RAW FACE as we walked along Kilbrannan Beach, the heels of my boots sinking into the damp sand as the seagulls screeched and swooped above the grey choppy sea. From inside a car, it would have been beautiful—the sweeping curve of Kilbrannan Bay, the dramatic foamy waves, the bright sunshine, the barnacle-covered rocks scattered over the yellow sand, and the spectacular mountains of the distant islands, pictured in a thousand Scottish calendars and shortbread tins, covered in a soft mist.

"Stop moaning, Karen," Carol said. "It's bracing and healthy and just what you need to blow away all the shite you keep talking."

I had been hiding in Anna's house in Clarkston for two days—I hadn't told her a thing, she'd never heard of Bobby Henderson, and we had had a great time going around the Art Gallery and Kelvingrove Park and having chats over hot chocolate and scones in lovely wee cafes, but I didn't tell her anything. Usually I would have. Anna and I had stayed close. She was a teacher too, Justin was a senior manager at the same bank, and our children were the same ages, but I needed more time to think about what had happened. I really couldn't believe I had done that. It felt so natural and so right and I wished I could feel guilty, even a little bit. I just wanted to see Bobby Henderson again.

The chilly walk along the windswept beach felt like a penance. I stuck my hands deep into my pockets as a low dark cloud covered the sun and cast a shadow over us.

Carol was trying to stay calm, but I knew she was really angry. She still didn't like Anna after all these years and would never meet up with her when I was home. She had hardly spoken to me since she met me off the train. "You slept with him, didn't you?"

"What if I did? And why would you say that?"

"My mum saw him come out of the house the next day, looking smug and strutting up the street. He even had the nerve to wink at her, the cheeky bastard. Then she saw you skulk into a taxi with your bag. He was smoking, and he had a *Glasgow Herald* under his arm. He can read, Karen, he just made all that up, and he does still smoke. It was all a load of shite that he told you."

"But what if he's the one, Carol? What if Bobby Henderson is the one for me, always was, and we missed our chance because of his dyslexia? How many people our age get a second chance at first love? This might be my destiny. This might be the universe giving me a second chance."

"Lovely day," called an old man in a thick parka and wooly hat as his little white Westie ran around in frantic circles chasing seagulls.

"Yes, lovely day!" we chorused.

"I mean really," I said. "I can't let this go. It might be our last chance."

"Oh, for eff's sake! First of all, Bobby Henderson is not dyslexic. He's a liar and a sleaze and you are a fool. You've made such an arse of yourself, Karen. Listen to yourself, it's embarrassing! Three days ago you were crying and snottering because Jack was flirting with Samantha, and you desperately wanted him to yourself. Now we're back in 1977 listening to this old shite about Bobby Henderson. Have you finished your French homework and tidied your room? Because you're not allowed to come out and play with me until you have. It wasn't first love. Until last night, you'd never even had a two-word conversation with Bobby Henderson. We've not even talked about him for about thirty years. He's not dyslexic; he made that up. He reads out the pub quiz in the Railway Club every week, and he smokes like a chimney. You must have smelled it when you were shagging him on my old bed."

I could feel my cheeks burning. Bobby had told me he'd stopped smoking twenty-five years ago. I looked down at the sand as we trudged along. Carol kept going, her feet stomping into the sand. She wasn't looking at me.

"It was a moment of nostalgia, Karen. That's all it was. This age can be depressing. We're getting older, the fine lines get deeper every day as the bank account gets smaller, people are blowing up planes, Afghanistan, Iraq, Iran, Darfur, the economy is tanking, property prices going down, the Euro is going down the drain and the pound is next, Uncle Jakey could run the country better than the prime minister, a fish supper costs a fiver and the customers moan about it every single day, and I really did see a fifteen-year-old policeman yesterday. Who wouldn't want to be sixteen again for five minutes? Who wouldn't want to relive the excitement, the hope, the innocence, the drama, the mystery, the perky boobs, the taut skin? But that's all it was, Karen. It's adultery."

That stung. Small cold drops of salty rain smacked against my face as the sun struggled to reappear.

"Lovely day," called an older couple wrapped in anoraks, striding along with their hands behind their backs.

"Lovely day!" returned Carol.

"What is wrong with people round here? How is this a lovely day? And you're wrong, Carol. I really felt something."

"Yeah, Bobby Henderson's willie."

I tried not to laugh. And so did she.

"I've never seen myself as someone who could have an affair, and Jack could never see past me. But something's changed. I saw how he looked at Samantha, and I can't bear the thought of him with anyone else. I am so jealous I could stab him. I can't stand it. The thought of Jack lying in his boxers next to someone else, it's unbearable. I just want things the way they were. Jack and I were great together. And I don't know if he's at it with her. If he's not, it's not because he doesn't want to. I saw how he looked at her. Then when I saw Bobby Henderson…"

"Torn between two lovers…"

"Stop it, Carol, it's not funny!"

"Sorry." She didn't look sorry. "But I do think you'll end up with Bobby Henderson. You'll be Karen Henderson."

Karen Henderson.

I had written that name a million times on my maths jotter, in my diary, on bits of paper, on my hand.

"Seriously?" I couldn't stop the huge grin that spread over my face. Me and Bobby Henderson. Karen + Bobby.

"Yes, he loves you, always has. He'll leave his wife and you'll leave Jack. The two of you will buy a bungalow here in Kilbrannan near his wee granddaughter. You've always secretly loved it here—the rain, the wind, the chip wrappers blowing up the street, the drunken fights on a Friday night.

His wife will be absolutely fine about it, she gave up her big Irish Catholic family to marry a British soldier but you and Sinead will become good pals and Jack will write you a big cheque and drive you to the airport in his BMW. Finn will have to stay in California until he graduates from college, but Eilish will be thrilled—you know how much she loves it here, she can't stay away. She'll be happy to give up her millions of pals, her high school, her indie band, snowboarding, her drama group, her swim team, the long hot summer. Kilbrannan Academy is just exactly like her high school. She'll adjust, no problem. And you, you can get a wee job in Tesco, make Bobby's mince and tatties at night and go down the pub with him on a Friday, have a wee drink, then get a kebab on the way home. You can catch up with *Coronation Street* again, and Buster will love the six months in the quarantine kennels, if he survives the journey. Then that same day, John Travolta will call you and finally ask you out—he'll wear his white bellbottom suit and ask you to go out dancing with him in the Railway Men's Club, and Nick Santiago will turn up at my door with a bouquet of roses, declare that the whole gay thing was a wee mistake. I saw how he looked at me last week. He'll ask me to marry him, and then I'll get a job as Beyoncé's back-up dancer and as the face of Lancôme..."

I looked at the sand, at the thick tide lines of dark green seaweed, at a crab scuttling for shelter. My feet were wet and cold. "What am I going to do?"

"Give yourself a shake. Rebuild your marriage. Don't tell Jack. Get rid of Samantha. Buy Jack a pair of boots and a U2 album. Get a grip of yourself. Let's run."

We ran along the sand, struggling for breath, the shells crunching beneath our feet.

"Lovely day," called a wee woman in a thick woolen coat, her old black Labrador hobbling along by her side.

"Lovely day!" I shouted back, breathless with exertion and cold and shame. Carol had forgiven me. She would never let me forget it, but she had forgiven me. Jack never would. If he ever found out, he would leave me, and I would have to live with that.

Then we saw them on the prom, both of us at exactly the same moment. He was wearing the same leather jacket and jeans. The boots. The woman was taller than me in her high boots, slimmer than me in her boot-cut jeans, gorgeous in her black polo neck, her thick dark hair in a loose high pony tail, her bright red lipstick perfect against her pale Irish skin. Between them they swung a curly-haired little girl bundled up in a red duffel coat, yellow Wellington boots, pink wooly tights and a hat with a huge pom-pom. She was shrieking with laughter as they swung her along the prom. The grandpa bent down, put his hands on either side of her round little middle and swung her round and round as she screamed in delight, then lifted her onto his shoulders. He held the child with one hand and with the other reached out and pulled his wife towards him. As Carol and I darted behind a bin, the woman leaned against him, slid her hands around his back and under his jacket as Bobby Henderson ran his hand over his wife's pert little bum and gave it a squeeze.

We huddled behind the bin in silence as the wind whipped around us. I had never felt so stupid, so foolish, so humiliated in my life. Tears of shame pricked my eyes.

"Looks like you'll have to pick John Travolta then," Carol said.

41. If I Can't Have You

THIS WAS WHAT I WAS GOING TO MISS MOST IF JACK AND I separated. If Jack found out about Bobby Henderson, or if he had succeeded with Samantha, then he wouldn't give me his air miles anymore and I would be up the back of the plane with everyone else, squashed into my tiny cramped plastic seat with my little foil carton of horrible overcooked pasta and stringy chicken. So I decided to make the most of my very final Business Class flight, my last time ever lounging on the soft leather bed with linen pillows and fine china and starched napkins and a menu of delicious choices. I never drank when I flew long-haul, but by the time the plane doors were closed at Glasgow Airport at 9 AM, I had had two glasses of Bucks Fizz and had ordered a gourmet cooked breakfast. Next time it would be a carton of Ribena and a packet of salt and vinegar crisps, so I was going to enjoy this. Then I did what I always did when I left Scotland—I reclined my seat, put the soft blanket over my head and cried quietly for seven hours. This was the only time I allowed myself to do this. Seven solid hours of silent weeping for what I didn't know I had left behind when I begged Jack to accept the scholarship

DENISE ALLAN STEELE

from UC Berkeley when I was twenty-one years old. Now I knew what I had given up so easily—a life with Carol and Marco, seeing them every few days, our children brought up as cousins, Marco's first day at school, his first guitar solo in the school concert when he was six years old. I wasn't there. My pregnancies and my children being born—Carol wasn't there. Carol never having any more children—I still didn't know if that was a choice. My mum and dad moving to Spain—I saw them every year for a month, but one year one of them would be gone and I wouldn't be there. Being normal, being able to speak without someone telling me that they loved my accent. Sometimes I just wanted to say something and have the other person answer, but every single day for the last twenty-five years my accent had been what people heard and not what I said. When I made speeches at graduations, I could see people smiling at the way I spoke rather than being impacted by my words. Sometimes I just wanted to fit in. But an immigrant doesn't fit in anywhere. I would never be fully American—I had never heard of the TV shows that my friends watched as children, I didn't quite catch all the cultural references, and it took me years to work out the tax system and the money and how to drive on the wrong side of the road with no gearstick, and to navigate friendships and dinners and coffees, making dozens of micro-adjustments every day so as to not draw attention to myself as different. The redoing it all the other way when I went back to Scotland, trying to orient myself with words and cadence. I had always admired immigrants who spoke English as a second or third language. At least I could read everything. It was the same language written down. I couldn't imagine living every day in a language that was not your own. I usually got labeled as an ex-pat rather than an immigrant, and the answer to why that was the case had

238

always bothered me. And foxgloves. I loved foxgloves, fairy hats, and had been trying for twenty-five years to grow them in California, under trees, in shady corners, watering them every day, but they just wilted in the dry climate. When I got the train from Kilbrannan to Glasgow I saw them, ancient layers and layers, thousands upon thousands of foxgloves in their beautiful natural luscious glory, growing wild and free along the railway embankment, all shades of pink, blue and purple, and I couldn't even grow one in my house.

And I didn't quite fit in in Scotland any more either. I was too American now, expected too much, expected it with a smile and right now. Scottish people thought I sounded American, and it could be exhausting to think about the right word to use in the right country, as the wrong word resulted in me sounding ridiculous/cute/a fanny.

Sidewalk/pavement, guy/dude, dollar/pound, biscuit/cookie, crisps/chips, petrol/gas, playtime/recess—it was a minefield and I sometimes wished that I could just be me.

I had to give up my teaching qualifications and start all over again in my thirties—and it was years before I had my own bank card or even a permanent resident visa in my own name. I cried for the simplicity of what I had left behind, of nice helpful free midwives and doctors and hospitals and schools and colleges, and for the views of the islands, and for the long magical days of June when it was light until almost midnight, and for the bright crispy September mornings when you could see your breath.

And I cried for old things—old walls with old ivy growing on them, old trees, old buildings, the old harbour—and I cried for the banter, where every Glasgow bus stop was a discussion group and every taxi driver a comedian. And I cried for my old long-haired Scottish boyfriend, Jack Logan. And I cried because Mrs. McKenzie had given me the bag of old records that Grandpa Jimmy had saved for me for thirty years.

By the time we landed in Newark, I had tidied myself up, removed the pounds in my purse for dollars, put my California driving license back in its place, brushed my hair, brushed my straight white American teeth, put my earrings back in, thanked the Lord for Lancôme, spritzed myself in Chanel Chance and I was American, feeling a little thrill when I saw the Stars and Stripes on the wall of the Arrivals Hall, then hearing the scary-looking Border Patrol Officer glance at my passport and say, "Welcome home, Ma'am."

"Thank you, Sir," I replied, and I meant it.

42. A Letter from America

October 2007

DEAR CAROL,

To make sure that you delete this email as soon as you read it, I am mentioning in every few lines the secret liposuction you had on your huge thighs the last time Dan was in Italy, when you told him the money was for a new exhaust for your car, and the fact that your real hair is grey, and that you fancy the Polish porter at your hospital.

Now I know that no one will ever see this, as you don't know how to edit, so you'll have to delete it.

I'm in the lounge at Newark Airport, halfway home, and dreading seeing Jack again. What if he knows? And worse—what if he knows and doesn't care? Liposuction.

I know we have a binding agreement never to talk about how I live so far away, and this agreement has served us well for almost twenty-five years of wrenching airport separations, but it is always just as hard and the truth is that I hate living so far away from you. We always thought we would bring up our children together and it is the worst thing in my life

241

that we did not. I loved having Marco here every summer and I love how close they all are but it's not the same. It's just not the same as popping in and out of each other's kitchens. Being away from you has been the hardest thing in my life. Liposuction.

By the time the captain put off the "fasten seatbelt signs," I had convinced myself of five things.

1. It wasn't really me with Bobby Henderson, it was the seventeen-year-old me, and that means that it doesn't really count, because it wasn't the real me, it was me in 1978. The real me would never have done that. And 1978 me would never have done that either. So it wasn't really anyone. Your real hair is grey.

2. He really did give my dad a letter for me, and my dad threw it on the fire—I called my mum from the airport. He really did. It would not have made a difference as I was so into Jack by then but Bobby Henderson gave my dad a letter for me.

3. However the not being able to read story is made up. You were right—he buys the *Glasgow Herald* every day from the newsagent. Mrs. Foster told me he had bought the last one when I went in yesterday. And he still smokes. That was made up too.

4. I am not going to tell Jack, ever. This will forever remain a secret between you, me, and probably your mum and Auntie Julie. They will not say a word, they never do, and Bobby Henderson will never tell anyone in case his wife finds out. Liposuction, liposuction, liposuction.

5. I am going to pretend that this never happened. The seventeen-year-old me thought it was fantastic, but the real me will live with the foolishness and humiliation and the fear of Jack finding out, and if he does I will have to deal with it.

And that is the last time I will ever mention this to you. You fancy the Polish porter.

As you know, Finn, my wee boy, was texting me constantly my last few days in Scotland. It appears that my husband Jack has finally decided to be a dad—when he got back from Frankfurt, he took two weeks off and did not open his laptop or look at his phone, not once. Looks like the lovely Samantha gave him the knock-back, thank God. After three days, he sent his moany parents to his brother in Vancouver on a one-way ticket—they are gone! He finally saw that my children do not like their grandparents and he could not put up with the moaning—I may never again have the annual month-long ordeal!

Eilish has not talked to me directly but every day she's been sending me videos of dogs making noises that sound like words—you know how much I love talking dogs. And she has brushed and walked Buster every day and is going to summer school to try to pass the two classes that she failed. There is hope.

And tell your mum again how much I appreciate Grandpa Jimmy's records—I can't believe he kept them for me for all those years. I really will treasure them forever.

Need to go—next flight being called—

K xx

43. Rewind

"LADIES AND GENTLEMEN, PLEASE FASTEN YOUR SEAT BELTS as we begin our descent into San Francisco."

Fasten my seat belt, indeed. The six-and-a-half-hour flight from Newark had felt like a week as I followed the journey on the map on the TV screen at my seat. Over Chicago, I enjoyed yet another Buck's Fizz, now called a mimosa, and a delicious cheese plate. By the time we were flying over a barren South Dakota, I started to feel a dread. Jack had known me since I was seventeen years old, and he would sense right away that I was hiding something. I thought about making something up, that someone I used to know had died tragically or that I was homesick, but I was the worst liar ever and always forgot what I had said, so that wouldn't work.

By Wyoming, I had had another two mimosas and was doing yoga breathing to keep myself calm as the display counted down the minutes to our destination. Two hours and forty-five minutes to sort myself out. If I could rewind a few days, I would have taken the Rod Stewart album from Bobby Henderson and the chocolate, given him a quick chaste Christian hug and closed Mrs. McKenzie's front door in his face. Then I could have wallowed in a warm, dreamy, teenage romantic cloud for a few days and it would be a funny story for Carol and for my California pals, and a huge boost for me to think that my high-school crush was still chasing me. But I could not rewind, and I had not closed the door and I had made a fool of myself and of my family and of the last twenty-eight years of my life.

Over Utah, two hours to go now, and I realised with a start that Jack might have already left me for Samantha and was waiting to tell me in person. Would I wait for a decent interval and join Tinder, swiping right for yes with nobody swiping back? Or Plenty of Fish—I'd heard that was quite good for older people—or even worse, like my coworker Julia had done and had met her handsome fiancé, would I sign up for Senior People Meet? Maybe I would be like my yoga partner, Cindy, and live a bohemian carefree life with dogs and candles and books and dinner parties for yoga ladies in my new lovely garden. Or would I be like Benyamin's mum, on endless dates with unsuitable men, looking for what she had thrown away?

When I asked for my sixth mimosa, the attendant brought me a cup of tea.

Nevada, nearly home, and I realised that for the first time in my life, there might be no one waiting at the airport for me. No one had asked for my flight time, and I hadn't even thought about it for one minute. Would I burst into the arrivals hall to no one? All those lovers and families with balloons and flowers and overexcited dogs squealing with delight when their person appeared at the top of the stairs. Maybe I was nobody's person any more.

I decided against asking again for a mimosa when I couldn't work out which shoe to put on which foot, as the passengers gathered their belongings and straightened their seats.

I would be brave, like all the other successful, confident single women. I would go home on the BART with thousands of other people, then get a taxi to the house. Yes, I thought, I'm a brave, confident successful woman as I stood up and fell along the aisle on my way to the toilet as my shoes actually were on the wrong feet.

"Turbulence," offered the kindly passenger in seat 1A, as she helped me to my feet.

It was also turbulent as I made my way off the plane, holding onto the walls of the gangway and clutching Grandpa Jimmy's precious records.

A wheelchair attendant, who with several others was waiting at the gate, touched my arm as I shuffled past.

"Assistance, Ma'am?" She was gesturing for me to sit in the wheelchair. "You dizzy, Ma'am? I take you."

"Oh, no thank you, dear!" I laughed. "I'm only forty-five years old. My heels are just a bit too high!"

She was an older Filipina lady with a kindly face and an instinct for helpless passengers who might cause a blockage in the efficient flow of San Francisco International Airport. "You sit, Ma'am. I take you."

She was standing right in front of me, blocking my path with the wheelchair. I flopped gratefully into it. Ninety-two gates might take me several hours. I was drunk for the first time in my life. Drunk on mimosas and shame. Marisol, my angel, pushed me right through the terminal as I hid my face behind my blue pashmina, an older lady pushing a fit, drunk, forty-five-year-old wife, mother, teacher and adulteress. After a few minutes, she stopped, knelt in front of me, took my shoes off and put them back onto the correct feet. It was shameful, but it did feel good to let this lovely woman take care of me, and I wished I could go home with her.

"Can I go home with you, Marisol? Or can you take me home and I'll get you a taxi back? You're really nice and I'd like us to be friends."

She patted my head, and I knew that I would be the story for her family tonight. "Well, Ma'am, wouldn't it be easier for you to get taxi home by yourself, and I stay here?"

As we entered the Baggage Claim, Marisol said, "Oh look, the man's singing! Look!"

Through my drunken confusion I saw a man playing a guitar and singing by the side of Carousel 6, and he was looking right at me.

As the light on the carousel blinked on and off and the beeping told us that our bags were on their way, the man was walking towards me. He was wearing jeans and boots and underneath his unbuttoned shirt, he had squeezed himself into an old faded black T-shirt that said "I Hate Maggie Thatcher."

"I really want to see you," he sang. Then he pointed at me and continued singing the song he had first sung to me in the street almost thirty years ago.

"That's my boyfriend, Marisol. That's Jack!"

I jumped out of the wheelchair to run to him, but my shoe got caught in the footrest and I landed on the floor of the baggage area with my foot still stuck in the wheelchair. Jack knelt down beside me while Marisol covered her face with her scarf to stop herself from laughing as she disentangled my foot. I could see a small crowd gather to film the scene as Jack knelt down beside me and took my one free hand in both of his.

"Karen Alexander." He laughed. "My girlfriend. Entertaining the public since 1962! I'm taking you home."

About the Author

DENISE ALLAN STEELE LIVES IN CALIFORNIA WITH HER husband and three large dogs, all of whom compete for space on one couch. Her children are grown and making their way in their millennial world, and her grandchildren are chubby and cute.

Denise taught in primary schools in Scotland for many years before moving to the San Francisco Bay Area, where she works with parolees entering the community college system.

She decided to write *Rewind*, her first novel, when her snow-boarding, hot-tubbing, drum-circling Californian teenagers asked her what it was like growing up in Scotland in the "olden days."

A Holiday Wish

COURTNEY J. HALL

WHEN I EMERGE FROM MY APARTMENT BUILDING'S LOBBY into the late October morning, I know it's going to be a perfect day.

There are several reasons for this certainty. For one thing, I'm headed to The Daily Grind. Already I can taste the rich flavor of their house blend. The one I've never been able to replicate at home despite buying the very same beans from their little gift area, grinding them—as needed, no more—in my ridiculously expensive coffee grinder, and brewing them in the coffee maker I blew almost three hundred bucks on. It just doesn't work. I can't stand to think of how much money I would save if it did. And if I learned to bake my own croissants. Then again, if I knew how to bake croissants like the delicate, flaky rolls of bliss behind the glass counter at The Daily Grind, I would be several hundred—okay, thousand—dollars richer but probably the same amount of pounds overweight. So maybe it's better that I'm as hopeless with butter and flour as I am with expensive coffee.

Second, it's a slow day. I have a few final details to take care of for two upcoming weddings and purposely scheduled only two new appointments. That will occupy my morning, so I can spend the afternoon studying magazines, vendor catalogs, and websites, fantasizing about the perfect wedding. It's outdoors, of course; September in a field at sunset, with fairy lights delicate as gossamer strands wrapped around the chairs and twinkling as the sun goes down. Fishbowl vases filled with water and floating gerbera daisy blooms in violet, tawny, and ivory stud the long, rustic wooden tables. Green grass is gilded by the setting sun, then polished silver by moonlight, while a groom in a classic tuxedo dances with a loose-haired bride. She wears an ivory gown that's strapless and form-fitting to the waist, but flares out over her hips in clouds of sparkling, beaded tulle. It's a wedding vision any of my brides would die for me to bring to life for them, but it's mine. All mine.

Which leads me to the third and biggest reason why I'm so convinced that today is going to be the kind of day high-school me would have recorded in painstaking detail in her diary—

Drew is home.

Finally.

I haven't seen him in nearly ten days. I miss him like crazy when he's away. Especially now, when we should be making plans for our wedding. We've been engaged for a year, and people are asking what the holdup is. We've been together for eight years, after all. Not only that, but I'm thirty, turning thirty-one in January, and he's thirty-two. Neither of us is getting any younger. In fact, two of the brides I'm meeting today are younger than I am. But today, after we're reunited over cups of steaming coffee and a plate of glistening croissants, after I drink in his curly blond hair and hazel eyes that crinkle to the point of closing even when his mouth just hints at a boyish smile, I'll show him everything I've come up with and we can get started.

The crisp autumn air smells clean in a way heavy, humid summer air never can. It bites at my cheeks and ruffles the edges of my burgundy scarf. Through leaves burnished gold and crimson the sun dapples the sidewalk and bounces off the shop windows as I hurry past. It's so nice out this morning that if it weren't for the promise of coffee, croissants, and Drew, I would have been a little disappointed to come to the end of the half-mile walk between my apartment and The Daily Grind, which is on a quaint tree-lined street just a few doors down from my own shop—Silver Bells Wedding Designs. It's a play on my name, Noelle Silver, and the fact that I specialize in Christmas weddings. They're my absolute favorite. Something about the holiday season just lends itself to gorgeous weddings. But Drew's the outdoorsy type and has his heart set on getting married outside. If he wasn't, we would definitely hold the ceremony at Christmas.

The bell on the door jangles a familiar welcome as I step through. I'm immediately enveloped by the best scent in the world—fresh-brewed coffee and things baking. It's a weird time; just nine o'clock, when high-school students are already in class and most working people are at their desks in offices scattered across the town. But there's a college campus just a few blocks away, and some of the tables are occupied by students buried in books, their lattes a permanent accessory like a backpack or pair of earbuds. I spot a two-top by the window and drop onto the chair, setting my canvas tote of wedding stuff on the dark wood floor beside me. I always prefer window seats to those buried in a dark corner. I like to watch life go by.

It also lets me see Drew the second he comes into view. He parks his black Prius halfway down the block, practically in front of my office, and gets out. He's dressed in dark jeans—every day is casual Friday at his office—and a hunter green button-down shirt, a blazer draped over his arm. The golden sunshine bounces off his only slightly darker hair, and even from here I can see how the color of his shirt makes his eyes more green than hazel.

Beautiful. I grin to myself. He's mine.

The bell jangles again as he opens the door and enters the shop. He glances around, looking for me, and even after eight years together my heart gives an erratic little *thump* when his gaze lands on me. I lift my hand in a wave. He hesitates, then smiles as he heads for our table.

I go to get up, to throw my arms around him, but before I can he puts his briefcase on the floor, drapes his blazer over the back of his chair, and leans down to peck me on the cheek.

"The usual?" he asks, and walks to the counter before I can respond.

I sit still, trying to ignore the little buzz of dismay that ripples through me. Seriously? Ten days apart and that's how he greets me? Anyone looking at us might have thought I was his sister, not the woman with whom he planned to spend the rest of his life.

He's probably tired. Jet-lagged. He'd been in Texas and gotten home so late last night he hadn't even wanted me to come and pick him up from the airport. Poor thing.

I watch him chat with the barista, a twenty-something guy with floppy blond hair who looks like he should be carrying a surfboard across a Hawaiian beach instead of serving coffee in a sleepy little suburban-Philadelphia college town. Drew turns around, a cup of coffee in each hand, and starts back toward me. He sets the cups on our table, but he doesn't sit.

"Croissants," he says by way of explanation, and goes back to the counter where he takes a plate from Surfer Boy.

I reach for my cup as the buzz becomes more of a rumble. Tired or not, Drew is never distant. But he's said three words since he arrived and none of them has been about how much he missed me and couldn't wait to get home to me. How jet-lagged could he be? Houston is on central time, only an hour behind us.

Finally he eases into the seat across from me and puts the plate in the middle of the table. I glance at it. Two croissants nestle together like lovers, and I'm hesitant to separate them. Instead I sip my coffee. It's black, the way I like it. No milk, no sweetener to muddle the flavor. It clears my head, sharpens my focus. What am I freaking out about? It's a beautiful day, and Drew is here.

I smile, set my cup down, and reach for Drew's hand just as he lifts his own cup to his lips. He grimaces. "No sugar," he complains, and jumps back up. He goes to the counter beside the pastry display case and grabs a few packets of sugar. Then a few more. He counts what's in his hand and puts a few back. Then he picks up one more, and a wooden stirrer.

What the hell is he doing? Unlike me, Drew requires sugar in his coffee. But just one packet—two if it's an extra large. Certainly not seven to nine, which, from my vantage point, seems to be the number clenched in his fist. Is he that desperate for an energy boost? Why not just dump an entire Red Bull into his cup?

The rumble starts to feel like someone's next to me with a jackhammer on full blast. I've seen Parkinson's patients with steadier hands than mine. Something is wrong.

Drew meanders back to our table with a quick pit stop to admire the display of travel mugs before he slides onto his chair. He tears open a packet of Sugar in the Raw and dumps it into his coffee. He stirs vigorously, his eyes trained on the whirlpool he's created inside his sixteen-ounce cup.

He doesn't look at me. My heart thumps, a bass drum in my chest.

"I missed you," I blurt out, unable to take the silence a moment longer. I force a smile. "Ice cream in front of *The Tonight Show* doesn't taste half as good without you."

He lets go of the stirrer, and we both watch it swirl around the cup of its own volition until the tiny coffee whirlpool fades and disappears. After a while, he meets my eyes.

"I missed you, too," he says.

Funny. I should feel relieved, right? I don't. He looks strange. Oh, he's still Drew—the broad shoulders of a high-school quarterback despite being only a year away from attending his fifteenth reunion, the smattering of freckles that have yet to fade even though summer's been over for six weeks, the curly blond hair and the innocent grin I so wish he'd flash at me right now. The package still looks like Drew. It's what's inside that's different.

I try another tack. "Did the trade show go well?" I know how high-pressure those things can get—he's told me. They sound a lot like weddings. Maybe something went wrong.

"It went fine." He rolls the empty packet of sugar between his fingers, making what looks like the world's tiniest joint.

Speaking of weddings... "I brought some things I want us to look at." Maybe talking about our own wedding will wake him up. I lift my bag from the floor and withdraw the binder inside, the one I've stuffed full of flower arrangements, menu options, and color schemes.

"What kind of things?" he asks.

I force a grin. "Wedding things."

It looks like he tries to smile, but fails. "Noelle—"

I plow ahead. "I know how you've always wanted to get married outside, and if we're going to do that, it has to be in late September or early to mid-October. Lots of venues will already be booked, and I might be able to pull some strings, but I don't want to if I don't have to."

"Noelle—"

I open the binder to the section labeled *Venues,* find my favorite—an old farmhouse just outside of town—and push it across the table toward him, shoving the plate of untouched croissants out of the way.

"What do you think of this?" My nerves vibrate like too-tight guitar strings. Why do I feel like I'm going to hate what comes out of his mouth once I let him speak?

He barely glances at it. "It's nice." He closes the binder, moves it aside. "Noelle, we have to talk."

And there it is.

He's not tired. Not jet-lagged. Not upset about a catastrophic trade show or how Surfer Boy forgot to put sugar in his coffee. Whatever his problem is, it has to do with me.

I swallow hard, making my throat muscles ache. I feel hot. I'm glad I left my hair down today because I can imagine how red my ears are—that's what happens when I'm nervous. They glow like beacons.

"Okay." I don't recognize my own voice. Since when do I squeak?

He sucks in a deep breath. Lets it out. The napkins on the table flutter.

"This isn't easy," he mutters.

Not easy? For him? Does he think it's cake for me, waiting to hear what he wants to say and knowing it's probably going to hurt?

"Noelle, I—we can't get married now."

Find out more at http://www.fivedirectionspress.com/a-holiday-wish.

Have you ever wanted to rewrite your favorite novel—fix the heroine's mistakes, win the hero's heart? Nina Pennington does. She is overjoyed when she lands the plum role as the heroine of *The Scarlet Pimpernel* in a class assignment based on a computer game.

Nina knows she can win—until she realizes her one chance for success requires an alliance with her least-favorite fellow grad student, cast as the Scarlet Pimpernel himself.

The game challenges Nina in ways she never anticipated, and that least-favorite fellow grad student starts looking better by the minute. But then, she has always had a soft spot for the swashbuckling Scarlet Pimpernel.

Now Nina has to choose: win the game, or take a chance on love?

http://www.fivedirectionspress.com/not-exactly-scarlet-pimpernel

THIS BOOK WAS TYPESET USING ATHELAS, A BODY FONT inspired by British literary classics, with headings in Homemade Apple and Stalker 2, commercially licensed display fonts selected for their schoolroom feel. The tape cassettes come from Wingdings 2.